ADVENTURES OF
THE JRACONER

Adventures of the Jraconer

The Tales of Tears and Joy

JOSHUA HIXON

Joshua T Hixon

First Printing, 2021

Prologue

In the northeast of a country named Koftan there is a village on the edge of a forest with no name. Not much is known about the village by the outside world. The forest however is known as where all Weres in the country come from. Werewolves are the most famous from the forest. They have started almost all wars on the continent which Koftan is on. The other Weres are only known in the village on the edge of the forest. Werecats are a little more famous of the other weres. They need males of other humanoid species. The other weres don't like to reveal much about themselves.

Koftan is famous for its export of "horse" meat. Horse meat isn't actually in its export of "horse" meat. The actual export is the meat of the slaves that do everything in the country. Humans are their preferred slaves. They may only live 100 years max, but their meat is so tender and juicy. Though the humans of the world of Jraconer aren't like the humans you may know. They are exclusively of the darker skin tone. Closer to that of the dirt they work in. The people of Koftan think that the humans are actually born of the soil which gives them their skin tone and their affinity for working in the dirt. Now the slaves aren't typically treated like the slaves you may think of. The human slaves were found working in their fields when the Green Skin goblins came across them. The goblins offered to buy their produce that they didn't need. When the humans started to die the goblins offered to buy the bodies as well and put fresh humans in the fields to keep the crops growing so that the food chain didn't stop because the farmer died. The bodies are then butchered and sold as "horse" meat or workhorse meat.

I feel I should explain that humans aren't just slaves. While all of them are what you may call black, they have many jobs. Blacksmithing is one job a lot of them seem to love to do. Though the competition with the dwarves makes getting into that field very difficult. They also love to be general store owners. Hardly ever like to do jobs that involve travelling far from home. This is due to their family-oriented beliefs and subsequent lifestyle.

There are in fact many different kinds of people that live all over Jraconer. Now Koftan isn't the only land mass on the planet. There are many but the largest one is what the planet is named after. It has its own massive inland sea the size of the Pacific Ocean. You have the people named after the country they originate from, the Jraconer. They live 1000+ years on average. None of them have been recorded dying of natural causes. Then you have the gnomes and dwarves who live underground. They gnomes prefer to build cities in natural cave systems in frigid mountains. The dwarves prefer warm weather mountain caves to call home. They like to dig till they find lava and build their cities around the lava. You have the Weres obviously but not much is known outside of the unnamed village. Some small pockets of kenku exist in Jraconer. Tabaxi also exist in Jraconer but they originate from an unknown continent. Satyr have small communities all over the place. Tiefling also have small communities in the major cities in Jraconer. Kobold run most of the mercenary rings all over the planet. Goblins in the country of Jraconer are seen as savages. However, in the rest of the world they run all slave rings including some of which is illegal to be mentioned here.

Chapter 1

In the middle of the forest in the north east of Koftan we find a young boy about 10 years old named Enoch following what sounds like a young girl panicking trying to run from something. Enoch manages to catch the girl who is running from something or someone. "What is wrong miss?" Enoch asks as the young girl collides with him.

"Get out of my way! If they catch me, they will rape me and then sell me to sex slave traders!" the young girl yells trying to get past Enoch.

"Miss, you are safe with me. Stay with me and I will protect you from them!" Enoch responds trying to calm the young girl down.

"How will you protect me? You are just a young boy!?" the girl exclaims still trying to get passed Enoch.

"Do you know where you are, miss?" Enoch asks trying to look the girl in the eye.

"The forest by my hometown, duh!" the young girl exclaims stopping and looking at Enoch like he has hit his head too many times.

"The forest of the Weres. I am a were. I can protect you against just about anything that dares enter the forest, miss." Enoch explains as he steps so the girl is behind him because he spots two adult human males finally get to the young girl.

"Give us the girl and we won't hurt you, boy!" The bigger human male yells brandishing a knife.

"Why would I give up my younger sister to two es-caped slaves!" Enoch responds exposing his giant ca-nine teeth as he is starting to get ready to turn into a werewolf.

"Oh, so this little werewolf thinks he can lie about this dwarven girl being his little sister. Haha!" The sec-ond human male laughs holding the rope to tie up the girl.

Enoch doesn't verbally respond just attacks the two without going full werewolf. After having ripped out the bigger human male's throat Enoch turns to the one with the rope.

"Aw, Fuck that I didn't sign up for this shit!" the hu-man male yells before dropping the rope and bolting towards the edge of the forest.

"Thank you, boy. May I ask my rescuers his name? My name is, Yennifer." Yennifer asks shocked.

"Name is Enoch. So where do you live, Yennifer?" Enoch responds as his teeth return to normal while wiping the blood from his face.

"Uh, I don't know if telling a werewolf where I live is a good idea?!" Yennifer exclaims with a hint of terror in her voice.

"I am not just a werewolf. I am half werewolf half werecat. I live in town so I should be returning home. Might as well escort you home to make sure you get there safely." Enoch responds showing Yennifer his hand which he has turned into the paw of a werecat.

"Fine I will let you escort me home. So, my family believes something I should warn you of..." Yennifer says trailing off.

"What is it, Yennifer?" Enoch asks looking into her eyes with his werecat eyes.

"I am in your debt. This is the major reason I didn't want you to escort me home. My parents will make me keep up the belief. I was out here trying to figure out how to survive on my own and you had to save me. They told me to not go into the forest or I would end up indebted to someone if I was lucky." Yennifer explains sheepishly.

"So, you want to learn to survive? Well I need an adventuring buddy. Adventuring is mostly surviving away from civilization. We can kill two birds with one stone by me teaching you to survive and you become my adventuring buddy. Do you like that idea, Yennifer?"

Enoch responds looking at Yennifer with a hint of excitement in his eye.

"Let's get headed to town. While we make our way back, I will think about it." Yennifer says sounding kind of defeated.

"One last bit of info about being my adventuring buddy is that it pays decent enough to live off of. After all we will be classified as mercenaries for the jobs we will be taking." Enoch responds adding in hoping that Yennifer will agree to it.

Now back in the village at the door to Yennifer's family home. Yennifer knocks on the door. Her mother comes to the door. "What is it? We don't want anything! Oh, it is just you girl! Get inside! You are grounded for running off like that!" Yennifer's mother yells angrily grabbing Yennifer by her right arm and practically throwing her inside.

"Ahem!" Enoch says clearing his throat.

"What do you want, boy!?" Yennifer's mother asks pissed off.

"I saved your daughter from some sex slave traffickers. She explained she would be indebted to me." Enoch explains confidently.

"So Yennifer, has a life debt to you! Well then take her!" Yennifer's mother responds grabbing Yennifer by her left arm and again basically throwing her out the door before slamming it.

"Well not quite what I imagined would happen. Do you have anything you needed from the house?" Enoch asks looking at Yennifer who is crying.

"All I own is what you are looking at. I now have no place to call home even." Yennifer responds looking up at Enoch with tears streaming down her face.

"Calm down, Yeny! I think my mother will let you live with us till I can get you earning enough money to afford your own place to live." Enoch whispers in Yennifer's ear as he pulls her in for an embrace.

"Please don't put me into the trade that my parents have been threatening to put me into!" Yennifer exclaims softly enjoying the embrace.

"Yeny, I am talking about what we discussed in the forest. Teaching you survival skills while also teaching you how to be a mercenary." Enoch says putting a hand on the back of Yennifer's head.

"Oh, ok. Let's get headed to your parent's house." Yennifer responds letting go of Enoch and wiping away her tears.

"So, uh you may end up either sleeping on the floor or something a little less comfortable." Enoch says warning Yennifer before leading the way to his house.

Now at Enoch's parents' house he doesn't bother knocking just opens the door and lets Yennifer go in ahead of him. "Who is this young girl, Enoch!?" Enoch's father asks partially slurring his words.

"Don't mind your father, Enoch. He is drunk as usual. Although I do want to know why you brought a girl home with you?" Enoch's mother chimes in.

"I am Yennifer. I am indebted to your son for saving me from two child sex slave traffickers in the forest. I was trying to teach myself how to survive before they found me. I am sorry if I impose. My mother threw me out when she learned of your son saving me from the traffickers. They had threatened to sell me into the trade many times before." Yennifer explains dropping to the floor and bowing to hide her tears.

"Get up young Yennifer. We don't have a room of your own to sleep in nor a place really. Unless our son has any idea where you could sleep." Enoch's mother responds after lifting Yennifer to her feet gently grabbing her under both arms.

"Well I do have that bed roll one of us could use to sleep on the floor and the other gets the bed. Yes, I realize her and I sharing a room may not be the best situation, but it is better than how I saw her mother treat her. I wouldn't be surprised if they made her sleep on the bare floor." Enoch says chiming in looking at Yennifer from behind.

"I did sleep on the bare floor. Hence all I own is what you see on me. Most of the stuff I was using to try and learn to survive on my own with was either donated or pilfered while no one was looking. I will admit I have thought of trying to steal from your house before. I didn't know any of you though, so it wasn't anything personal. I wouldn't complain about sharing a room with your son if you don't mind." Yennifer responds fighting tears.

"I will give Yennifer a bath while you set up your room to house the two of you. Hopefully, Enoch can help you, Yennifer." Enoch's mom says looking at Yennifer with a look of compassion.

A little while later Enoch is sitting on the bedroll on the floor when Yennifer comes in wearing what looks like one of Enoch's shirts as a nightgown. "I would feel much better if you slept on my bed, Yennifer." Enoch says looking at the girl who just got out of a bath.

"I am sorry that I am wearing one of your shirts but...!" Yennifer exclaims before being interrupted.

"I completely understand why you are wearing one of my shirts. I have no problem with it. Climb on my bed please. I want to see if you will be able to sleep there without an issue." Enoch says interrupting Yennifer.

"Wait you actually want to give up your bed for me?" Yennifer asks shocked as she sits on the bed.

"Yes, I would rather you enjoy some luxury you haven't had from what you have said. Ahem! Cross your legs if you are going to sit on the edge of the bed. I don't need to see your parts down there." Enoch responds turning his head waiting for Yennifer to cross her legs.

"Sorry! I-I-I!" Yennifer exclaims before just starting to cry from embarrassment.

"Yeny! I didn't mean to make you cry. I just don't need to see you down there. Maybe in the future if we decide we want to be together but as we are both children, I don't want to think of you like that right now." Enoch says jumping from the floor to sit next to Yennifer and giving her a gentle squeeze from the side.

"I've never worn something like a dress before. I have been given pants and shirt to wear. Not even feminine styled pants and shirts either. Like my parents wanted a son and not a daughter. I don't know how to act while wearing clothes like this. I am sorry if I offended you with me showing you my personal bits." Yennifer responds looking over at Enoch.

"You didn't offend me, Yeny. You just flashed me is all. As I have said I don't want to see you like that now. But when we are both older, I may not be opposed to us having a relationship where maybe seeing you like that is normal. Let's go to bed. Get comfy and I will cover you up. I will be on the floor if you need me." Enoch says trying to calm Yennifer down.

"I know I am indebted to you, but can I ask a favor?" Yennifer asks sheepishly.

"Just because you have a life debt to me doesn't mean I won't do things for you, Yeny." Enoch responds chuckling softly.

"I have never had an opportunity to share a sleeping space with someone. Could you share the bed with me tonight?" Yennifer asks still sheepishly.

"Ok, just don't try anything inappropriate. We aren't supposed to be sharing a bed, but I want to make you comfortable. I feel bad for getting you thrown out of your family home." Enoch responds moving to lay down close to the edge of the bed.

"Thank you. I won't do anything weird. Just want to know what it is like to sleep close to someone." Yennifer says laying in front of Enoch as he pulls the blanket over the two of them.

Chapter 2

A few years have passed since that day. Enoch is just waking up in his and Yennifer's tent with her nowhere to be found. While the duo are working with another group of people as mercenaries Enoch made sure their tent was a little ways away from the others because despite his best efforts to keep Yennifer clothed in the mornings while outside she keeps trying to walk around naked. "Where could she be? I think she will show up if I start cooking our breakfast." Enoch says aloud to himself.

Yennifer walks up while Enoch is cooking. She is completely naked. "Why you have a problem with me being naked when we're alone?" Yennifer asks looking down at Enoch who is now 15 while she is a week from turning 15 herself.

"Well let's see. You're 14 going on 15 may be the truth but you being a dwarf you are a bit short so people think you're an overly developed child and if I don't keep you dressed people may think I enjoy relations with children. Mmph hpmm!" Enoch starts to explain before Yennifer moves so his face is buried in her sternum between her massive bosom.

"Ssshhh enjoy my warmth." Yennifer says smothering Enoch between her breasts before he pushes her a step back.

"If we were in a private place like a room in a tavern, I'd gladly indulge you. However, since we are outdoors in a public place, I urge you to at least put the gown on I make you wear just before bed for now. If you would wait a little over a year to do this kind of thing, I would indulge you in public like we are now. Yennifer, I do love you, but I just don't want people thinking I am a pervert who likes children. You may be close to 15 but until you're 16 you don't have the papers to back up that you are in fact old enough to consent to inappropriate contact." Enoch responds at first a little ways away from Yennifer but halfway through talking embracing her and whispering in her left ear.

"You ... you ..." Yennifer says shocked freezing trying to process a 4-word statement Enoch said to her.

"You're shocked that I admitted I have feelings for you? Despite you nearly getting me banned from ever leaving my family home 4 almost 5 years ago when you decided to not only ask me to join you on my bed your first night in my family home you decided to strip so you were naked cuddling with me I do in fact have feelings for you. Kind of hard not to when we have saved each other from massive injury at least once every six months. Plus let's not forget the 2 years we spent lost in the Untamed Jungles in the middle of Koftan some 600 miles off course from where we were supposed to be. Seeing you naked everyday for those two years I really started to enjoy what I was seeing. Granted we were only 11 when we got lost and 13 when we made it out of the jungle. I have come to love you for who you are not for your body over the past 2 years since then." Enoch explains looking into Yennifer's slightly pink eyes.

"I love you too, Enoch. I have been telling you that I love you for a while now. I was about ready to give up on us. You finally have admitted you have feelings for me. If you would let go of me, I will go get dressed as you requested, Enoch." Yennifer responds smiling with tears gently sliding down her cheeks.

While Yennifer is in the tent getting dressed the other mercenaries come over. "When will you two be ready to make the last leg of the journey back?" The Human male lead mercenary asks semi annoyed.

"Sorry I woke up only like 10 minutes ago. I am cooking Yeny and I our breakfast. She was supposed to wake me up but she wandered off to do who knows what before returning. She is currently getting dressed. Give me like 15 more minutes and we should be ready." Enoch responds embarrassed.

"We leave in 30 minutes. You need to figure out how to get that girl to keep her clothes on. It wouldn't just look bad on you. It would ruin our employability as well if we were caught with a nude female minor in our group. When we get back to town don't expect us to ever join on jobs with you two again. She is too much of a liability. Understand!?" the male human explains annoyed.

"Understood, sir!" Enoch says sighing.

"What was that about, Enoch?" Yennifer asks sitting next to Enoch fully clothed with a stumped look on her face.

"Just another group that sees you and your constant insisting on being naked as a liability so we will be on our own again when we get to town later. I guess I will have to reveal the surprise earlier than I had hoped." Enoch responds all happiness gone from his demeanor.

"You mean the house you have been keeping secret from your parents for the past several years? I can finish cooking go get dressed for the day." Yennifer says looking at Enoch who seems defeated.

"Why should I be surprised you already know about it? You don't seem to leave me alone back in the village. Even when I ask you to leave me alone you follow me. I have been trying to set the house up for you and me so when you turn 16, we could move out from my parents' house so we wouldn't have to worry about our activities upsetting my mother. Just don't burn it please. I love you, Yeny." Enoch responds defeated.

"I am sorry. I just wanted to spend time with you outside of our missions and your parents' house. Over easy?" Yennifer asks somberly.

Enoch doesn't say anything just nods before moving to stand up and kissing Yennifer on the cheek before heading in the tent.

Now entering the perimeter of the unknown village the group are met by their employer on the border of the town. "You two!" the boss yells pointing right at Enoch and Yennifer.

"Let me guess. We aren't allowed to work for you after this job?" Enoch responds defeat slipping into his tone.

"That girl of yours needs to learn to wear clothes. I run a business of repute and rumors of a minor dwarven female walking around naked while I am employing them are ruining my reputation. No one wants to employ either of you in this town because of her refusing to wear clothes. Here is your pay! I can't kick you out of town, but no one here wants to employ either of you. Her for not wearing clothes all the time, you for not making her wear clothes. The others in the group I am sorry your reputation here was ruined by being associated to these two." The boss says pissed off throwing the pouch of coin at Enoch.

At the local pub Enoch is slouched over on the bar with Yennifer sitting next to him. "I am sorry, Enoch! I didn't know my actions in the field would ruin our chances of working in our hometown!" Yeniffer exclaims looking at Enoch who is slouched over like he just lost his dog.

"You didn't know? More like you didn't think! Now that house I have been building and setting up for us serves no point. I can't work in my own hometown where I had it built. I used to refuse to believe my parents that maybe the tribal life would have been better for me. Now I am starting to see they were right. Now of course it is too late I have imprinted on you a non were so I am forbidden from entering the tribe as we can only imprint on one person in our life. Well until the previous person dies of course then we can imprint again. Your kind live what 400 years? My kind are lucky we live 100 years! Hell 25 years is lucky with the constant combat with the other tribes! I don't even have money to buy supplies to make it to a town where I pray, they haven't heard of you and your refusing to wear clothes. The coin we got for that job was severely reduced compared to our agreement. Feels like he wanted to cancel the contract and refuse to pay us, but he took pity on the fact we are now more or less doomed to become homeless if we can't make it to another town far away from here. I need time to think, go to our room in this tavern if that is still allowed for us."

Enoch responds fighting the urge to scream and make a scene.

"I love you, Enoch." Yennifer says meekly as she stands up.

"Love you too, Yeny. Now leave me be for a few hours." Enoch responds looking at Yennifer from the side as she starts to cry before heading towards the stairs.

Enoch has left the pub and wandered into the forest where he is wandering aimlessly when he hears what sounds like a scuffle between two weres one in their human state the other in their were state. Wanting to help one of them he rushes to the source of the sound to find a girl fighting for her life against a werecat. "Permission to help you, miss!?" Enoch yells picking up a dropped spear.

The girl just nods as the werecat tries to attack her. The girl is severely injured she is trying not to collapse so the werecat can't kill her.

Enoch gets between the werecat and the girl pointing the spear at the werecat. The werecat knocks the spear from Enoch's grip causing Enoch to have to grapple the werecat. Pulling out a knife Enoch holds it to the werecats throat. "I can either slit your throat or I can release you and you walk away and leave this girl alone. I don't know what has caused your conflict don't really care to. Just care that you leave her alone whether that is because I have to kill you, or you do the smart thing and leave with your life." Enoch says in the werecats ear before the girl grabs him from behind.

"Don't kill her. She will leave. You have bested her in combat." The girl exclaims as she grabs Enoch from behind.

"How do you know that, miss? Never mind that, how badly are you injured?" Enoch asks turning around after releasing the werecat.

"Just some cuts from their claws. Though the bleeding may become an issue. My name is Maria. What is yours?" Maria responds as she sits on a rock.

"Name is Enoch. Let me patch you up, Maria." Enoch says pulling bandages and a bottle of high proof alcohol to disinfect the wounds.

Enoch is just finishing with patching up Maria when he hears what sounds like a familiar gasp and the breaking of twigs under foot. Enoch just tosses his supplies in his bag and bolts towards the source of the sound.

Now back in the village Enoch witnesses a figure rush in Yennifer's parents house and slam the door. Due to his manners he knocks on the door. "What do you want heartbreaker!?" Yennifer's mother asks.

"I would like to explain the situation to Yennifer! It isn't what she thinks!" Enoch exclaims not even remotely out of breath.

"She doesn't want to speak to you ever again!" Yennifer's mother yells trying to slam the door before Enoch stops her.

"Then give her this." Enoch says coldly holding out the pouch of coin he received hours prior from their ex-boss. "If she decides she wants to assess the situation of our relationship that we've been working on for the past 5 years she knows where to find me." Enoch adds before letting the door close.

Now at the pub Enoch is on his usual stool at the bar when a short, cloaked figure walks up and struggles to climb on the stool next to him like a familiar dwarf. "Need any help?" Enoch asks in a cold disconnected tone.

"Not if you don't want to give me any help." Yennifer responds fighting sobs.

"I will help if you will let me explain the story." Enoch says turning to Yennifer.

"That is why I am here. I wanted to hear your story at my parent's house but well you were there, so you know how my mother is. Thank you, Enoch." Yennifer responds as Enoch helps her up on the stool.

"As you know from our countless arguments over the years, I go to the forest to clear my head of the bad emotions and think clearly on our issues. I was doing my usual loop when I heard what sounded like two weres either fighting or fucking. Was hoping the former as walking in on the latter is not a good thing to do. It was the former except one were was in her human state the other was in their werecat state. Both of them are werecats. Obviously the one in their were state is but the general build of the other one is a female werecat. I fought off the one in their were state. Offered to patch up the one who was being attacked. She let me patch her up which you witnessed me finishing up with that. So, what do you say honey?" Enoch explains looking Yennifer dead in the eye.

"Can we talk please? Is it ok I order some alcohol?" Yennifer asks kind of meekly.

"Warning I don't have much money. All the platinum I had was in the pouch the ex-boss gave me which I gave to your mother. I imagine she kept it." Enoch responds leaning forward to kiss Yennifer on the cheek.

"What would you like, Miss?" the bartender asks looking at Yennifer.

"Wow no question if I am old enough? Uh what ever he is having." Yennifer responds looking over at Enoch.

"Both the food and beverage or just one or the other?" The bartender asks confused.

"Get her both, Bill." Enoch says slightly annoyed with Yennifer.

"You sound annoyed, Enoch?" Yennifer asks meekly.

"Let's see you got us basically black balled from the mercenary business in our hometown. You followed me on my walk to clear my head, then when something unexpected happens and I follow my nature and heal an injured person you assume I am doing something inappropriate with her. You run to your mother who abandoned you five years ago because you have a life debt to me which was repaid many times over a long time ago. Now you come to find out what really happened and when I reveal it you don't tell me if things are ok between us. How could I be annoyed at any of that?" Enoch responds getting more and more upset at the same time getting louder and louder.

"I – I – I ..." Yennifer says meekly scared to say what she's thinking.

"You what?!" Enoch asks resisting looking right at Yennifer revealing he is crying.

"I am sorry. If you want to leave me here, I understand. Just remember as you are bound to me, I am bound to you. I may leave this town to find work, but I won't move on emotionally to other men." Yennifer says fighting tears herself.

"Yeny, I need time to process. I don't think you are the only female I have imprinted on. I do believe I imprinted on the girl you saw me patching up. So, I may move on, but I will always remember you are my first love. I can't give you a time or place for us to meet and see if we want to continue with us. I love you, Yeny. Here is the coin for her food and drink. I am leaving the area for an unknown amount of time." Enoch responds getting off his stool before hugging Yennifer and kissing her on the cheek one last time before walking away.

"I love you too, Enoch." Yennifer says before slouching forward and bawling her eyes out.

Chapter 3

About a decade has passed Enoch is back in the unnamed village and he is in the forest looking for Maria when he hears what sounds like a girl screaming in agony. Rushing to get to her he finds a naked girl trapped in a bear trap with some form of poison on the teeth. "Permission to touch you to help you miss?" Enoch says crouching next to the trapped female.

"Go ahead! Just don't even think of cutting my leg off I need it!" the girl yells in agony.

"Wouldn't think of it miss. May I ask your name? There I have got your leg free. Looks horrendous." Enoch says as the girl gets up and attempts to bolt before tumbling from the agony of trying to run on her injured leg.

"Fuck! Why should I tell you my name?! Maybe you put this trap to try and get a were to imprint on you!" the girl screams as she fights back tears due to the pain.

"See this?! I am a were myself! I haven't been in this area in 10 years or so. It would have been a decade if I had gotten here a week from now. Can I finish what I was trying to do?" Enoch responds pulling out some vials and bandages.

"I can't run, now can I? Name is Alice. My little sister said she was helped by a guy with that same necklace. I don't know, I was trying to kill her about a decade ago in my werecat state when a kid threatened to kill me if I didn't leave her alone. She saved my life..." Alice says looking at Enoch slightly scared.

"So, did he threaten to kill you with this knife?" Enoch asks tossing the knife he had held to a werecats throat a decade ago.

"Yes! How do you have that knife?!" Alice responds terrified.

"I am the guy who held that knife to your throat. Could you hand it to me so I can cut these bandages to fit you? I don't hold past emotions against you. I only interfered with Maria and your fight because my conscience wouldn't let me ignore it. Same as right now I am only patching you up because I couldn't ignore your screams of agony." Enoch explains looking down into Alice's eyes.

"So, I am guessing with you being gone you don't know about the war? No one who isn't connected to my kind are allowed to enter the forest anymore."

Alice says looking up at Enoch after handing him the knife.

"Would explain why I was looked at funny when I walked up to the forest. They must have seen something on me marking me as who I am as they just let me walk through." Enoch responds looking at the bandages he just finished putting on Alice's leg.

"May I ask who you are?" Alice asks looking up at Enoch still kind of scared.

"Does the necklace not tell you enough. My mother is a werecat, father is a werewolf. I am the half and half that was used as a peace treaty." Enoch explains trying to help Alice to her feet.

"Didn't know if the necklace was actually yours or you stole it from the actual owner. Your mother died in the war as did ..." Alice responds trailing off while looking right at Enoch from her right side.

"As did who?" Enoch asks looking at Alice.

"My sister died right about here a year ago in the war. Her death from a trap lead to the peace talks. I miss her. Wish I hadn't fought with her so much. Tried to kill her every chance I got. I was the last person to see her alive. I found her here she told me to go get some help. I went for help came back and she was gone but the puddle of blood was enough that she shouldn't have tried to leave. It's my fault for not trying to help patch her up." Alice responds crying.

"Let's talk about this once we get you some-place safer. Where is your tribe? I am getting the vibe we're being watched. Don't know if it is wolves, cats, or boars." Enoch says slight bit of fear in his voice.

"It is my fellow tribe mates. You can leave if you don't want to address the fact you imprinted on not just my sister all those years ago but me as well." Alice responds as a werecat comes up behind her so she could sit on her back.

"I thought I could only imprint on one per-son. Here I am having imprinted on three females. One is dead, don't know where the other is. I will come with both to move forward and to give my condolences to your tribe about your sister." Enoch responds helping Alice to sit on her tribe mate's back. "I am going in as my most easily identifiable form." Enoch continues be-fore transforming into his grim form.

"Wow so you did get your father's grim abil-ity. He almost killed me in that form. He is dead as well. Sorry for killing him." Alice says adjusting so she is seated like she is riding a horse.

Now at the entrance to Alice's tribal den. The guards initially point spears at Enoch but Alice motions for them to lower their weapons. "He saved me. He also protected Maria from me almost 10 years ago. He chose his most identifiable form." Alice says looking at the guards.

Inside the main den Enoch turns back to his human form. The alpha looks right at him. "So, the prodigal son returns after his absence started a war costing thousands of lives on all sides of the war! What made you want to return now!" the alpha yells looking at Enoch with a death glare.

"I didn't return for Maria or to reintegrate with the were tribes. However, here I am. So why do you say I caused a war? Because I couldn't make money in the village anymore, so I left to survive on my own. I honestly would rather have nothing to do with the tribes. Sorry if that hurts to hear but considering I am the last living of my family I don't feel a tie to the tribes. I'd rather find my old dwarven female friend and leave this town behind." Enoch responds looking around him.

"You don't want to go forward with the fact you imprinted on me. Even though I am the alpha's daughter you don't want to go on with me?" Alice asks looking at Enoch surprised.

"No, I would rather avoid the were tribes. I have been doing it for the past 9 almost 10 years so why should I change that now. I don't particularly enjoy being told how to live my life. That is all I dealt with when I thought the tribes were my only way forward. Then I saved a dwarf girl from being sold into the sex slave trade and I got to experience life outside of the tribal lifestyle. I fell in love with life away from the tribal lifestyle. Then I threw it away by saving Maria from being killed by Alice here." Enoch explains looking right at Alice.

"How dare you accuse my daughter of trying to kill her sister?! Take him to the dungeon!" the alpha screams.

"WAIT! He is telling the truth. He stopped me from killing Maria all those years ago! He held an iron dagger to my throat and threatened to kill me if I didn't leave Maria and him alone! I have the scar to prove it! He didn't cut me intentionally, but the blade was sharper than he realized is my guess!" Alice exclaims getting off the werecat she rode back to the den on.

"He held a metal knife to your throat! Send him to the dungeon!" the alpha screams.

"Why do you want to send him to the dungeon? He defended your youngest daughter from me with a weapon I would like to guess he didn't know was highly destructive to us weres. He was raised in the mortal society so his parents may have not taught him about what metals do to us. If you are sending him then you are sending me as well." Alice says standing next to Enoch and grabbing his hand.

"Fine! His trial will be in the morning. Take him to your room where the two of you will be held till morning when the two of you will be tried." The alpha responds defeated.

Now in Alice's room of the den Alice transforms into a werecat and back. "Why did you do that?" Enoch asks sitting on Alice's bed.

"Because I don't think you should be punished!" Alice responds sitting next to Enoch.

"Thank you, but I meant the transforming if you were going to quickly transform back." Enoch says looking at Alice.

"You don't know much about us weres do you?" Alice asks sighing.

"Not really. My parents ... well no mother was just starting to teach me when I saved the female dwarf and then proceeded to basically leave home and never comeback. Why are you climbing on my lap?" Enoch responds shocked.

"You are my counterpart. When a were is injured if they transform to their other form it will heal the injury completely without leaving any scarring." Alice explains looking into Enoch's eyes.

"Oh. Uh, I am not too comfortable with what your doing sitting on me like that and all. I didn't even let the dwarf do this even though she was my first imprint. I just wish I could find her. I miss her. Life without her has been boring and bland. I haven't had much enjoyment these past 10 years." Enoch says meekly.

"Fine just trying to follow tradition of bonding with my counterpart." Alice responds huffing.

"I am a little hungry. Any chance I could get some food?" Enoch asks meekly.

"Hold on. Hey, can you bring us some of the roast that was cooking over the central fire pit please!?" Alice yells poking her head out of the doorway.

A few minutes later the were who Alice rode in on comes into the room with a giant platter of meat with a couple potatoes and carrots. "Here. Enoch is it? I hope the alpha decides to be nice to you two. If she does please take care of Alice. She ..." the female says before Alice cuts her off.

"Ahem! He doesn't need to know about that! Thank you for the food. Did my mother try to stop you, swee... Marley?" Alice chimes in interrupting Marley.

"He should know about our relationship if he did actually imprint on you all those years ago! Yes, she tried to stop me, but I brought up our relationship and she let me bring the two of you food. Will you please take care of her, Enoch?" Marley responds looking right at Enoch.

"If the alpha shows me mercy, I will do what I can to protect Alice, Marley. This is delicious." Enoch says looking from Marley to Alice.

"Thank you. Both for the compliment and saying you would protect Alice. Madison required me to get that affirmation from you before technically I could let either of you eat. Let me report this back to the alpha and then I will stand guard at the door to the room." Marley responds before getting up and leaving the room.

"You do realize your initial claims of not wanting anything to do with the tribes are now in question with you saying you will protect me?" Alice asks turning to Enoch.

"Let me guess I just started the formal process of my imprinting on you?" Enoch responds pausing eating.

"Basically. You were right this is delicious. I forgot how well Marley can cook. Haven't really been here since Maria's passing. Too many emotions being here. With you here though they don't seem to be bothering me." Alice says looking at Enoch.

"Ahem! So, I have heard that Enoch is willing to protect Alice! Why the sudden change of heart, Enoch?" the alpha asks entering the room.

"It wasn't because of the food. If you show me mercy, I am technically in your debt as you have no reason to show me mercy. I figure agreeing to keep by Alice's side is the best thing I can do if you show me mercy." Enoch explains standing up to meet the alpha's eyes.

"In the morning your hearing has been changed to the beginning of the formal process of you imprinting on my only remaining daughter Alice. My name is Madison by the way." Madison says holding out a hand to Enoch.

"Marley kind of let your name slip when she brought the food in. Just figured I wasn't supposed to know it quite then, so I pretended I hadn't heard it. Thank you for showing me mercy. Alice is either my second or third imprint. If the chance to finalize the first one ever arises, I will take the opportunity. Doesn't mean I will quit caring for Alice however." Enoch responds shaking Madison's hand.

"As much as that isn't the most desirable agreement I do understand. You are a male half breed, so your werewolf side is capable of breeding with non-tribal people. If the dwarf you spoke of is your first imprint, then I can't argue against your connection to her. Just don't completely blow Alice off if you find your first imprint please." Madison says nodding.

"I wouldn't blow her off. I am just starting to actually like Alice. Not to keen on how her and I imprinted on each other or her accusations that I laid the trap I found her in today but I can't change how she feels when she is in agony. Any clue what this poison is and how to neutralize it by the way? It was on the trap I found Alice caught in." Enoch responds pulling a vial of the poison he got off the trap earlier.

"Where was the trap?!" Madison asks demandingly.

"Where I found Maria before she passed on?" Alice chimes in still seated with a ham bone in her hand.

"Could someone have reset the trap Maria was caught by?!?" Marley exclaims from the doorway.

"No, I destroyed the trap after she disappeared. I go to that spot often to reminisce on different things. It seemed to be her and my favorite spot to fight and argue. Oddly enough the same place Enoch saved her from me. When the poison first entered my veins, I felt hazy. Like the world was closing in on me. But as more got into my body I felt hyper and the pain from my injury was amplified. Enoch found me not to long after I entered that state. I – I..." Alice says trailing off like she zoned out before she starts seizing.

"What's going on!?" Madison yells.

"She is having a seizure. I don't know if it is the poison or the meat, I hadn't gotten to the stuff still on the bone. I am going to do everything in my power to keep her alive!" Enoch responds lifting Alice on the bed while she is still seizing.

"Lock up Marley! She got the food!" Madison yells turning to the door.

"No! Don't! It isn't the meat! Her leg wound has started to reappear! She went werecat and back to normal. Her leg should be healed if I understood what she explained properly. In my bag is the trap I found her in. Any markings that would indicate who could have placed it!" Enoch explains holding Alice trying to get her to quit seizing.

"We can't touch the trap! It must have been laid by a human! It is made of metal!" A guard yells looking down in Enoch's bag.

"This is an act of war!" Madison screams.

"Hang on mother! Do we have the forces to fight a war so soon!? Yes, they made the first attack, but we can't just jump into a battle we aren't properly equipped for." Alice says sitting up from Enoch's embrace.

"She is right, Madison!" Marley chimes in as she fights free of the other guards hold.

"Actually, I wasn't right where Maria died. So that trap could date back to the war that just ended. Does it look a little rusty?" Alice asks looking at the guard with Enoch's bag.

"It does look a little rusty." The guard responds.

"Ok then I walked where I shouldn't have. It was slightly buried under dead leaves so I didn't see it." Alice says leaning back into Enoch's arms.

A little time has passed Marley got Alice the antidote to the poison. The two have finished eating. Alice has left to take a bath and Enoch has returned from outside and Marley is still standing guard of Alice's room. "Can you and I talk for a few minutes? Just you and me in the room?" Enoch asks looking at Marley.

"About what, Enoch?" Marley responds relaxing a little and grabbing her right arm as if to show she is a bit shy.

"You and Alice's relationship. I haven't dealt with the were tribes much, so I am curious with what you mean you and her had a relationship." Enoch explains looking at Marley as he sits down on the bed.

"It was a literal relationship. We have had what would you call it ... Lesbian relations. When an alpha's daughter is imprinted and the person who imprinted on them runs off the alpha to be is assigned a female plaything if you will. You ran off so to speak so both Maria and I were assigned our own playthings. Maria didn't use hers. I took advantage of mine as much as I could. Marley knows how I like my parts stimulated pretty well." Alice says walking in completely naked.

"Oh, you're back! I should be on guard ...!" Marley exclaims getting up to rush to the door when Alice grabs her halfway and kisses her square on the mouth. "We can't do that anymore! Your counterpart is here! I am nothing more than a guard for you now!" Marley says pushing Alice away.

"I doubt he cares. He only agreed to go forward with the imprint to save his own ass. My emotions and needs mean nothing to him. You at least get me." Alice responds looking over at Enoch coldly.

"I was actually asking Marley about your relationship so maybe she could give me tips on how to handle you. Both in bed and in life. I want to do this right. I don't want you to hate me more than I have already made you do." Enoch says getting up and walking to the two.

"I can't really teach you how to handle her, master. You are different than me. You have to figure out how she likes your parts on your own. As for in life it is the same that I can't teach you anything. Your personality is different than mine. You have to figure how to balance your needs and wants with her needs and wants." Marley responds meekly.

"You don't have to call me master. Just call me by name. I'd still like some advice as using my hand on her parts can't be too different than you using your hand on her. Same with my mouth down there. Plus, any quirks of Alice's would be nice to get a hint ahead of time. Maybe she hates the smell of lavender and I like it. Things that save me from getting a pissed off cat trying to kill me." Enoch explains blocking Marley from escaping from Alice.

"Let me free please!" Marley exclaims quietly.

"So, what is the policy on an alpha to be keeping their plaything if their counterpart returns?"

Alice asks as Enoch pushes Marley into Alice's embrace.

"I don't know! The counterpart rarely returns after running off! Please let me go back to my post! Enoch, please quit joining in on Alice's perverted game!" Marley responds panicking.

"I wasn't joining in on anything if you'd turn around, I was going to thank you and then guide you back to your post." Enoch says softly in Marley's ear.

Marley turns around and Enoch hugs her. "Thank you for your service to Alice while I wasn't around." Enoch whispers in Marley's ear.

"Why are you such a killjoy, Enoch?!" Alice asks annoyed with Enoch.

"She was looking flustered and I don't want to make her job any harder than it needs to be. Plus, tonight and tomorrow are about you and me not you and her. I want to get to know the girl I have imprinted on in this room." Enoch responds turning to face Alice.

"By her facial expression when you pushed her into me, I think you may have imprinted on her as well." Alice says smirking at Enoch.

"I can't be imprinted on!" Marley exclaims blushing as Enoch turns to her.

"She can be imprinted on. With a normal person I would only have to worry about them imprinting on one of my tribe members. So tomorrow we will get the formal process started then we will be sending Alice and Enoch out of the den to explore the world and maybe finish the process. I can't have him imprinting on my whole tribe. As for Marley she will remain here. I can't give up the best member of my guard. If she wants to snuggle with you, Enoch, let her please. You two need to get to sleep. You are being too loud!" Madison chimes in walking up to the doorway.

"Enoch, could you hug me before you head to bed with Alice?" Marley asks meekly.

"Sure thing, Marley." Enoch responds hugging Marley.

"I am sorry if I make things difficult for you. I didn't think you could imprint on non alphas." Marley says softly in Enoch's ear.

"It's ok, Marley. I need to head to bed. As Madison said if you want to join us just don't push one of us out of bed." Enoch says giving Marley a gentle peck on the cheek.

A few hours have passed as Enoch and Alice have passed out. Marley is trying to climb in front of Enoch because Alice moved behind him. "Huh? What is going on?" Enoch asks softly as Marley lays on his arm waking him up.

"She is taking you up on your offer to join us. She almost fell asleep standing watch." Alice whispers in Enoch's ear.

"Oh ok. Come closer, Marley. It is okay to put your back against my front." Enoch says trying to pull Marley in closer.

"Your part is stopping me. It is sticking straight out." Marley responds meekly.

"Sorry I will deal with it you get closer. Don't be afraid of it." Enoch says as Marley moves into his embrace.

Chapter 4

Sometime later Alice and Enoch are wandering through the streets of the port city of Chaffington on a job with a new employer when Enoch is pulled down a side street by a cloaked figure. His disappearance goes unnoticed. The cloaked figure holds a finger in front of what Enoch assumes is their mouth. This figure is of a familiar height and body type. "Reveal your face." Enoch says softly.

The hooded figure pulls their hood down only revealing the top of their head. "I can't here." The masked individual says trying to hide their familiar voice.

"Yeny? You realize I am not upset with you anymore?" Enoch asks crouching to the masked figures level.

"There are people in town who I owe money to. I can't get a job here. Apparently, our old employer ruined my reputation all over Koftan. I see you have moved on." Yennifer responds looking into Enoch's eyes.

"Seemingly moved on but not really. Alice knows if I find you, I am not refraining from going back with you. I would like to explain to you the circumstances you find me under. Is there a safe place for us to meet?" Enoch says trying to pull Yennifer's mask down.

"I have a house down by the dock. Here is my address. Come alone. I can't take the mask off in public." Yennifer responds handing Enoch a slip of paper before pulling her hood up and heading down the alleyway she dragged Enoch into.

"You okay, Enoch? You look like you have seen a ghost?" Alice asks entering the alleyway as Yennifer disappears from sight down the opposite end of the alleyway.

"I found Yeny. The dwarf I imprinted on in my childhood. I need to stay in town till tomorrow morning. I have a meeting with her that I have to go to alone tonight." Enoch responds trying to give as little detail as he can.

"Good! The intel I got back in Cloughton was correct. I set up a fake job in hopes we'd find her. You seem so mopey lately so I thought maybe finding your first love might cheer you up." Alice says smiling.

"You aren't to meddle in my love life!" Enoch yells before bolting out of the alleyway passed Alice.

The sun has gone down. Enoch is at the address Yennifer gave him. He knocks on the door. "Coming!" Yennifer hollers from a distance it sounds.

"Hey, I don't think I was followed. Can I come in, Yeny?" Enoch says as the door opens revealing a warmly lit kitchen with Yennifer at the door.

"Only if you brought as I instructed in the note. I don't have money for food I can't scrounge. Sorry that I made you spend money on me again." Yennifer responds stepping aside so Enoch can enter.

"Yeny, you are the first person I have imprinted on. Been three others since but I can't control that. One is dead and the second is who you ran from, third is a guard in their tribe. So, what is for dinner, Yeny?" Enoch says setting a bag on the counter for Yennifer.

"What I can afford to make. So how have the years treated you?" Yennifer asks looking in the bag.

"Meh. Been looking for you for about 5 years now. Wish we had set a place to meet. May have never found out about the second person I imprinted on beside you. Which if I never found that out I wouldn't have imprinted on the third. How about you? How did you afford this place?" Enoch responds watching Yennifer zoom around the kitchen.

"Remember that old box I kept in my bag?" Yennifer asks as she turns to face Enoch.

"Kind of not really." Enoch says sheepishly.

"Every time I made a few platinum coins I would put a few in it. Well 250 platinum buys you a house on the docks here. Can't afford to live but at least I have an untaxable house to live in." Yennifer responds moving so she is standing directly in front of Enoch.

"Ah. May I ask you something?" Enoch asks looking into Yennifer's eyes.

"Ask away. I am an open book for you." Yennifer responds smiling at Enoch.

"Do you consider sharing a bed while you sleep nude infidelity?" Enoch asks sheepishly.

"If you weren't a were, I would say yes, however as you are a were, I can't really say that as it is how weres sleep isn't it?" Yennifer responds as a kettle starts whistling. "Tea?!" Yennifer asks before turning to go grab the kettle.

"Sure. I bought the good stuff I remember you absolutely loving when we last went on a mission together." Enoch responds enjoying watching Yennifer move around the kitchen floor.

"Any other questions?" Yennifer asks looking at Enoch as she pours him a cup of hot water for him to put his tea bag in.

"You never finished with how the years have treated you?" Enoch responds looking at Yennifer with a loving gaze.

"The past 10 years outside of buying this house have been absolute shit. No one wants to be associated with a female who made the mistake of refusing to wear clothes in her teenage years despite not doing that in a long time. With that finding a job is impossible. No one even wants to be friends. It's like there are posters with my face saying to avoid me that I haven't seen." Yennifer says fighting sobs.

"You haven't seen them because of your height. They've been at the average person's height. When I was getting close to your house, I just started following them and your house is covered in them above your height." Enoch responds pulling a poster Yennifer just described out of his pocket.

"You could have said something, Enoch. Not even my own soulmate can be honest with me!" Yennifer exclaims before trying to bolt to her bedroom.

"Yeny, this is the first I have seen you in a decade. I was planning to ask if you knew about them, but you brought them up. I care about you enough that I have a bag full of ones I took down before the local fat boys threatened to arrest me if I didn't stop taking them down." Enoch responds grabbing the back of Yennifer's shirt collar and dragging her back to the kitchen.

"Wait you care enough to want to risk getting arrested for removing posters about me? I should get cooking. Take your cloak off and relax. I do see this as both of our house actually. Weren't for you keeping me employed in my youth I couldn't afford this place."

Yennifer says as Enoch walks up to the counter next to her.

"Need help, Yeny?" Enoch asks washing his hands.

"It would be nice to have assistance in the kitchen for once. Any ideas what to make with this stuff?" Yennifer responds as Enoch starts chopping up the vegetables.

"You cut the meat up. Got any animal fat we could use to fry this stuff up?" Enoch asks looking over at Yennifer.

"No, I don't. Been unwillingly vegetarian for a while now. Couldn't get my hands-on meat." Yennifer responds meekly.

A couple of hours have passed, and the duo have just finished eating and cleaning up. Retiring to the den Enoch is seated in front of the fireplace after having just lit a fire. "You want to sit and talk?" Yennifer asks standing behind Enoch.

"Sure, come sit next to me. What do you want to talk about?" Enoch responds as Yennifer sits next to him and kind of leans on him.

"Why did we even separate to begin with? I know I saw you patch up another girl but why didn't we work it out? Why was separating with no way of knowing if we would ever see each other again the only option? Why is it now after 10 long years we finally reconnect?" Yennifer asks as Enoch puts his arms around her.

"Let's see I couldn't find a job in our hometown because of your annoying insistence on being naked all the time. You listened to your mother on relationship problems when she was famous around town for cheating on your father with every man who would look at her with any expression other than disgust. Again, your mother. We didn't discuss a place to meet sooner in our lives. Hell, I am only here because Alice got sick of me moping, so she went about tracking you down. Your nudity reputation made it easy to find you I am guessing." Enoch responds kissing the top of Yennifer's head.

"Want to head to bed? No sex tonight. I am not the most presentable down there right now. It isn't a good idea for me to go swimming for a couple of days." Yennifer says meekly while enjoying the embrace.

"Let's wait till the fire gets closer to going out on its own so there isn't a concern of the house igniting in our sleep." Enoch responds as there is a knock at the door.

"Who could that be?" Yennifer asks kind of jumping in Enoch's arms.

"Alice. Only were I know of in town other than myself. Yes, we weres can detect those around us. If you don't mind, I would like to answer the door so she will leave me alone for the night." Enoch responds looking at Yennifer.

"Let her in. We made too much food. Don't want it to go bad or a rat to smell it and to make its way in and make itself home here." Yennifer says getting up and rushing to the door in front of Enoch.

"Oh, Enoch you actually made it here. I followed the posters, so I figured she lived here. Is she home?" Alice asks looking at Enoch but not looking down.

"Down here ditsy! I am a dwarf, so I am a wee bit shorter than you two!" Yennifer exclaims annoyed.

"Oh, sorry! I forgot that you are a dwarf. Nice to meet you! I am the alpha's oldest daughter of the tribe back home. So, uh any place for me to crash?" Alice responds meekly.

"Why can't you crash at the tavern?" Enoch asks annoyed.

"Some how they know I am a were and they don't serve weres." Alice responds still timid.

"You reek like a typical were does. I bath often for a reason. Can she crash Yeny?" Enoch says before looking down at Yennifer.

"Good once she is done eating, she can watch the fire to make sure the house doesn't ignite so that we can head to bed. No worries of hearing him and I going at it. It isn't the safest time for me to go swimming at the nearest beach for a couple more days." Yennifer responds somehow sounding chipper while talking about being on her period.

Enoch doesn't say anything just starts loading a bowl of food for Alice. "Here. While it isn't anything like the roasts you have had the luxury to grow up with. It tastes great to Yeny and I." Enoch says setting the bowl of food on the table in front of a chair.

"What are you two planning on doing tomorrow?" Alice asks meekly.

"I don't really have a plan. Maybe I can get Enoch to buy me breakfast at the local pub down the dock. Though he will probably be confronted to pay off my debts." Yennifer responds with a hopeful tone in her voice.

"I only have a handful of platinum, Yeny. I don't keep much liquid on me." Enoch says sighing.

"What about this?" Yennifer asks handing Enoch a box.

"What's in it? You have it locked so I can't just look inside." Enoch responds semi curiously.

"Oh shit! Forgot I locked it. Got paranoid for a while." Yennifer says pulling a key from down her blouse before handing it to Enoch.

"Was this under your bosom? It is really warm." Enoch responds unlocking the box.

"Why does it matter if she hides a key under her boobs? You are going to be having naked relations with her sometime in the near future." Alice chimes in annoyed.

"I was picking on her. Yeny and I pick on each other when we are in good relationship status. Wow the key and deed to the house in our hometown. I gave these to you in case you needed either money or a place to stay." Enoch says looking at Yennifer.

"What crawled up your snatch and died?!" Yennifer asks looking right at Alice.

"I will try and teach her about personal hygiene this week so we could have the house to ourselves when you are off your natural bodily functions." Enoch says handing Yennifer the box with the key and deed to his old house.

"What do you want me to do with this?" Yennifer asks looking up at Enoch.

"I gave you possession of the house when I gave you those two items. They are yours not mine." Enoch responds looking down at Yennifer.

"Would you two just go to bed already?!" Alice asks sounding even more annoyed.

Now in the upstairs bedroom Enoch and Yennifer are in bed. "Why is she such a cunt?" Yennifer asks trying to be quiet.

"No, clue. She wasn't like this at all on the way here." Enoch responds as Yennifer tips him on his back.

"So, I may have lied to you. Yes, I am unwashed down there, but I got off my period yesterday. Was planning on getting cleaned up before I spotted you in the street. So, do you want to have some naked fun time before we go to sleep?" Yennifer says grinding against Enoch's hip area.

"I'd like to have bathed before I have some fun. I can smell myself and doubt if I could get it up that it would last long with how bad I am stinking." Enoch responds as Yennifer sighs.

"Fine I was hoping you would get me to a roaring climax and maybe upset the cunt downstairs." Yennifer says trying to climb off Enoch.

"If you really want to have some fun just say something, Yeny." Enoch responds grabbing Yennifer's hips.

Chapter 5

About a month later Enoch and Yennifer are roaming the streets of Chaffington when Alice runs up to her. "Why won't you go back out on adventures yet? You keep saying you want to leave the continent. Why?" Alice asks upset trying to get Enoch and Yennifer to stop walking.

"Yeny can't find a job in this country. An old employer dragged her name through the muck in this pitiful country. Honestly want to return to my hometown to literally drag him through the muck but that would start another war for your people. If you don't want to leave the country with us, then go back to your tribe den. I am not going back there. Only people who I have any connection two who can make a living in this country are you and Marley. As much as I love Marley, I haven't finalized my imprint with anyone other than Yennifer." Enoch explains as him and Yennifer round a corner in attempt to lose Alice.

"That was kind of harsh, Enoch." Yennifer says softly.

"With weres there are two ways for them to get your message. Either with tooth and claw or with harsh words. Only way I got her mother to not declare war on non weres after I found Alice caught in a trap." Enoch responds as he hears sobbing from behind, so he stops.

"So, you don't want to keep your agreement with my mother about me?" Alice asks trying not to make a scene.

"Do you want to leave this country?" Enoch responds with a question as he turns to face Alice.

"No, I would prefer to stay here, but if you offered to pay for my fare to go with you I would. I don't want to go back to scissoring with Marley and no chance of getting what I keep hearing you give to Yennifer. I want what I was promised when I was a child if I ever got imprinted on by a male I could reproduce with. I want a life outside of going on patrol of my tribal area. I have tasted that life and I don't want to lose it. How would you feel if you got a taste of a better life and then just like the seasons change you lose it because someone else says they want something different!?" Alice explains still trying to not make a scene but failing.

"Alice, come here." Enoch responds calmly.

"WHY!?" Alice asks raising her voice.

"I want to talk to you in a little more reasonable of a tone." Enoch answers just slightly louder.

"Fine!" Alice exclaims walking so she is right in front of Enoch.

"Do you see why I was opposed to your mother forcing me to continue with the imprint? I love this life and she was talking of taking it away from me. I currently don't have the money to pay for the three of us. I can only afford Yennifer and myself at this moment. Unless someone buys the house, I gave to Yennifer I can't afford to bring you. Trust me I wanted to. You are an amazing warrior. Having you on my side fighting monsters was amazing." Enoch explains touching Alice's face.

"Wait so you do want me to come along? How much is fare for the boat?" Alice asks looking up into Enoch's gentle hazel eyes looking down into her purple eyes.

"I need 100 platinum per person. That just covers getting on the boat not even food. I could more than afford all three of us but not enough food to last us the 2 months or so we would be on the boat." Enoch responds sighing as he watches the gears in Alice's head start to move.

"I could afford the food potentially if you will pay for my ticket. Please?" Alice begs looking up into Enoch's hazel eyes as they go a little more grey.

"We'll talk about it. So can Yeny and I get back to our date please?" Enoch responds kissing Alice on her forehead.

"Is this an honest we'll talk about it or a you give up we'll talk about it?" Alice asks trying to keep Enoch's attention.

"Did you not feel the ass grab?" Enoch responds.

"I don't understand why you think gripping my ass communicates anything other than a mixed message!" Alice exclaims.

"Was it a super firm ass grab or a gentle ass grab he was more like brushing your ass?" Yennifer asks finally speaking up.

"Super firm I would have to guess." Alice responds confused.

"He meant what he said then. We kind of developed the ass grab system in our time lost in the Untamed Jungles." Yennifer explains in a reminiscing tone. "Speaking spent water where a simple either ass or boob grab doesn't spend as much water." Yennifer continues.

Yennifer and Enoch are now sitting at a table outside of the tavern of their choice eating. "So, did you really mean you wanted her to come with us on our journey to my motherland?" Yennifer asks looking across the table at Enoch over her bowl of local seafood soup.

"No, I even lied with the grab system because she always asks and I have always told her to figure it out herself but you and I haven't communicated on that yet, so I knew you would explain it and if I went with the truth you would tell her that I didn't mean what I was saying." Enoch responds smiling at Yennifer.

Some people out of nowhere knock the duo out and pull bags over their heads.

Chapter 6

Months have passed when Enoch and Yennifer wake up with bags on their head. Well it feels like months it could have been a couple of hours. The duo can't speak as they have been bound and gagged. "So, you are probably wandering why I have had you brought here. I have been paid to bring you here for a once in a lifetime job. You are not to know where you are or anything of that nature. If my underlings will remove the cloth from your jaw what do you say?" a cloaked man asks in a dark room as the bags are removed from the duo's heads and Enoch's gag is removed.

"I would have to decline. By kidnapping us you have declared war on me. Do you even know who I am? I don't know your names but almost all of you are weres. The guy directly behind me may smell like one but he isn't a were. The young lass standing behind you is a bit of an oddity. She gives off an aura similar to mine.

Which is impossible I have been told I am one of a kind. I am the only half werewolf half werecat in existence. Who is paying you to take me against my will?!" Enoch responds with his eyes still closed.

"I wasn't informed I was acquiring a were let alone my daughter's replacement. Yes, my daughter is a half breed just like you. She however is a female and the treaty required a male like yourself, so she was cast out from the tribe and her mother and me were also cast out for creating her. Someone from your past who is also a were paid us to locate you. However, your associate is unneeded so she should be killed as she knows too much." The man says coldly.

"Touch her and everyone in here will die. She is my mate. I don't know anyone from my history who could be in Jraconia as I have never been in my memory." Enoch responds as he gently drops his bindings to the floor after finishing cutting them.

"She isn't from around here she has told me. She is from Koftan like yourself. Your associate is unneeded so why should we keep her alive. You imprinted on my associate first." The man says even colder.

"The first person outside of my family I had contact with is to my right. She is the first person I imprinted on. Whoever is telling you otherwise is lying to you. My second imprint was 5 years after my lover to my right. That individual died around a year ago. The third and fourth person I imprinted on are back in Koftan.

One is the older sister of the deceased, the other is her assigned plaything. So, if someone is claiming to be one of my imprints, I would like to know their location so I can punish them for false information. Now if you don't mind my lover and I will be leaving." Enoch responds standing up and starting to untie Yennifer.

"So, you think I am actually dead!?" Maria asks bursting through the door letting light in.

"Your entire family thinks you're dead. You're not my first imprint. Not that it would matter as I have finalized my imprint with my lover in front of me. Let's go sweetie." Enoch responds helping Yennifer to her feet.

"How can you imprint on more than one person while the previous is still living?!" A female voice asks from behind.

"As a half breed, I figured you would know, miss. You are older than me from your energies. So, you should have some knowledge about how our kind work." Enoch says not turning to face the source of the noise.

"My daughter hasn't left our tribal den before today. She agreed to remain quiet if I allowed her to leave just this once! As you are the only free roaming half breed you are the only one to know you can imprint on multiple women at a time." The man responds annoyed.

"Don't get upset with her. Her question is one I have pondered greatly in the last 10 years between being separated from my lover and finding her again. And to your daughter that question is one I don't have an answer." Enoch says as he gets to the door next to Maria while holding Yennifer's hand.

"Where do you think you are going?!" Maria asks demandingly.

"Somewhere my mate can see for one. Also, someplace I am not being assaulted by the stench of a wannabe were." Enoch responds forcing the door open for him and Yennifer.

Yennifer and Enoch have seated themselves at the bar in the tavern. Maria is being really annoying. "Would you quiet her down she is scaring away my regulars?" The bartender asks looking at Enoch.

"She is pissing me off as well. If I knew how to shut her up I would. If you have people to break up fights could you have them throw her out? I would pay them a platinum for their troubles." Enoch responds sighing.

"I'd gladly do that for free, Boyo." A male voice says from behind Enoch before you hear Maria yelling for him to let go of her. "Stay out no one wants you here, lassie!" the man says as the door slams.

"Thank you kindly, sir. Name is Enoch." Enoch says offering to shake the man's hand.

"My name is Angus. Angus Draconer, the dragon slayer!" Angus responds shaking Enoch's hand.

"Dragon slayer? So, you think dragons are real?" Enoch asks chuckling.

The bar goes completely quiet. "I take it you aren't from around here, boyo? Dragons are as real as weres like yourself. Your kind are rare around here. As for your lassie there next to you they are aplenty around these parts. Now if you want a job around here, I am the guy to ask. Though if you want the high paying jobs you are really going to have to work your tail off doing jobs that pay barely a brass piece for about 6 months nonstop to get to the jobs that pays silver. Then it's another 2 years before you will be allowed to know of the jobs that pay gold. 10 years for even a whiff of a single platinum. That's if you were to have bitten your tongue on dragons. But you didn't so it will take you about 100 years to work your way to making platinum from me. 200 from anyone else if they know to listen to me." Angus says in the most serious tone you will ever hear from a guy who hasn't been sober a day in the past 150 years of his miserable life.

"You just had to voice your mind again didn't you, Enoch!" Yennifer yells slapping Enoch upside the head.

"So how much is a trip to anywhere on the sea other than Koftan?" Enoch asks meekly as Angus sits on his left.

"How much you got?" Angus responds with the same tone and a dead cold stare.

"300 platinum." Enoch says meekly.

"Boyo, if you hadn't made the mistake of making fun of my profession I would take you anywhere in the world ocean for 25 platinum, but for your mistake not even 10,000 platinum could get me to take you anywhere other than a long walk off a short pier." Angus responds with the same tone and expression.

"Kid, he is fucking with you! We don't expect outsiders to believe about dragons. Though if I was you, I would apologize for laughing at him when he said his profession. Though thanks for the laughs as I got to watch your face as he gave you the piss." The bartender chimes in before turning around to hide his face while he laughs.

"You couldn't let me mess with him just a little longer! I was so close to making the poor kid wet his trousers!" Angus says laughing.

"I'm sorry I laughed at your profession, Angus." Enoch meekly says trying to calm down the urge to wet himself.

"You aren't the first outsider to think I am a daft old man for saying dragons are real. Definitely won't be the last either. So, I overheard you in the back room. Would you like a job? It isn't like what I said at all. Hell, I struggle to think of a task that anyone would only pay brass for." Angus responds patting Enoch on the back.

"There you two are! Why did you leave without me! More importantly why did you lie both on the price and the length of the journey!" Alice yells as she gets behind Enoch who pisses himself from the shock.

"You just made the poor lad wet his trousers!" Angus exclaims laughing.

"Alice, we didn't come here of our own volition. We were kidnapped by ..." Yennifer starts to explain before Enoch interrupts.

"Some member of the local were tribe thinks I want to marry his daughter who is apparently my predecessor when it comes to the peace treaty." Enoch interrupts quickly.

"Why did you lie about how long it takes to get here?!" Alice asks still upset.

"I have a fear of heights. I can't consciously fly because of that. We were knocked out and brought here while still unconscious. You would have happened to pack Yennifer and I some clothes or maybe grabbed the bag we had in our bedroom?" Enoch responds with a slight bit of hope in his voice.

"You are lucky I did grab that bag. Why do you need it?" Alice asks confused.

"Angus here just got done scaring me for making fun of his profession and then you come in and scream behind me bitching me out. I wonder why I would ask about a bag with more clothes in it not just because I messed myself, but I am in a foreign land earlier than I expected to be." Enoch responds annoyed.

"Oh, wait he wasn't kidding you wet yourself!?" Alice asks fighting laughter.

"We didn't want to bring you Alice." Enoch says coldly.

"You absolute ass!" Alice yells before bolting out of the tavern crying.

"Is there an indoor bathroom? Heck how much is a room here?" Enoch asks grabbing the bag with his and Yennifer's clothes.

"2 gold for the week. Bathroom is in the suite for the price I just said." The bartender says still fighting to stop laughing.

A little while later Enoch comes downstairs and sits between Angus and Yennifer. Someone taps on Enoch's shoulder from behind. "What is it now?" Enoch asks defeated before turning around on the stool when a female hugs him.

"Thank you for still being here. My father told me if you weren't still out here, I would have to be doomed to never have a chance with the guy who imprinted on me." The girl says softly in Enoch's ear.

"Another one. What is your name, miss?" Enoch responds putting his hand on the girl's side.

"Jennifer. But you can call me Jenny." Jennifer says letting go and standing up.

"Well this is going to be confusing. What makes you think I have imprinted on you?" Enoch asks sighing.

"You didn't imprint on her today. You did it when you born in this very town 26 years ago." The cloaked man says walking up to his daughter and Enoch.

"I haven't been to this country before in my life." Enoch responds annoyance coming into his voice.

"You have son. Your mother and I were sent off before you were born just in case you were a girl like Jennifer here. When you were born, we went back to Koftan to raise you. It however was my idea to keep you from growing up in the tribe directly." Enoch's father says coming from the room that Enoch came to in.

"Next thing I know you're going to reveal that I am actually Jennifer's little brother." Enoch responds getting mildly upset.

"No, we are not related. Though your dad has been here about as long as Maria has. He in fact brought her here to try to save her from the poison on one of his tribe's traps." Jennifer says looking at Enoch.

"So how did Enoch imprint on her when he was a newborn little baby?" Yennifer asks confused as she turns to face Enoch's father.

"You see while he couldn't be imprinted on, he could imprint on those old enough to be imprinted on. Which Jennifer was old enough for him to imprint on her. Though he shouldn't have any worries of him imprinting on anyone new since he says you two have well Y'know." Enoch's father explains not slurring his words once.

"Dad, I have a question." Enoch says confidently.

"Ask away, son." Enoch's father responds.

"Are you actually sober?" Enoch asks looking at his father funny.

"Have been for 14 years. Since you left home and had no sign you were ever coming back. Probably didn't help with your mother and my relationship that I got sober once you left but not while you were home. You leaving for the 10 year stint without any form of contact caused the war that cost many of their lives. Which sadly included your mother." Enoch's father responds stroking his jaw while pondering.

"Sorry about the leaving but I was chasing the first person to imprint on me. Yes, even when we spent every day together for the almost 5 years I was chasing after her. I wanted to have fun with her so bad, but I was trying to respect her belief of wait till she was an adult. God only like a month ago we finally went from being imprinted to finalizing our imprint." Enoch says kind of quietly because he is ashamed of his prior actions.

"Well Jennifer's father and I should be headed back to the local den. Can Jennifer stay with you?" Enoch's father asks.

"I would rather she return with you. But before she leaves." Enoch responds as he stands up and hugs Jennifer and kisses her on the cheek.

"Please let me stay with you." Jennifer asks softly as Enoch holds her.

"Go with your father. Tomorrow Yennifer and I can come to your den and talk things over. Well if Alice doesn't decide to be a pain in our butt. She can't find out Maria is still alive. Love you, Jennifer." Enoch responds giving Jennifer one last squeeze before letting her go.

Now it is just Yennifer and Enoch at the bar when Angus comes back to the bar. "Why did you leave the bar?" Enoch asks looking at Angus funny.

"Too many weres. I realize you are a were yourself, but you don't smell like one. It is like they don't know how to clean themselves." Angus responds as the bartender slides him a beer.

"Yeny, you seem off? Other than being kidnapped is everything okay?" Enoch asks glancing over at Yennifer.

"I am exhausted. I don't know whether it is potentially from a concussion or what, but I am ready to head to bed." Yennifer responds yawning.

"Can we talk about a job in the morning, Angus?" Enoch asks looking over at Angus.

"Sure thing, boyo. Rest well. Warning the mattresses here can be a little different than you are used to." Angus responds nodding.

A few hours have passed as someone is trying to sneak in the room when they step on a creaky floorboard. "Who is it?" Enoch asks aloud annoyed from being woken up.

"Can I join you two?" Alice asks meekly from across the room.

"Close and lock the door then come join us. Yennifer is behind me. She likes to be behind me for some reason." Enoch responds sighing.

"It is so you can protect me. How many times do I need to tell you that?" Yennifer whispers in Enoch's ear.

A little while later not even an hour there is a gentle knock on the door. "May I come in?" A voice that sounds like Jennifer asks on the other side of the door.

Getting up Enoch unlocks the door and steps out into the hallway. "I thought I told you to go with your father, Jenny?" Enoch asks leaning on the wall next to the door.

"My father told me if I wasn't serious about trying to pursue you, I would never see you again. He figures you are planning to slip out of town tonight to avoid having to get involved with me. I seriously want to finalize the imprinting process with you." Jennifer explains meekly.

"Come here." Enoch says holding his arms open to Jennifer.

"Why do you just offer me a hug when I confess something to you?" Jennifer asks hugging Enoch.

"I figure letting you hold me while I tell you what I want to say will show you I mean what I am saying. I plan to come with you some time tomorrow. We never agreed on a time, did we? I have a meeting about getting money flowing my way in the morning tomorrow. So how does afternoon sound for our little meeting. I don't really have a place for you tonight. Alice came back a little while ago. I would love to see if you could imprint on me, but I would need space for you to sleep in the bed. I want to be wrong about me being unable to be imprinted on. I feel bad that as a baby I marked you and when I meet you as an adult you can't imprint on me because I finalized my imprint with the first person, I remember imprinting on." Enoch explains still hugging Jennifer.

"You actually care about my daughter?" Jennifer's father says from the shadows.

"You had to bring your father, Jenny?" Enoch asks annoyed.

"I didn't bring him! He must have followed me. But I echo his question. You actually care about me?" Jennifer responds looking into Enoch's eyes.

"I am half naked letting you bury your face in my body hair. I kissed you earlier. Yes, it wasn't on the lips, but I don't know about non weres here, but they don't like it when a man kisses another woman other than the one that is known he is with where I am from. I could have just ignored you or told Alice to answer the door if I didn't care. What did I do? I pulled my arm out from under Alice and walked to the door to greet you. I feel bad for the one imprint of mine that is back in Koftan. I care for all of my imprints. Yes, Maria makes me extremely angry but what do you expect she assumed she was my first imprint." Enoch explains running his fingers through Jennifer's long blonde locks while she rests her head on his chest.

"Could you find a place for me to sleep with you and the others on the bed, please?" Jennifer asks lifting her head from Enoch's chest to look him in the eyes.

"Fine. Can I see your preferred were state?" Enoch ask letting go of Jennifer.

Jennifer turns into her werecat state looking up at Enoch.

"Do you ever take a bath when in were state? Your fur looks disgusting. I say this because I have a hard time when Alice refuses to clean the viscera from her fur and it dries, and she tries to climb in bed with me in the dried viscera covered state. Makes my skin itch like mad. Yeah, I could go were mode and it wouldn't bother me but one of my imprints isn't a were, so I try and stay in this state for sleeping." Enoch explains looking down at Jennifer before she transforms back to normal.

"I have never had anyone to share a bed with, so it really hasn't mattered if my fur was messy. Maybe Alice could go were and I take in front of you as a human state?" Jennifer responds meekly.

"That might work. Sir go home. I am working on figuring how to fit all four of us on the bed." Enoch says looking right where Jennifer's father is standing in the shadows.

Back in the room Enoch locks the door behind them. "Alice please go were state for the night. Jennifer's were state is worse than yours has ever been. Her father is a persistent old guy. I get Jennifer is what 30 years old, but I planned to try and get her to imprint on me tomorrow but as assurance she is here and needs a place to sleep." Enoch says quietly as he slaps Alice's leg.

"How did you know my age?" Jennifer asks shocked.

"If I was able to imprint on you when I was born you had to be around 4 years old when I was born. I will lay down you climb in front of me and Alice will curl up on my feet." Enoch explains climbing in bed.

"Do I lay with my back facing you?" Jennifer asks meekly.

"Whatever you feel most comfortable. Breathing what I exhale isn't the greatest idea though." Enoch responds as Jennifer lays on his arm with her back to his front.

"So, I hope you don't mind that I got comfortable." Jennifer says meekly as Enoch realizes she is naked.

Enoch doesn't say anything as the smell of Jennifer's hair sends him into a wave of memories, he didn't know he had. Jennifer flips over to face Enoch as he lays so he is flat on his back with his eyes wide. "Are you okay, Enoch?!" Jennifer asks climbing on top of Enoch not thinking of certain things causing him to 'impale' her. "Crap my father is going to be upset if he finds out I lost my innocence before I imprinted on Enoch!" Jennifer exclaims.

"No, he won't hear that, Jenny. My reaction was you imprinting. You just need to learn to not climb on top of me when I have a naked Yennifer behind me and you naked in front of me. My laying on my back was a reaction to memories from the moments after I was born. So, the smell of your hair reminded me of what your hair smelled like when you held me when I was just born. You actually didn't just imprint on me. I just remembered when you imprinted on me when I was a baby." Enoch explains putting his hands on Jennifer's hips.

"So, I wasn't your first imprint?" Yennifer asks groggily while moving to rest her head on Enoch's shoulder.

"Apparently not. So, um Jenny, can we finish this tomorrow? I want to go to sleep right now. I do want to fully finalize our imprint but not right now." Enoch responds still holding Jennifer's hips.

"Can I do something while I am here on top of you?" Jennifer asks meekly.

"What is it, Jenny?" Enoch responds loosening his grip on Jennifer's hips.

"First, I would like Yennifer to move her head, so I don't put my breast in her face. I would like to kiss you on the lips." Jennifer says looking down at Enoch who is lit by moonlight from the window next to the bed.

"Go ahead. Yennifer can move if she feels like it. I don't control her. Just like I don't control any of the females I have imprinted on." Enoch responds before Jennifer kisses him on the mouth while wiggling her hips a little.

Jennifer doesn't talk when she stops kissing Enoch just keeps moving her hips around before moving to a slight up and down motion.

"Don't wiggle your hips like that, please. May not be able to keep control of my urges if you keep it up. I would prefer to save this for later. When I can freely move around the chosen location and have my way with you." Enoch says gripping Jennifer's hips again to stop her movement.

"You are no fun!" Jennifer softly exclaims laying flatly on Enoch.

"No, he is plenty of fun if you let him do it his way." Yennifer says from Enoch's right shoulder.

"Don't think Alice is enjoying her view of our parts." Enoch chimes in chuckling looking at Alice over Jennifer's back.

"Forgot she was down there." Jennifer responds meekly.

"Can we finish this later? I want to sleep now have fun later." Enoch says rubbing Jennifer's back.

"Sure, I am guessing go back where I was?" Jennifer asks lifting herself off Enoch.

Enoch just nods before going back to the position he was in before this one.

Chapter 7

Next morning Enoch wakes up to what sounds like a female sobbing in the bathroom. He looks around to see who it could be. Alice is missing from around his feet, Jennifer is comfortably in his arms asleep, Yennifer is starting to wake up behind him. "Jenny, I need to go check on Alice." Enoch says softly as he taps on Jennifer's shoulder.

At the bathroom door Enoch knocks on the door. "Go away!" Alice exclaims still sobbing.

"Alice, Sweetie. What is wrong?" Enoch asks turning the handle and gently pushing on the door.

"Oh, you just naturally think you can fix everything that is wrong in your 'imprints' lives!" Alice responds raising her voice slightly.

"What is this about, Ally cat?" Enoch asks through the door.

"So, you think giving me a cutesy nickname will fix the situation?!" Alice yells through the door.

"No, not at all. I want to find out what you are upset about and try and remedy it. I can't really do that if you won't tell me what is upsetting you. I would also like to be able to sit next to you." Enoch responds still pushing on the door.

"I will let you in if you promise to do what I ask." Alice says standing up allowing the door to open.

"What is it you would like to do?" Enoch asks coming in the bathroom.

"I want to finalize my imprinting process soon. Before the next full moon." Alice responds crossing her arms across her chest.

"When is that?" Enoch responds scratching his chin.

"Last night was new moon. So, like what 2 weeks or so. Is that okay, Enoch?" Alice asks looking at Enoch.

"It is doable. I just want to get the four of us a house of our own too. A bigger bed is a must. I don't like having to require you or Jenny to go were state so the other can be in my arms. I am sorry I call all of you my imprints. I don't know what to call you all to be honest." Enoch explains holding his arms open to Alice.

"So, can I ask if you've seen a girl who looks like Maria around here?" Alice asks hugging Enoch.

"Why do you ask about that? I thought she was dead." Enoch responds trying to sound like he knows nothing about Maria being alive.

"So, did I but I saw a guy that looks like your father as well. I remember killing him myself. Why are you trying not to look me in the eye!?" Alice asks starting to yell.

"Because they are both alive apparently. I didn't know this till last night. Your sister commissioned Jennifer's tribe to get me here. They kidnapped Yennifer and I from the tavern we were eating at before we awoke in the back room downstairs last night. I wanted to tell you, but I knew you probably would not believe me even though I am telling the truth that I didn't know they were still alive to last night. Later today Yennifer, Jennifer, and I are headed to their tribal den where I believe your sister and my father live." Enoch explains looking right at Alice as she pushes him away from her.

"So, you expect me to believe that you had no clue she was alive!? Why do you seem to think I am stupid? You have seemed like you have been hiding something from me since I found Yennifer for you!? I worked myself to the bone to find her for you hoping you would realize that I care for you more than that dwarf does, but you seem to think I am a waste of your time!? I am done trying to make you happy!?" Alice yells tears streaming down her face.

"Do you want me to ruin the surprise I have been keeping from you?" Enoch asks somberly.

"What could you possibly offer me that would be worth keeping it a secret?!" Alice yells still crying.

Enoch drops to one knee. "Will you marry me Alice?" Enoch asks holding a ring attached to a chain around his neck.

"Wait you want to marry me? Are you fucking with me?!" Alice responds shocked.

"No, he isn't messing with you. He can't marry me by his upbringing. He could however marry you. We have been looking for a ring that better fits what he thinks of you. That is what we have been keeping secret from you since you found me for him. That ring is his ring." Yennifer explains leaning on the doorway of the bathroom.

"You have been planning to try and marry me?! Why would you keep this secret and not just tell me?" Alice asks dropping to Enoch's level.

"You kept that you were trying to find Yennifer for me a secret, so I wanted to keep the fact I want to marry you a secret. I realize now that you are too paranoid to keep secrets from." Enoch responds looking into Alice's purple eyes.

"I hate surprises. You should know that!" Alice says punching Enoch's shoulder causing him to start to fall back which he grabs her hand and pulls her down with him.

Landing with a thud the duo is just lying on the ground when there is a pound on the door of the room "WOULD YOU QUIET DOWN!" The owner of the tavern yells through the door.

"Enoch, Why do you want to marry me and not Jennifer? You have gone further with her than you have me?" Alice asks meekly while playing with Enoch's chest hair.

"Who was there when I needed someone to cover me against a shadow bear? Who has kept me warm when we got lost in the frigid plains in the northwest of Koftan? Who did all the leg work to reunite me with Yennifer?" Enoch responds with a question playing with Alice's jet-black hair.

"I was and did. What does that have to do with the fact you've been with her?" Alice asks still having her head on Enoch's chest.

"Ok so what I have been with her. My reason for wanting to marry you was that I haven't been with you and I want to marry you before I am with you. I want a semi normal life with you. Granted normal doesn't come to us weres but I sure as hell am going to try." Enoch responds still playing with Alice's hair.

"You want to marry me because of the fact we haven't been in bed together yet? Why do I not feel surprised of this?" Alice asks sitting up just enough to take her top off before laying back down.

"Ahem! We need to get a move on if you want to start making money, Enoch." Yennifer chimes in looking down at the two on the floor.

Now downstairs Enoch and Yennifer are at the bar as Angus walks in. "So how many people do you want to employ under me?" Angus asks sitting to Enoch's right.

"Well just three of us. I expect one of my imprinted weres to stay in her home den. Yennifer, Alice, and I to be honest." Enoch responds meekly as Alice and Jennifer walk up behind him.

"You don't want me to go on adventures with you?" Jennifer asks from behind Enoch.

"I want you to learn to be the alpha of a tribe. I don't want to be in this town forever. I want to move somewhere else and bring the three of you girls with me. I want to start our own tribe. If you don't want that future well guess you shouldn't have picked me up when I was a newborn. You doomed us to be bound together if that isn't what you want. I hate being near the ocean. I prefer somewhere past the first set of mountains." Enoch explains not turning around to face Jennifer, so he doesn't crack from seeing her facial expression.

"So, you think I want to be in charge of a tribe?" Jennifer asks tears streaming down her face.

"No, I don't think you want that at all. I only say I want somewhat of a tribe, so my children have the discipline of being raised in a tribe without the hassle of actually being in a tribe. My parents tried to replicate it, but I am the opposite of a tribesmen. I hate being in a pack of other men patrolling the perimeter in the most dangerous section of the territory. I want to take you with, but most squads are a max of four people unless Angus here wants to not do the adventuring and let the four of us do the jobs then risk his reputation. I also would be risking my reputation as I haven't seen you on a mercenary job. The two I said have saved my skin more times than I can count on jobs where we fought off shadow bears and hordes of rabid green skins." Enoch explains turning to face Jennifer.

"Actually, with two weres in the group I was going to let you find a final member. I don't particularly want to be associated with so many weres." Angus chimes in trying to not upset the group.

"So, Jennifer it is up to you if you want to go adventuring but before we can do that we need to head to your tribe as I promised your father. When will we have to head out for a job Angus?" Enoch asks slightly scared.

"Well I need to find some clients first so how about we meet up in a couple of weeks and see if I have found any clients." Angus responds thinking he got off scot free for his racism.

"Let's get headed to the tribe den. Jennifer you lead." Enoch says getting up.

Now outside. The girls are around Enoch. "You are just going to work for that racist pig?!" Alice asks severely upset trying not to cry.

"Can we not do this in public? I don't know how much of this town has the same view as him." Enoch responds calmly.

"Enoch is right. This town does have the same view as him. Let's get moving." Jennifer says looking at Alice.

"So, we are just going to ignore how he treated us?" Alice asks trying to get the discussion done now.

"Ally cat, do you want to be chased out of a town for something beyond your control? This town doesn't exactly like our kind. Let's not make a scene so they have a reason to throw us out before we have the finances to leave." Enoch responds grabbing Alice by her face and trying to talk to her.

"Are you even phased by the racism?" Alice asks meekly.

"I absolutely hate it. I just know when a battle is worth fighting. Right now, this battle isn't worth fighting. Let's get a move on and we can lament about this later." Enoch responds kissing Alice on the lips.

Now at Jennifer's den the group arrive to spears drawn and threats of violence. "You are not welcome here!" the guard yells pointing a spear at Enoch.

"Why is that? I was invited by Jennifer's father to your tribal den. Unless he was lying to me on me being welcome. If I needed, I could classify this as a declaration of war on the tribes back in Koftan and have them here to wipe each and every one of you off this planet." Enoch responds not even budging as the spear keeps getting closer to his throat.

"You should be welcome. Let me go see what is going on." Jennifer says trying to pass the line of guards.

"You aren't allowed to cross! Stand back!" The guard yells stabbing Jennifer's shoulder with a spear.

"You just fucked up!" Enoch screams before going grim state and biting the guards throat out. Enoch doesn't stop there he kills every guard that comes running and when his father comes running out Enoch is too far gone so he just growls at him and attempts to lunge at him.

"Down son! What is going on!?" Enoch's father asks dodging his son's attacks.

"The guards wouldn't let us through. One stabbed me and Enoch lost it." Jennifer says showing the wound on her shoulder.

"So, he is in protection mode. Why did he have to choose his grim state to go into protection mode?" Enoch's father asks annoyed.

"Wait! There is a werewolf grim? I thought it was reserved for the Werecats!?" Jennifer responds shocked.

"Crouch down Jennifer. Let him lick your wound. He needs blood of his dearly beloved that caused him to go into protection mode. There is a grim for both werecats and werewolves. I used to be the werewolf grim. Then he got old enough to use it so I lost my ability to use it." Enoch's father says still dodging attacks.

"Come here, sweetie. You need to calm down if you want to finalize our imprint." Jennifer says as she kneels down to Enoch's level.

Enoch starts licking her wound while pushing her over, so she is laying on her back. Once Jennifer is knocked over and Enoch is hovering over her he returns to his human state. "I am sorry I went overboard. That has been building for a while. I haven't let my were state go crazy in a long time." Enoch softly whispers in Jennifer's ear while embracing her.

"You have been ignoring your were states boy?!" Enoch's father says annoyed.

"I have been avoiding all things were related for the past 10 years. I didn't want this curse. I was born to a curse that is two times worse than yours. If I could, I would give up this curse in a heartbeat. I hate that if I let my secret slip in most mortal towns, I will be run out of said town. I don't want to be homeless because of something beyond my control. I hate being a were." Enoch responds standing up and pulling Jennifer to her feet.

"Not again!" Alice exclaims angrily.

"How much of what you said last night was a lie?!" Jennifer screams facing Enoch.

"My love is for your personality not for your abilities. If you don't see your were abilities a curse, then I don't see them as a curse for you. I have lost many jobs because my status of a were gets revealed. I have lost thousands of platinum because of the fact that I am a were. I don't like being known as a were despite I avoid letting the monster loose. Only time I let that monster loose is to kill off a few weres who upset me to the point my chains holding him in crumble." Enoch responds calmly.

"Wow! You really hate our kind. Can I go inside?" Jennifer asks turning to Enoch's father.

"I have nowhere to go. Can I follow her?" Alice asks meekly.

"Go you two. You are not welcome here till you can come to terms with the were inside of you. Take your dwarf with you." Enoch's father says before turning back to the entrance of the den and going in.

"You really had to tell them how you feel now of all times. Now we are out two people for our team." Yennifer says facing Enoch.

"I – I – I... Welp what do we do now?" Enoch asks defeatedly.

"We rented that room for a week. We have the rest of that week to figure out what we do now. In that time, you can either come to terms with your demons or chalk up the whole were community as a loss and move on with me. I plan to find a way to leave this town and continue our search for my ancestral home. Let's get heading back to the tavern." Yennifer responds before turning to the way they came.

"I am sorry that I have failed you." Enoch says meekly.

"You haven't failed me. You failed those two girls. Only way you fail me is if you ditch me for your kind." Yennifer responds not turning around.

"WAIT! WHY ARE YOU LEAVING?!" Maria screams trying to follow the two who just keep walking ignoring her as Alice and Jennifer come running after her and drag her kicking and screaming back into the den.

Now back at the tavern the duo are at the bar. "I heard you have been cast out from your kind for expressing how you feel about your abilities. You still want a job here?" Angus asks sitting down next to Enoch.

"I want a ship out of this country. Don't care the destination just anywhere but Koftan and as far from here as possible." Enoch responds no emotion in his tone what so ever.

"Enoch! What about us!?" Yennifer yells from the other side of Enoch.

"I feel dead inside. I think of our future I feel nothing. I don't agree with imprints at all. However, I lost my other half due to my words today. I felt complete with one of those girls around. Now I feel empty. No emotions. Nothing but emptiness. I am sorry I pulled you into my actions. I don't feel anything for you. Haven't since we had our first moment of intimacy a couple months ago." Enoch says colder than the tops of the Shivering Mountains.

"Enoch! Please say just kidding! PLEASE!" Yennifer yells as tears start streaming down her face.

"I feel nothing when I think of our future." Enoch says turning to reveal his eyes have gone almost black from being so dark of a brown.

"I can't do that Enoch. You have issues you have to deal with here. I don't offer people an escape from their problems if I know they have problems. You are on your own boyo." Angus chimes in before walking away.

"I can't believe I thought you actually cared but no it was just a façade so you could use me for your benefits. I wish I hadn't bumped into you in that forest all those years ago. Think my life would be better as a sex slave. Bartender! How much for a small room with a single bed?" Yennifer responds to Enoch before turning to the bartender.

"1 silver. I am sorry for your loss." The bartender says looking at Yennifer.

"Enoch, can I have all my money?" Yennifer asks looking at Enoch as he gets up and handing her his only coin bag.

"Where I am going, I don't need it. Take my room. I am going to figure out my life. Goodbye, Yennifer." Enoch says before leaving the tavern with his only bag of stuff.

Chapter 8

Eleven months have passed, and Enoch has just arrived in a little village known by the locals as OxenDe-Valley. Sitting in the local pub Enoch is sitting at the bar when he feels a tap on the shoulder. He looks to his shoulder. "Over here old man." A woman says sitting on the opposite side.

"I am not old." Enoch responds softly.

"You look older than me. Name is Maria. You new here too?" Maria says offering a hand to Enoch.

"I don't give my name out that easily. Been ran out of town just for saying my name." Enoch responds ignoring the woman calling herself Maria holding her hand out.

"You sound familiar. Like a gentleman who saved my life when I was less than 10 years old. I am 19 now. Last I saw him he was walking away with a dwarf like 11 months ago while my sister and someone else dragged me away kicking and screaming." Maria explains staring at the door on the other side of the bar.

"Why are you following me? I need time to figure out who I really am. I have only the money to afford myself a meal every couple of days so I can survive when I am in a town." Enoch responds glancing at Maria revealing his eyes to her.

"Why do you look like you have nothing left to live for? You have imprinted on 5 females 3 of which wish you would return to us?" Maria asks looking right into Enoch's eyes as the black seems to be getting darker.

"I have nothing to live for. I hate what I was born into. I felt nothing when I finalized my commitment with the dwarf. I haven't felt anything since then. Only feelings I have are hatred and sorrow. Haven't felt happy once in my life." Enoch responds as an orc sits on his other side.

"If I were you two, I would take that conversation elsewhere. Your kind aren't actually too popular round here. My kind aren't liked but we haven't caused issue in this town unlike your kind." The Orc says before grabbing his beer and walking away.

"I have a room upstairs. If you want a soft bed to sleep in just say something." Maria says getting up before Enoch grabs her arm.

"Please." Enoch says looking right at Maria.

Now up in Maria's room. "The main bed is mine. You can have the smaller one if you aren't comfortable sharing a bed with someone of our kind. I do still care. That is why I have been looking for you. I heard this place is the mercenary capital of the region so I figured you would end up here at some point." Maria explains as Enoch walks up to the smaller bed.

"Thank you, Maria. You've changed a lot in these past 11 months. I didn't recognize you." Enoch says taking his shirt off revealing his scar covered back.

"You haven't changed much visually. I will be downstairs for a little while. Too early for me to sleep. Sleep well, E." Maria responds before leaving and closing the door.

Sometime later Enoch wakes up with Maria climbing in the bigger bed making noise. "Thank you, Maria. If you want to join me just say something." Enoch says just loud enough for Maria to hear him.

"If you want some company just come up here. That mattress is too hard for me." Maria responds patting the spot next to her as she hears Enoch get up.

"You are the one person I was kind of hopeful would find me to be honest." Enoch says lying down next to Maria.

"Thank you, E. I was hoping I would find you before the other two. They want to kill you." Maria responds sliding up behind Enoch and spooning with him.

"Why are you calling me just the first letter of my first name?" Enoch asks as he feels Maria trying to put her left arm under his head.

"You brought up being chased out for your name being said." Maria responds before snuggling with Enoch.

"Let's get some sleep." Enoch says melting into Maria's embrace.

Chapter 9

The next morning Enoch awakes to a nude Maria standing in the doorway to the bathroom of her room. He is for the first time in over 10 years is seeing Maria completely naked. "Where did you get the scar on your back?" Enoch asks climbing out of bed.

"Punishment for chasing after you the last time I saw you. You want to take a bath, E?" Maria asks turning to face Enoch as he gets to her.

"Sure. I am sorry that I have caused you so much pain." Enoch responds touching another one of Maria's scars.

"That one is from the war. Also, technically your fault. Most of my scars are side effects of your actions. Kind of weird you have caused me literal pain, yet I would give up everything to be with you in a way you have probably written off as never going to happen with anyone of our kind. I just wish things had gone down differently." Maria explains looking up at Enoch with her azure eyes.

"I haven't written off all of our kind. If you had expressed interest last night when you came to bed, I would have agreed to it. Doesn't mean I would say no now because you didn't take the opportunity last night. I just would ask we hold off on the bath till after the fun. Now I think we should make our decision. Fun now or get on with our lives. I need to make some money so I can head out of this town. I am looking to leave to the northern inland sea. I don't want to be down here if they are looking for me here." Enoch responds gently moving a strand of hair out of Maria's eyes.

"I was hoping we could travel together. I don't want to lose you again, E." Maria says as a tear falls from her right eye.

"I know I said I travel alone but you may be the best companion in this point in my life. If you want to stay with me then maybe you can show me where to find a job here that accepts our kind." Enoch responds before kissing Maria on the lips.

"Well that knowingly accept our kind there are none to my knowledge. Which is why we both need to take a bath. You hated me 11 months ago for faking my death against my will and now you reveal that you would go to bed with me." Maria says letting out a slight chuckle as Enoch puts a hand on her lower back.

"I didn't hate you. I was terrified of if your older sister found out you were very much so alive. I have seen your grave. If they knew you were alive, they would exile anyone who knew on top of exiling you and make all those who got exiled kill on sight. I didn't want to die for knowing you are still alive. At this point if I do die, I want you by my side. I realize we all die alone but at least I can do it with someone I love by my side." Enoch explains giving Maria a loving squeeze.

"Let's get taking our baths. Fun can wait till we're on the road. By the way the scar on my right breast I keep spotting you looking at was to mark me as an enemy of the were tribe here in Jraconia. So, no I don't see us doing the naked tango as finalizing my imprint. I just see it as an opportunity to show that I love the man I am giving my virginity to." Maria responds smiling as she releases Enoch so they can take a bath.

"Can we take our baths at the same time?" Enoch asks meekly enjoying the view of Maria's naked body in front of him as she bends over to check the water temperature.

"Sure, E. I think you should just refer to me as M from now on. They might have spies listening for both of our names." Maria responds knowing that her bottom is being watched by a very horny Enoch.

Sometime later the freshly bathed couple are seated downstairs in a dark room waiting for the boss to come in when the door opens. "The boss doesn't feel like doing his meeting in here. He is at the bar." A male dwarf voice says from the door.

Now out at the bar. "So, I will employ you two one last time to get you enough money to move on from here." The orc from last night says sitting on the other side of the bar.

"Wait you are the boss here?!" Maria asks shocked.

"I thought you have been working for someone here?" Enoch asks looking right at Maria.

"She has with my underlings who didn't realize she is what she is. I wouldn't have realized if it weren't for you last night and your stink. She has been working here for past 2 months doing small jobs around town to cover her room fare and bar tab. This job will pay in coin. 50 platinum each. You can take it and split or do whatever you two want with your lives as I don't care to interfere." The orc explains looking right at Enoch. "Ok not true. I know what it is like to have your face on wanted posters and have those who you think won't rat you out do just that. I saw a young girl putting posters up outside the tavern with you two's faces on them. I had my employees take them down on my property, but I can't protect you two anymore. Here are some masks. Wear your cloaks with the hood up and keep your face covered as best as you can. In the bag with the item you are to transport is your pay. Don't come back. Deliver the product and keep moving. Go where they hopefully won't find either of you. I would

normally send any outgoing mercenaries with someone to help if a fight arises but for this situation that
is probably the worst thing, I can do right now for you
two." The orc continues sliding everything across the
bar.

"Thank you, boss. Any chance of us getting some
food?" Maria asks meekly.

"Not this time sorry. For your safety I would get
everything you can carry from your room and get out
of town as soon as possible. I have reserved the whole
tavern for the next hour. So, you have that long before
people to potentially rat you out show up. M and E
good luck!" the orc responds with a hint of worry in his
voice.

Now on the outskirts of OxenDeValley the duo are
walking as Enoch's stomach grumbles louder than a
shadow bear roar. "We need to get food, or your stomach is going to give our position away!" Maria says with
a slight bit of panic in her tone.

"Let's hope we don't attract a dragon." Enoch responds meekly as his stomach pain is just about reaching crippling levels of pain.

"You actually believed that old coots lie?!" Maria
asks before bursting out laughing.

Maria is laughing as a dragon flies over their head
and it turns around to potentially attack the duo.

"You were saying?!" Enoch says pulling his spear off
his back.

"You think a spear is going to kill that thing!?" Maria asks fear rising in her voice.

"I have killed a dragon or two with this. The scar I felt you staring at last night is from my first round with a dragon. I didn't manage to kill it, but I did cut off a leg. Made this spear out of its bones." Enoch responds as the three-legged dragon lands in front of them.

"So, is this the dragon who you stole it's leg?" Maria asks terror showing in her voice.

"Maybe I am going to run right you go left if it follows me then it is in fact the one that these bones belong to." Enoch responds bolting right which the dragon does in fact follow him blasting fire balls at him every couple seconds. Enoch stops to send a blast of his own at the dragon drawing the magic from the bone spear. The blue fire ball Enoch lobbed at the dragon makes contact causing the dragon to let out a roar of agony as its front left leg separates from its body with a shower of bloody mist. As the dragon inhales to lob another fire blast Enoch sends another blue fire ball in its mouth causing its throat to explode separating its head from its body.

"When did you learn magic?!" Maria asks as she gets showered in dragon blood.

"When I killed my first dragon, I learned to draw the ability to use magic from the bones I use as a spear." Enoch responds as he starts cutting away at the dragon carcass.

"What are you doing to the corpse?" Maria asks looking at Enoch like he grew a third head.

"Their meat is some of the best I have ever had the privilege to eat. When you are wandering aimlessly and you down a dragon you will eat whatever you can get your hands on. I have no problem eating meat of the workhorse. I prefer the meat of the human work-horses." Enoch explains as he continues cutting off chunks of dragon meat and tossing them in a bag.

"Workhorse meat?" Maria asks confused.

"Some would call me a cannibal. However, as I said you will eat whatever you can get your hands on when you are starving. Never eaten were in my human state. As a were when I rip out another were's throat I tend to just swallow it. I haven't gone were in 11 months though. I hate how I feel as a were." Enoch explains as he ties of his bag of meat.

"We need to get you out of the savage mindset. You can't go around eating the other races just because you got hungry" Maria responds shaking her head.

"Have you ever been stuck in the lost village in the Shivering Mountains and all the meat on sale is workhorse meat?" Enoch asks looking at Maria like she hasn't ever suffered from starvation before.

"You found the lost village? Rumors are it is like an oasis in the mountains where all food grows just fine so why would they have a lack of animals to eat? I don't think you found the village if you couldn't buy animal flesh." Maria responds skeptical.

"The rumors of the place being able to grow enough food to feed the animals is as false as it gets. They only still live there because of the non-stop blizzards. I made it out because I couldn't survive staying there." Enoch says waiting for Maria to get moving.

Now at their delivery location. "What is the password?" The recipient asks.

"Move on, M. Escape away, E." Enoch responds seriously.

"Ok hand me the bag. Then you two follow the password." The recipient says as Maria hands him the bag.

Now near the northern shore and the second sun is getting ready to set. "What do we do now that we are at the lands end?" Maria asks as if she has no clue.

"See that boat? I paid for an individual in the time I have been travelling here to get me a boat with the supplies to make it anywhere on the coast of the inland sea." Enoch responds smiling at Maria.

"Well I guess let's get a move on. Maybe we should spend the rest of the night on the boat and set off just as the first sun starts to rise." Maria says running to the boat.

Now on the boat the duo are in the captain's quarters laying on the bed with Maria on top pinning Enoch to the bed. "I didn't think we would actually make it out of OxenDeValley. I would have figured they would have found us." Maria says looking down at Enoch in the lantern light.

"I figured the dragon would try to kill you before me. So where should we go tomorrow? I honestly hope the person I asked to buy me a boat and the supplies isn't here tomorrow. I don't know what she'd think of you and I." Enoch responds moving his right index finger in circles on the small of Maria's back.

"Who did you have buy you the boat?" Maria asks dreamily as she yawns fighting the urge to doze off.

"Yennifer. I gave her my coin purse with a note asking if she could do this for me. She was to leave the key to the door in a secure location in OxenDeValley. I got the key before I went to the tavern." Enoch explains also yawning. "Do you want to have some fun tonight?" Enoch asks after finishing yawning.

"I think sleeping would be a good idea. Can you spoon me tonight?" Maria asks sliding off Enoch.

"Sure thing, M." Enoch responds rolling on his side to embrace Maria.

Chapter 10

The next morning there is a pounding on the door waking the duo up. "Mask on, E." Maria says quietly reminding Enoch.

"Hey, may I ask what you are doing in my boat?!" Yennifer asks not recognizing Enoch.

"Yeny, I have the key you left for me in OxenDeValley." Enoch responds holding the key up.

"Oh, it is you. I heard a female voice that didn't sound completely familiar." Yennifer says embarrassed.

"That would be, M." Enoch responds patting Yennifer on the shoulder.

"Who?" Yennifer asks confused.

"With Alice and Jennifer looking for me I can't use full names of those who help me." Enoch explains looking down at Yennifer.

"So is M ...?" Yennifer asks still confused.

"M is the individual you witnessed me patching up and overreacted about." Enoch explains looking around. "If you want to keep talking come in." Enoch continues.

"If it is ok with M I would honestly like to join you on the voyage." Yennifer responds meekly.

"I am not even going to ask her because I don't want you coming along myself. I am on a journey to find myself. I realize I am bringing someone from my past with M, but I didn't really know her, so I am getting to know her along the way. It is like I never really knew, M." Enoch says trying not to upset Yennifer too much as she did do as Enoch asked.

"I understand. It was worth a shot asking. Good luck you two. I hope to bump into you in the future, E." Yennifer says before leaving.

Chapter 11

The duo are coming up on the port city on the coast of West Jraconer. "Land, ho!" Maria exclaims excitedly.

"Get dressed, M!" Enoch yells as he throws the anchor overboard to slow the ship.

"Will do, Captain E!" Maria exclaims excitedly before running below deck.

Now moored up and Enoch is heading down the gang plank with his mask on as he felt like something was off when a masked individual keeps blocking his path down on to the docks. Enoch gets backed up onto the deck. Enoch not wanting to allow the individual to progress drops to his knees and puts his hands behind his back. "You aren't that hard to find when you betray your ex lover's trust." The masked individual says crossing their arms across their chest.

Enoch doesn't speak as he doesn't want to give to much away.

"We know there is another were on your boat! They might as well just come up and join us in the conversation since you refuse to speak." The individual says the annoyance showing in their voice.

Maria has detected that there is trouble. "Stay down there. Lock yourself in our room." Enoch says telepathically.

"If she isn't coming up then I will just send someone who would love to get their hands on her. Can't promise she'll survive." The individual says as annoyance turns into anger.

Maria doesn't listen to Enoch as she comes up on deck and takes the same position as Enoch. Maria is wearing her mask as she knows keeping her face covered may do nothing if it is in fact Alice and Jennifer here on the dock, but it will help if it isn't.

"Good the estranged sister has some smarts after all. Alice, get them!" the masked individual yells excitedly.

Alice grabs the duo's hands and forces them to their feet. "You two should have just turned yourselves in at OxenDeValley. Or at least let the dwarf come with you. She ratted saying Enoch failed her when he chose Maria over her." Alice says twisting the duo's hands to get them to walk.

Enoch makes a noise in agony from his wrist being twisted. He coils a little knocking Alice off balance. Maria breaks free putting a dagger to Alice's throat while holding her right arm in a position if she struggles her wrist will break. Enoch dodges the masked individual's attempts to grab him. Placing the tip of his dagger in the individuals back between the fifth and fourth lumbar. Grabbing the masked individual's shoulder and pulling so the blade is starting to dig into their flesh.

"Why did I think the two relatives could get the fugitives under control!?" Jennifer yells walking up the gang plank.

"One more step and I will cut her throat!" Maria screams pressing the dagger into Alice's throat.

"You would kill your own flesh and blood?!" Jennifer asks stopping.

"I won't but he will permanently paralyze his father from the waist down." Maria responds initially faking out by lowering the dagger before she changes her mind and slits Alice's throat.

"BITCH!" Alice screams before collapsing and dying.

"You said you wouldn't do that?! Why did you slit your own sister's throat?!" Jennifer asks screaming.

"My sister would have flinched at me putting the knife to her throat that doppelganger didn't even flinch." Maria responds licking the blood from her dagger.

"Release your father and we can talk. That was your sister you just killed." Jennifer says tossing the shackles she had on her hip in the water down below.

"Meh one less person to compete with for E's affection." Maria responds sheathing her dagger as she looks up from her sisters gasping corpse.

"Why should he trust you?" Enoch's father asks knowing what his son was about to say.

"I wasn't going to kill either of them and you know that Zeke! There is another war started by casting him out! He must have sent a letter to the Koftan tribes!" Jennifer yells pissed off.

"I haven't done anything of the such though they were expecting Alice and I to return so they probably started gathering the forces to invade when we didn't return from a mission on the coast of the ocean Jraconia and Koftan share." Enoch responds pushing his father away.

"Thank you, son." Zeke says meekly as he stumbles forward.

"Why are you thanking me? M is the crazy one between us. I may be considered a cannibal, but I can't kill another person unless they harm those I love." Enoch responds with a dead stare.

"C-Cannibal?!" Zeke asks terrified.

"When the only meat available is workhorse meat you eat what is available or you starve. Go to the market and ask for the cheapest meat they have, and they will probably sell you the meat of a dead slave labeled as workhorse meat or worse as horse meat. I specify workhorse so they know I am not going to make a stink if I find a finger." Enoch explains still with a dead stare.

"I am working on him for that. What is the issue that makes you drop wanting to kill us?" Maria says rushing to Enoch's side.

"A war back in my home turf. This time he was easy to find. Follow the improperly disposed of dragon carcasses. Plus, betraying Yennifer made her more than willing to rat on him." Jennifer responds smiling.

"I never told her where we were going. Mostly because we didn't even know where we were headed. Also didn't really trust her. In the eleven months she could have made a deal with you to rat me out when I showed up. Which she must have done if she told that we left South Jraconia." Enoch says zoning out mid thought.

"I never agreed to anything prior to you failing me. That is right you failed me Enoch of the unnamed Village on the edge of the forest of the weres." Yennifer says walking up the gang plank.

"I have failed somebody..." Enoch says softly dropping his dagger on the ground before staggering back tripping over Alice's dead body and landing square on his back bashing his head on the deck of the ship.

"No, you haven't, E!" Maria exclaims rushing to Enoch.

"I have failed. I failed Alice, Yennifer, Marley, Jennifer, you, most importantly my own mother. I shouldn't have run off in the first place." Enoch responds still on the floor as a purple glow starts emanating from him.

Alice all of a sudden gasps before coughing up blood. "Why are you laying on my legs?!" Alice asks looking at Enoch.

"How is she alive?!" Jennifer yells.

"I wasn't alive?" Alice asks confused as Enoch stands up as the glow fades.

"I brought her back so that I haven't failed her and Marley." Enoch responds offering a hand to Alice.

"Wait you can use magic?!" Jennifer asks yelling.

"Quiet about it. It is against the law in most places around the world. Don't know about here but I would assume it is also illegal here." Enoch says softly as Alice hugs him.

"So, you do care?" Alice whispers in Enoch's ear.

"This past year has taught me many things. Not just what one will do when you are hungry enough but that I may hate my were doesn't mean I should hold it against other weres for not hating theirs." Enoch responds quietly enjoying Alice's embrace.

"So, does this mean you will come back with us to the den?" Alice asks releasing Enoch.

"No, I will however write a message to go back with you stating that I have left of my own accord. I want to work on myself some more. M you are welcome to come along." Enoch responds smiling at Alice.

"I am not leaving your side!" Alice exclaims with a pouting look on her face.

"Now that I think of it, I don't think you can safely until you go were. Your body is filled with the essence of the undead currently. Could you go were for me?" Enoch responds looking at Alice funny.

"I don't want to leave your side. I didn't think you cared enough to commit a crime against the gods which you just disproved me. I am as I was prior to my little sister killing me. The memory just took a minute to process because of how successful she was at cutting my throat. I don't want to go were. I haven't since you left that day a year ago." Alice says meekly.

"Not putting your weres energy to use is dangerous. That is why I use the powers of the occult. I use my were energies to do things like I just did with you." Enoch responds looking at Alice worriedly.

"Ok fine!" Alice exclaims before going werecat. Her fur is now completely black unlike the mostly white she was prior, and her eyes are so red they look like they are glowing.

"Uh is she supposed to look like that?" Jennifer asks kind of terrified.

"No, she is not supposed to look like that. What did you do?" Zeke responds looking at Enoch.

"I called in a favor with gods of life and death. They don't exactly like to listen every time if you don't offer something of equal value. I offered a part of my were powers. They seem to have taken my grim and made it a werecat grim for her." Enoch explains cutting his hand and holding it out to Alice.

Alice takes Enoch's whole hand in her mouth. "Don't!" Maria screams unsheathing her dagger and getting ready to kill Alice for a second time.

"Leave her be! Ally Cat, please let me keep my hand. I know I haven't treated you the best, so you have every right to bite my hand off, but I know that is not what you want to do with your renewed life. You would much prefer to return to your normal mode and continue with your life." Enoch says softly brushing Alice's fur.

"No, I would rather finalize my imprint. NOW!" Alice says telepathically.

"I can't do that. I have given up on the were path. I was hoping they would take the ability to go were away from me completely." Enoch responds as Alice bites down on his arm causing a crunch and a spray of blood across the deck of the ship before Maria does as she wanted and slits Alice's throat again.

"Can you pull your mangled arm out of her?!" Maria asks scared.

"Yeah She didn't get it to completely detach." Enoch responds in agony.

"I know you hate being a were, but you need to transform if you want to keep your arm, son!" Zeke yells looking at his son who is rolling on the floor in pain.

"He is right, E." Maria says looking into Enoch's eyes as they are tearing up.

"I am trying but I don't think I can!" Enoch yells as a glow leaves Alice's corpse. Enoch inhales and the glow enters his mouth. He instantly turns into his grim state, kind of. He is a werecat grim with glowing yellow eyes.

"Wait he is supposed to be the werewolf grim I thought?!" Jennifer asks scared.

"He has dabbled with the arcane he could have messed up his were states." Zeke responds as Maria cuts her hand and holds it out to Enoch. Enoch licks Maria's hand and pushes her over before turning back into his normal mode.

"Why would you stick your hand out for him to potentially bite it off!" Jennifer yells rushing forward before Enoch turns normal.

"I have had relations with him, so he is attuned to me. To my knowledge him and Alice hadn't done it yet. Plus, it wouldn't be the first time his actions have harmed me. I just keep letting him do things that cause me physical harm." Maria responds enjoying Enoch's embrace.

"What does she mean it wouldn't be the first time he has hurt her?" Yennifer asks chiming in.

"If E will let me get up, I can show you the scars I have received for his actions in one way or another." Maria responds running her fingers through Enoch's hair before he starts getting up. Now standing up she turns away from the group and drops her cloak to the floor before taking her shirt off revealing the scar on her back. "I received that for chasing after you two when he said he hated his were. The one on my leg is from the trap I got caught in because of the first war that Zeke saved me from death. Then I have a bunch of scars I would prefer not to show off in personal places from various things for being linked to him. There is one I can show on my front here on my right breast is because of me insisting on not wanting to find and kill E but instead wanting to help him." Maria continues showing each place she talks about including turning to face the group with a mix of her shirt and hands covering her nipples when talking about the scar on her breast.

"If his actions keep hurting you why do you keep running to him?" Zeke asks surprised.

"Why do you his father keep single despite his mother is dead if you absolutely hated her?" Maria responds with a question.

"Because I was bound to her by tribe law. That isn't why you run back to my son." Zeke responds annoyed.

"I keep coming back to your son because I believe in fate. Every time we get separated some force brings him to me. Why fight that force?" Maria says as Enoch hugs her from the front, so she quits holding her bosom as it is hidden behind him.

"M I don't mean to hurt you. I am sorry for the pain I have caused you. I love you." Enoch says meekly in Maria's ear.

"We have talked about this, E. I wouldn't change a thing in this world with our relationship. I am happy to be yours. I don't know what I would do if you hadn't saved me from Alice all those years ago." Maria responds embracing Enoch.

"Can we get that letter written so we can leave you two to yourselves?" Jennifer asks looking at the scene of the two holding each other and confessing their feelings.

"You guys go down onto the dock. I will help Maria get her shirt back on." Enoch says lifting his head, so it is no longer resting on Maria's forehead.

Now down on the dock the three are watching as Enoch has Alice's corpse on his shoulder. "Why are you carrying her?" Jennifer asks annoyed.

"Her body needs to make it back to Koftan. Here is a note to include with it. Father, could you deliver it? Oh, and give this note to her assigned bed buddy." Enoch says handing his father Alice's corpse with some notes which have who they go to written on them.

"He can't return to Koftan or he will be killed!" Jennifer exclaims.

"Not if he mentions his brother is a part of your tribe. He was severely injured, so he went to be with his brother to recover and he forgot he needed to return back to Koftan." Enoch says coldly.

"You think more like an alpha than you let on, don't you?" Zeke asks looking at his son.

"Well considering three of the 4 weres I have imprinted on are daughters of their tribe's alpha I kind of pick things up." Enoch responds just as cold as ever.

"Why are you so cold even to your father?" Jennifer asks kind of annoyed.

"Have you witnessed the death of someone you love? Twice?" Enoch responds looking right at Jennifer but not really it is like he is looking through her.

"No, I haven't witnessed anyone I care about die. What does that have to do with being a dick to your father?" Jennifer asks confused.

"Stare death in the face someday. You will lose the ability to feel anything other than despair and anger." Enoch responds as he starts walking towards town.

"Slow down I didn't know you were going to start walking." Maria says struggling to keep up.

Now in the nearest tavern Enoch and Maria are wearing their masks as the other two are bickering over who is going to write the note down. "You realize that unless it is in my writing, they probably aren't going to believe it?" Enoch asks annoyed with Yennifer and Jennifer fighting.

"Why didn't you say that sooner?!" Jennifer asks pissed off.

"Because you two came in arguing like an old couple. I assume my father is disrespecting my wishes for Alice's body." Enoch responds sighing.

"No, he went to the person who brought us here to return to Koftan. He doesn't want to disrespect you even though you are his son." Jennifer says meekly.

"I am closer to becoming alpha than you will ever be. You forced your way onto me that night. M and I had relations willingly. He sees that I am the most likely to take the alpha seat of the weres here. Now while I refuse to return to Koftan for fear that I will be pulled into the alpha seat if M wanted to go back to Koftan I would accompany her gladly." Enoch responds grabbing the piece of paper and the quill. "Do you have any ink?" Enoch asks quickly.

"No, we don't." Yennifer responds watching as Enoch takes the sharp point of the quill and stabs the tip of his left index finger and starts writing.

"Dear alphas,

I am very much so on this journey of my own accord. I would like it if you would quit wasting the lives of weres thinking they cast me out. I am on a journey of self-discovery because I realized what I want, and my actions didn't exactly line up. Please quit declaring war because I decide I want to go off on an adventure.

Sincerely,

Enoch."

"There take this to the front line. I am for this moment in time done dealing with the whims of the tribes." Enoch says handing Jennifer the letter.

"It was nice doing business with you. Sorry for your loss." Jennifer says getting up and bowing to Maria.

"Can I come with you?!" Yennifer asks desperately.

"No, please go to your ancestral home like we once planned to. I am going to keep journeying with M." Enoch responds getting ready to leave the tavern with Maria.

Now back on the boat Enoch is scrubbing the deck trying to lift the blood. "I thought you wanted to try being a mercenary here?" Maria asks confused.

"I do but I need to process my emotions on Alice actually being dead. I made a deal with the gods of life and death to revive her and she still ended up dead. That hurts to know I couldn't do anything to keep her alive. I thought I could save her. She was the one I actually wanted to try and be an alpha with. She was the first were I thought I had a future with. I realize I met you first, but you disappeared and were presumed dead. I mourned you. However, it didn't feel like you were actually dead. I saw Alice die twice today. I know she is dead. I just can't believe I lost her. I loved her. I will miss her. I don't know what to do now. Life without her in this world is something I had hoped to never have to experience." Enoch explains as tears are streaming down his face.

"I miss her too. But we need to get moving with our lives." Maria responds trying to comfort Enoch.

"You miss her? You didn't show any regret when you slit her throat the first time let alone the second time?! How can you say you miss her when you didn't show any emotion when you are the one who killed her the first time for no reason?!" Enoch asks raising his voice pushing Maria away from him.

"She was my sister. There are negative emotions between siblings. In the moment I was full of hatred for her hurting your wrist." Maria responds defensively as she tries not to fall from being pushed.

"She didn't hurt me. I acted that way to get free. You killed her without hesitation. I get the second time she was trying to destroy my arm. The first time she was at your mercy and you said you weren't going to kill her, yet you did it anyway. Why do you lie to me about your feelings for your sister?!" Enoch asks as he keeps walking towards Maria as she keeps backing up.

"Do you want to know how she treated me after you disappeared before the war?!" Maria responds finally getting angry.

"How did she treat you that made her deserve to die?" Enoch asks looking at Maria as he stops walking forwards.

"The most common thing she said was that I would not see you ever again. That you didn't want me because you thought I was a non were in trouble and you only patched me up once you found out I am a were because you didn't want to seem like a horrible person. Honestly I had started to believe her when I decided to set off to find you and prove her wrong which is how I ended up in the trap that she found me in then when I sent her to get help your father bloodied and battered got my leg free and took me to see his brother for help to try and help me both to survive and to find you. I have more emotional scars caused by her because I wanted to believe you would return for me. Honestly after almost a decade that wears on a person and they start to resent those who have repetitively been belittling them and when the opportunity to take all that pent-up rage out on their tormentor comes, they take the chance. I did anyway. I don't regret doing it either!" Maria responds as she starts screaming pushing Enoch with each breath she takes.

"I am sorry I upset you. I didn't realize just how horribly she treated you." Enoch says dropping to his knees in the spot where Alice collapsed when Maria first slit her throat.

"Why is it whenever you get yelled at you drop to your knees?!" Maria asks angrily.

"Whenever I got yelled at on the streets as a child, I would be physically assaulted, so I drop to my knees to take my beatings." Enoch responds looking at the ground beneath him.

"Get up! Finish cleaning and let's figure out our strategy to make a living in this highly foreign land." Maria says holding a handout to Enoch causing him to flinch.

"Sorry thought you were going to hit me, M. Can we just take a day to relax? I realize that is basically all we did on the way here, but I am emotionally drained today." Enoch asks meekly as he takes Maria's hand to help him get up.

"I am fine with that. Today was a lot more hectic than we expected." Maria says hugging Enoch.

"I expected them to find us but not for what happened to happen. I just want to have some stew and to cuddle and hang out with my, M." Enoch responds enjoying Maria's warm embrace.

"I wouldn't mind some nice dragon stew and a bottle of mead or two. Maybe some activities that don't require clothing. Maybe even some exercise to see who is more fit before some more exercise where we make sure the other feels good. Maybe falling asleep in each other's warm loving embrace." Maria says meekly while playing with some of Enoch's chest hair that is sticking out of his shirt.

"I would love that, M. Almost as much as I love you." Enoch responds looking at Maria's face causing her to blush.

Chapter 12

The next day the duo are at the tavern trying to find a job that allows weres. "So, I hear you two are looking for an employer? What would you two bring to a team?" The bartender asks while polishing a glass.

"We are both weres." Enoch says bluntly.

"So, what. I am a were." The bartender responds setting the glass down and turning his fingertips into the claws of a werecat.

"I am both a werecat and werewolf." Enoch says trying to turn his hand into the werewolf hand, but it turns into the werecat grim hand as his eyes turn into the glowing yellow eyes.

"That is just one. Nice eye trick though. How did you do that?" the bartender asks intrigued.

"Permission to go full were?" Enoch asks ignoring the bartender's inquiry.

"Granted." The bartender responds annoyed his request was ignored as Enoch goes werewolf grim with glowing blue eyes.

"He didn't ignore you on the eyes bit. He doesn't know." Maria says chiming in as she unwraps her injured hand and cuts in the same spot as yesterday before holding her hand out for Enoch.

"What are you doing?!" The bartender asks shocked.

"Ever heard of a grim? He went to his werewolf grim. They need blood to return to their normal state. His grim state has taken over both werewolf and werecat states." Maria explains as Enoch licks her hand before returning to his human state.

"What about a full werecat state? You promise both but don't do both?" the bartender asks polishing another glass.

"Give me a minute. The grim state is tough on your body. I have a theory why my eyes glow, but I won't divulge that out in the open like this." Enoch says before going werecat grim with the glowing yellow eyes and jet-black fur.

"Another grim?! Ugh?!" Maria responds unwrapping her injured hand out for Enoch to lick so he can return again.

"Wait he is grim for both? Where are his normal states?" the bartender asks as Enoch transforms into normal state.

"Don't know if I can do normal were states anymore. Again, not explaining that in the open." Enoch responds annoyed as he staggers when he tries to take a step towards the bar.

"Don't fall, E!" Maria exclaims getting ready to catch Enoch in case he falls.

"What is special about you, miss?" the bartender asks looking at Maria.

"Nothing really other than I know how to control him when he is in that state. I am just a werecat alpha's daughter. We are both from Koftan." Maria responds as Enoch collapses into her arms. "Don't worry, E. I've got you." Maria continues softly as she holds Enoch.

"Is he okay?" The bartender asks worriedly.

"Don't know. He has never gone grim twice in such a short amount of time. Last time he went grim it was to heal an obliterated arm. He thought it smart to stick his hand near a hungry shadow bear's mouth and it tried to eat it." Maria responds bending the truth.

"Squirrel and hare stew please?" Enoch asks stumbling over his words.

"What did he just say?" The bartender asks confused.

"2 orders of squirrel and hare stew with 2 pints of mead to go with them." Maria responds helping Enoch onto the stool he was sat on earlier.

"So, if you two are both weres does that mean you two have Y'know?" The bartender asks filling two glasses with mead.

"Yes, we have imprinted. We however have left the were tribe life behind, so we don't care that we are bound to each other. Also, yes we have finalized that as well." Enoch says downing his mead in one gulp.

"Holy! No one has done that before! Your order of stew will be right up." The bartender exclaims shocked.

"Going grim once is draining enough to devour an eight-course meal in 10 minutes and still be starving. Especially if you didn't eat anything in the grim state. Now twice in less than 5 minutes you might just want to bring a pot of that stew for me and start making a fresh pot." Enoch responds as his eyes start looking like they are smoking.

"Uh your eyes they are smoking?!" the bartender says slightly scared as someone from the back does as Enoch said.

"Probably a side effect of the two grim states being used so rapidly. M if you want any you had better get some before, I start ladling some into the bowl they gave me." Enoch responds as his eyes return to normal when he talks to Maria.

"The bowl is for her." The bartender says chuckling.

"Oy! I may be a were, but I am not a savage. Could you give me a bowl?!" Enoch responds angrily as the employee from in the kitchen brings a bowl out.

"Sorry, sir! I couldn't carry everything in one trip! Please forgive me!" the female elf worker exclaims scared.

"What is your name miss?" Enoch asks going from a harsh tone to a gentle tone.

"Ysrafaild. I am sorry if I have angered you enough to make you want me fired!" Ysrafaild responds terrified before she starts slapping her head.

"Oy! Stop that miss! It's not like that at all! You just look familiar like someone I knew back in Koftan. An elven slave girl back in the tavern in my village." Enoch says grabbing Ysrafaild's hand stopping her from hurting herself anymore.

"I used to have a master there!" Ysrafaild exclaims scared.

"Miss, you can take the rest of the day off. You will get your full pay." The bartender says chiming in.

"What did I do to get let off work!?" Ysrafaild asks worried.

"You haven't taken a day off once in the past 6 years you have worked for me so I figured one of your old acquaintances showing up would be as good of reason as any to give you a day off. Talk with him and be happy. Sounds like he cared for you back then." The bartender responds chuckling.

"Ysrafaild, I wouldn't mind catching up with you. I missed you once you had paid off your debt to the tavern owner back in Koftan." Enoch says putting his hand on Ysrafaild's shoulder.

"I paid off her debt and brought her here with the offer if she could find one dish my menu was missing her debt would be paid if she would be the one to make if for a single year. Here we are 6 years later she refuses to take her pay and she still thinks she is a slave. I like to end the cycle of slavery. She was young and shouldn't have been enslaved just because she was born into it." The bartender explains sliding Enoch a slip of paper on how much the bartender is holding for Ysrafaild.

"Ysrafaild, I will buy you a meal if you sit and talk with me. Obviously eat while talking but that is implied." Enoch says looking the young elf in the eyes.

"Why haven't you mentioned an elf girl from your youth prior to this, E?" Maria asks as she finishes her bowl of stew.

"I thought she was sold to someone somewhere I would never end up going. Basically, I figured I would never see her again." Enoch responds as Ysrafaild sits next to him.

"Could I have some of the stew in that pot? I may be the one who introduced it here, but I still love it." Ysrafaild says meekly.

"The pot is kind of empty already. When you weren't looking, I finished it." Enoch responds sheepishly.

"Oh ok. I guess I won't take any food then." Ysrafaild says sadly.

"Wow you are so gullible. While yes the pot is empty, I did save you a bowl. I remember this being your favorite dish when I was young." Enoch responds sliding Ysrafaild a bowl of stew as the bartender hands her a spoon.

"Well I did introduce you to it when you didn't like how I was being treated so you offered to buy me food and asked my recommendation. You showed me kindness which gave me hope which one thing lead to another somehow I caught the bosses attention when he was visiting our old town and he wanted to hear my story which made him want to pay off my debt." Ysrafaild says digging into the stew.

"So, whenever you two want to meet the team just say so and we can talk about you working for me. Now we don't kill dragons here. I mention that because Enoch's spear looks to be made of dragon bone. My name is Alexander Hazington." Alexander says turning away into the kitchen.

"Wait Hazington! Of the Chaffington Hazington's!" Enoch exclaims standing up at the bar.

"Yes, sir! Sadly, an injury kicked me out of my family's team in the league. They gave me a pretty lump-sum of money to set up a life somewhere and well I chose here. Who were you a fan of?" Alexander responds chuckling.

"I wasn't really a fan; however, I was offered a chance at joining the team and ditching the last nameless life. Eventually my prior engagements got in the way. Life of a mercenary called me back to the life of exploring for money. Would I change my decision? No not at all I love how my life turned out." Enoch says rubbing Maria's shoulder after he sat down.

"You must have been really good if they were thinking of giving you the last name. They only do that for people who can play better than their opponents can. Good you have what you want out of life is what matters most. I was starting to hate the lack of a life I had being the driver for the team. If there wasn't a game, I was either training or sleeping. I could at one point run the ball at a speed of 50 miles an hour. That was in the form you see in front of you. You can't be a driver and use your were state. My teammates could transform whenever they wanted. My brothers and sisters didn't have to train as much as I had too. On top of being the driver I had to keep track of the team's finances. Learning to keep track of the books is what made running this place so easy. Now keep what I have just revealed to you a secret please. I don't have anything clarifying that I am connected to the family so I don't have people coming in just for autographs taking up seats that customers who actually live in the town could sit in and enjoy a drink after work or maybe eat their breakfast, lunch or dinner." Alexander responds giving Enoch a cold glare.

"Alexander, I am not going to tell anyone about your past. That is your job to do. I don't tell anyone mine if I can help it. Telling people someone else's is a waste of my time. Food is delicious. Thank you for paying off Ysrafaild's debt." Enoch says bowing his head to Alexander.

"When will the mercenaries be in?" Maria asks quickly.

"They are already here. They are the individuals on the back wall cloaked by shadows. Meeting is whenever you two are ready. Just let me make the new batch of stew. Food is on the house. I have enjoyed talking with you two enough that the coin doesn't matter. Plus, I made Enoch go grim twice in rapid succession." Alexander responds pointing to the back wall.

"I should get back to work!" Ysrafaild says getting up.

"Go home! Ysrafaild I told you to take the rest of the day off and to relax! I will stop you from entering the kitchen!" Alexander yells blocking Ysrafaild from entering the kitchen.

"You aren't going to win, Alexander. She is persistent. Just let her work. She comes from a family of slaves. All they know how to do is work." Enoch chimes in looking over his shoulder.

Sitting across from a dwarven male snoring away. "So, you guys the mercenaries who work for the owner of this place?" Maria asks looking from the dwarf to the Tabaxi female.

"Aye! We are. A wee bit intimidated having witnessed the lad's abilities from a far." The dwarf responds opening his eyes.

"Nice to meet you!" The female Tabaxi says holding a handout to Enoch.

"Pleasure is mine. Name is E." Enoch responds shaking the Tabaxi's hand.

"Just a letter seriously!" The dwarf exclaims.

"Have you ever been run out of a town for telling someone your name?" Enoch asks looking at the dwarf with a glare colder than the vacuum of space.

"That I have not, and I doubt you have." the dwarf responds chuckling.

"I was run out of OxenDeValley in South Jraconia when I just even refused to say my name to M here. I was ran out of town because of my face. I am starting to think I am doomed to never be able to settle down. I will probably only be able to be here for only a couple of weeks before the war that seems to follow me comes here for me." Enoch says as his eyes start to glow again before they start to smoke again.

"I thought we got rid of the war that follows you?" Maria asks confused.

"I don't trust them to actually deliver the letter to the war front. Much like I don't trust my father to deliver your sister's dead body to the tribe back in Koftan." Enoch responds as his voice starts to sound more and more gritty.

"What is this about a dead body not making it to its destination, boyo?!" Zeke asks walking up behind Enoch.

"What are you doing here father? You should be back in Koftan?!" Enoch responds turning to his father as his voice gets even more gravelly.

"Woah, son! What is up with your eyes and voice?!" Zeke asks backing away from Enoch.

"What about it?!" Enoch responds getting angrier.

"Uh I think he is about to go grim state, M!" The Tabaxi exclaims.

"Crap!" Maria yells as she unwraps her hand getting ready to cut her hand again.

"Hug him, M!" Alexander screams from the bar.

Maria just hugs Enoch causing his eyes to return to normal and his snarling to stop. "Why are you here, father?!" Enoch asks looking at his father with hatred.

"I took Alice's body back and they told me to leave immediately. So, I came back to where I know the others were. Where are they?" Zeke responds kind of scared.

"Back in South Jraconia." Maria says as Enoch turns around to hold her properly. "E when you start getting upset please remember I am here for you. I don't want to lose you because you lose your cool and end up getting killed in the brawl that follows." Maria continues enjoying Enoch's embrace,

"I am sorry, M. I think my dabbling has ruined my ability to control my were states. I wish I hadn't dabbled as much as I have." Enoch whispers in Maria's ear before he lets out a little snore implying that he has fallen asleep on Maria.

"Oh, crap I can't hold you up, E!" Maria exclaims trying not to fall over.

"I am awake. I don't know why you had to yell. I am just enjoying holding my mate." Enoch responds as another sound similar to a snore comes out.

"Are you trying to purr?" Maria asks as Enoch lets out another snore like sound.

"He isn't aware of the sound he is making. He is in his savage state. Has he gone grim today?" Zeke asks looking at the duo hugging.

"Twice less than 5 minutes apart. Once as a werecat the other as a werewolf." Maria responds looking up at Zeke.

"Yeah he is so tired he is more or less a were just not in form. He will more than likely be utterly useless for the rest of the day." Zeke explains looking at his son with a look of concern.

"Well I guess we can't set off today. Name is Geoff Balderk." The dwarf says getting up.

"My name is Cumulus Nimble Foot." The Tabaxi says remaining seated.

"Why aren't you getting up?" Geoff asks a wee bit annoyed.

"We need to talk with these two even if we can't set off today. We should get to know our teammates." Cumulus responds sticking her tongue out.

"I will try to pay attention since, E is incapacitated." Maria says helping Enoch sit down and then sliding a chair right next to him before sitting down so Enoch can lean on her shoulder.

"Oy! I can pay attention!" Enoch says before letting out a sound much like a snore yet again.

"Sure, you will, E." Maria responds smiling under her mask.

"So why are the two of you wearing masks?" Cumulus asks meekly.

"We were at one point being hunted with our faces plastered around the cities of South Jraconia on wanted posters. When you are on wanted posters hiding your face is the smartest thing you can do. Well that and get as far away as you possibly can. Which is why we are here. Well it was why we came here then we were found when we arrived. A struggle happened and well my sister was killed in the process." Maria responds as tears come to her eyes.

"Quit crying about you killing your sister!" Zeke exclaims chiming in as Enoch's eyes shoot open.

"Alice would still be alive if you all wouldn't have hunted us down like a bunch of savages!" Enoch yells getting up and facing his father with his hand on his sword hilt.

"Keep your guard dog under control, miss." Zeke says calmly looking at Maria.

"E calm down! You triggered him! He is emotionally sensitive about Alice's death. Did you witness someone you loved die in front of you?" Maria responds grabbing Enoch's wrist to try and calm him down without getting up.

"Father go back to your tribe. You are not wanted here. Or should I quit calling you something you never bothered with." Enoch responds.

"That is harsh, E." Maria says softly.

"No, he is being honest. In his youth I was nothing more than an alcoholic who said he would never amount to anything. He has amounted to more than I ever have. He is the most qualified to be an alpha even though I am the son of an alpha. Because of the treaty I was stripped of the title of heir to the alpha. I will return to my brother. Good luck, son." Zeke explains with a straight face.

"So, what should we talk about?" Cumulus asks a little while later as the group have settled into their seats and Zeke is long gone.

"Well why are you two seeking jobs as mercenaries?" Geoff asks looking right at Enoch who has his eyes closed.

"I have worked as a mercenary since I was a teenager, I am 27 now. I just prefer how much the adventure of it pays." Enoch responds without opening his eyes.

"You are 28, E." Maria says meekly.

"You sure? Then again I quit counting when I started my journey to find myself after I patched you up and lost Yennifer." Enoch responds opening his eyes when he looks at Maria.

"Losing a friend because you patch up a stranger is bullshit." Yennifer says walking up behind Enoch.

"What are you doing here?" Enoch asks staying seated but grabbing Maria's hand to try and calm him down.

"Well a tribe that despises you wouldn't let the dwarf that was with you in the moment you left causing the war join their ranks. Why don't you get up to greet your oldest friend?" Yennifer responds throwing her arms open.

"Because I would much rather run a sword through you than to so much as touch you." Enoch says as Maria climbs on top of him to try and calm him down.

"What is that little life stealer doing to you?!" Yennifer yells getting ready to grab Maria and throw her to the ground.

"She is protecting you from me. I have a hatred for you and the alpha's daughter you ratted us out to that overrides my control of my were states." Enoch responds embracing Maria.

"So, I have wasted ten plus years of my life on you!" Yennifer yells grabbing Enoch's shoulder.

"Miss, no fighting in here! Especially not with a were!" Alexander hollers from the bar getting ready to vault over it.

"Oh, you have a lot of people protecting you. Coward!" Yennifer says angrily.

"No, I am protecting you. He is an anomaly. He not only can go both werecat and werewolf they are both grim." Alexander responds grabbing Yennifer's shoulder.

"So, he did mess up his were states when he ...?" Yennifer gets out before Maria jumps up.

"Yes, it messed him up horribly. I need to get back to him, but don't tell anyone about that!" Maria says interrupting Yennifer.

"What is going on?" Geoff asks curiously.

"We can't tell you here." Enoch responds his voice getting gravelly.

"What is up with his voice?" Yennifer asks slight terror in her voice.

"He is losing to his grim state. Which one I don't know he would have to open his eyes." Maria responds climbing on Enoch in the chair again.

"Wolf!" Enoch says his voice returning to normal. "I can tell by his hunger. The werecat is more of a sexual hunger. Werewolf is more of a literal hunger." Enoch continues fighting the urges of the werewolf.

"Why not let him loose in the woods?" Cumulus asks curiously.

"Too dangerous I have no control over the grim. I fear I may end up killing a child or worse someone I actually care about. I just wish I hadn't done as Alexander had asked." Enoch responds as his voice starts to return to normal.

"I will get her away from you four." Alexander says dragging Yennifer out the door.

"Can we hurry this up I think E and I should get back to our boat so he can rest and hopefully get his were under control." Maria says as Enoch starts rubbing her back.

Chapter 13

The next day the 4 have met up in the back room of the tavern when Alexander comes in looking at the 4. "How is E doing?" Alexander asks taking a seat.

"I am doing okay. I don't feel the hunger I was feeling before. Though the hunger I am currently feeling is because we slept later than we would have liked so I am literally hungry." Enoch responds as his stomach growls as loud as a dragon.

"We can get food when we get outside of town. Where are we headed boss?" Maria asks ignoring the loud roar like noises coming from Enoch's stomach.

"Ysrafaild! Get this gentleman a bowl of your famous stew!" Alexander hollers.

"You don't have to." Maria says as Ysrafaild comes in with the bowl of stew.

"His stomach is too loud for me to think." Alexander responds as Enoch digs in.

"Thank you. Ysrafaild, here." Enoch says before handing a slip of paper to Ysrafaild.

Ysrafaild doesn't say anything just reads the piece of paper before she starts to cry.

"What's up?" Alexander asks worriedly.

"My family is proud that I made it out of slavery and wishes for me to visit them in their family home back in Koftan. Enoch, did you write them?" Ysrafaild responds excitedly.

"Yes ma'am. I thought they should know how their daughter is doing. Specially considering they are free because I kept my tips, I wanted to give to you and them. Many years ago, I paid their debts and handed them the leftover coin told them to build a homestead so if I ever found you, I could send you back to them even just for a visit. Slavery is wrong." Enoch explains as he finishes the bowl of stew. "Could you take this back to be washed?" Enoch asks holding the bowl up to Ysrafaild.

"Yes, sir. Thank you!" Ysrafaild responds tears in her eyes as she hugs Enoch.

"When did you send the letter?" Maria asks confused.

"Last night while you were asleep. They live in Chaffington." Enoch responds as Ysrafaild lets go of him before she takes care of the bowl.

"Wait you fell asleep before I did?" Maria asks confused still.

"My were state was asleep. I was more or less unconscious all day yesterday. I had brief moments I was able to control myself. Never again am I going grim. Not unless I absolutely have to. I am thinking of calling my variation demon grim. The pure hatred he exudes is demonic." Enoch responds leaning back. "So, what is the job?" Enoch asks putting an arm around Maria's chair.

"Well there is a monster wreaking havoc in the western edge of the country on the shore of the ocean that acts as our border between us and the rest of the world. Uh I hope you two know how to swim. Most weres don't. The monster is a water-based monster. Like a sea serpent. I want to say that I have heard from the mercenary ringleader in Koftan and your reputation is massive, E. Not so much for Maria. Did you not work as a mercenary in Koftan?" Alexander explains as there is a serpent that forms from the flames of the candle being followed by the smoke.

"Did you do that?" Maria asks excitedly.

"Uh you aren't going to report me for using sorcery, are you?" Alexander responds cautiously.

"No, she won't. She hasn't turned me in for my dabbling." Enoch says sitting up.

"So, what do you do?" Cumulus asks curiously.

"Depends what is your opinions on playing god with life and death?" Enoch responds as his eyes glow a mix of purple and blue.

"That it is extremely dangerous and for that stupid." Alexander says giving Enoch a wary look.

"That is a good opinion of it. I gave up my were states to revive M's sister Alice yesterday. She went demon grim werecat and obliterated my arm which caused M to kill her again. Then a warm feeling hit me, and I regained the ability to go were but only demon grim were. Prior to that just your typical offensive attacks." Enoch explains as the glow in his eyes dissipates.

"A glowing wisp left Alice's body and you inhaled it then went demon grim werecat." Maria says shuddering.

"You have dabbled with death and rebirth magic, yet you center around deathly magic? Is that correct?" Alexander asks looking dead at Enoch.

"Sums it up pretty well. Gained the ability when I killed my first dragon. Not the dragon my spear comes from. That would have been the first to attack me and the last I have killed. Cleaved its leg off and it got me pretty bad. Almost died all alone that day. Felt like some force was keeping me alive. Like I have a guardian or maybe I wasn't destined to die that day. Felt kind of the same way when Alice destroyed my arm and I regained the ability to go were." Enoch explains staring off into space.

"Is he okay?" Geoff asks worriedly.

"Oh, I am just fine. Just a side effect of making a deal with the gods of life and death. I sometimes space out." Enoch responds spacing out again.

"No that is a side effect of dying and being brought back by the powers that be. I should have died in the incident that ended my career so long ago, but I woke up as if I had only been injured like I broke my leg. I remember feeling my neck and most of my skull crunch off the uneven pitch at 50 miles an hour." Alexander says as his eyes glaze over.

"What is the pay?" Maria asks as she is getting a little bored.

"Oh, uh two hundred gold a person. If one of you dies your next of kin will get the pay. For M that would be E and vice versa." Alexander responds zoning back in.

"Most important question. When do we need to be back by?" Enoch asks snapping his fingers.

"Uh I don't put a time limit on missions like this. Don't want to make you feel like you need to hurry and then you make a mistake and end up dead." Alexander responds zoning back in again.

"Let's get a move on. Tell Ysrafaild he is in here. She knows how to get him back to normal." Geoff says chiming in.

Now on their way to the west coast of the continent the group encounter a giant scorpion which notices them right away and starts trying to attack them.

Enoch knowing his spear is of no use starts firing blue fireballs at the scorpion. One of his fireballs hits the base of the scorpion's tail cleaving it off so it looks but it just blew it down towards the ground. "I have no clue how to kill this thing. I have never encountered one of these!" Enoch hollers a hint of terror in his voice.

"Wow such a small country boy! Watch this!" Geoff yells as he catapults Cumulus so high into the air, she grazes the lowest layer of clouds.

Cumulus pulls her maul off her back and swings it towards the ground causing herself to spin a little bit before she comes down on the scorpion shooting its blood everywhere. "Tada!" Cumulus exclaims standing up in a massive whole in the scorpion.

"Wow! That is one way to do it. Is this edible?" Enoch asks drooling at the thought of how much meat is in this thing.

"Is he always so hungry when a beast is killed?" Geoff responds concerned.

"Yes, he is always hungry. Should have seen him when he killed the dragon that almost killed him previously. He left it just a skeleton on one side. He would have taken all the meat if his bag would have held more. He loves eating weird meats." Maria explains as Enoch runs at the corpse with a knife in one hand and a bag in the other.

"Well as long as he cooks this it is safe to eat. I would take a piece of shell with the meat, so you have something to cook it on. If he doesn't cook it, he runs the risk of poisoning all who eat the meat. Now we don't know how poisonous this beast was as none of us were stung thank fully. Well we don't know unless Cumulus got a taste of its venom on impact. She knows how to tell that." Geoff explains chuckling.

"It is very poisonous. It was a shadow scorpion. So, he better not take the shell otherwise he is wasting the meat as the shell will put poison into the cooked meat. I knew to keep my mouth shut on impact with this one. I could tell by its markings that it is highly toxic, and I have nothing to neutralize this one's poison in my supply kit. Though if he is worth his salt at cooking this will be extremely delicious. Almost wild boar belly level delicious. What do the more civilized people call it? Bacon!" Cumulus says smiling.

Enoch has returned with a bag of meat. "I was tempted to bring some shell to cook it in but when I put a flame underneath it started filling with a purple venom looking fluid. Don't want to risk death from that stupid of a mistake." Enoch says smiling at Maria.

"You are like a kid in a candy store when you find a meat to cook. I love you, E." Maria responds chuckling at Enoch's simplicity.

"If it keeps me from eating workhorse meat, I figured you would be happy!" Enoch says sticking his tongue out at Maria.

"Why are you talking of cannibalism?" Geoff asks scared.

"When you are starving you will eat whatever you get your hands on. I'd buy it before I kill someone, I know to eat them." Enoch explains going cold in expression.

"I lost a brother to slavery and found his face in a bag of horse meat back 5 years ago." Cumulus says shuddering.

"I am sorry to hear that. M is trying to keep me from eating the stuff. It is easier here in Jraconia than in Koftan. More monsters to carve into and eat." Enoch responds somberly before shuddering.

"Let's get moving again." Geoff says annoyed.

Now close to the west coast Enoch's stomach is growling very loudly again. "We have to stop, or he is going to alert the sea serpent. So, can you weres swim?" Geoff asks showing that he is very annoyed.

"I can. Fell overboard a couple times on the way here across the inland sea." Enoch responds meekly.

"When did that happen?" Maria asks worried.

"You liked to go to bed before the moon was very high in the sky. I can't sleep that early." Enoch responds pulling out his skillet and meat bag.

"Just because you are a werewolf doesn't mean you have to sleep like one." Maria says giggling at Enoch's folly.

"You are a werecat you don't feel the urge to howl at the full moon among other things. Found out why the inland sea is salty. When the full moon is over head werewolves are very ... horny." Enoch responds giving the wood in front of him a quick blast of fire.

"Eeeeeewwww!" Cumulus exclaims gagging.

"What's her problem?" Enoch asks giving Cumulus a glance.

"You said the reason the ocean is salty is ... spunk." Geoff responds also gagging.

"How do you like your food cooked?" Maria asks looking at the two gagging individuals.

"How are you not triggered by what he said?" Cumulus asks ignoring Maria's question.

"He is my soul mate. We think a lot alike. We are both very perverted. I had to urinate over the railing of the ship a lot. So, excrement causing the saltiness isn't an odd thought considering fish urinate, defecate, fornicate in the water. Again, I ask how you would like your food cooked?" Maria explains sighing as the duo across from her and Enoch both barf at the same time.

"Well looks like I am cooking just for the two of us, M." Enoch says looking over at Maria.

"Give us a minute. We've swam in the inland sea in the past week. Hrrph!" Geoff chimes in before projectile vomiting.

"Oy! don't put the fire out with your getting sick!" Enoch exclaims sending sparks in Geoff's direction.

"He is very protective of the cooking process." Maria says chuckling at Enoch.

"You two are way too messed up." Cumulus says wiping her face on a scrap of cloth from inside her medicine bag.

Some time has passed the team have eaten. All stomachs have settled, and the crew is on the shore of the world sea. "So how do we get the monster to come out?" Geoff asks stumped as Enoch is sobbing loading a small bag with the leftover uncooked scorpion meat. "What is up with him?" Geoff asks confused.

"He is loading the bag with bait." Maria explains.

Enoch doesn't speak just strips stark naked and slings the bag over his shoulder before diving into the ocean. "What is he doing!?" Cumulus asks terrified.

"Again bait! He may be a few cards short of a full deck, but he has always ended up correct with his actions." Maria responds watching Enoch paddle further out as a dark shadow starts following him in the water.

The dark shadow surfaces to reveal it isn't a sea serpent but an underwater dragon. Enoch doesn't notice till it fires a ball of fire in front of him. When he sees that he whips around and starts swimming right at the dragon. As it goes to try and swallow Enoch, he stomps on its head launching himself in the air and hurling the bag of Scorpion meat mixed with a jug of its venom in the dragons mouth along with a timed blue ball of fire without the aid of his spear. The food lands on its tongue immediately followed by the fireball which hits the parcel detonating it vaporizing the poison which the dragon slams its mouth shut on. As Enoch splashes down from a height of twenty plus feet in the air the dragon becomes enraged. Enoch is panicking as he swims towards the dock. "SPEAR! NOW! M!" Enoch yells hoping he is heard as Maria tosses his spear to him. Enoch is now facing the dragon holding his spear he uses his magic to propel himself towards the dragon and jams his spear in one of its eyes but he is going at such speed him and the spear kind of both end up in the dragon's eye socket.

"He is crazy taking it on all by himself! Should we help him?!" Geoff asks getting ready to start stripping.

"Leave him be! He knows what he is doing! He is venting his hatred over recent issues in his and my life!" Maria responds putting her hand out in front of Geoff.

"How do you know he can do this alone?!" Cumulus asks confused.

"He isn't doing it alone! He is drawing energy from myself!" Maria responds looking at the other two revealing her eyes are glowing as she clutches a necklace in her left hand.

Enoch has finally climbed out of the eye socket as the dragon is breathing purple flames into the air. The purple is coming from the poison Enoch made it inhale. Its flames were your standard orange flames previously. Enoch is started to get too tired to keep the fight up so he pries the dragons mouth open and just keeps firing blue fireballs down its throat hoping it will sever its head like the last dragon he fought. Getting worried he can't kill this thing on his own Enoch decides this is a good time to let the demon loose. Turning demon werewolf grim Enoch is struggling to keep a hold of the dragon. Enoch plummets into the ocean at this point is a 100-foot sink to the bottom. Enoch is now terrified that even his grim state can't save him and kill the dragon.

"Why did he go grim!?" Maria asks screaming fighting the urge to jump in after Enoch.

"Maybe we should help him!" Cumulus exclaims.

"If anyone is going in after him it's going to be me!" Maria yells stripping down to her birthday suit and diving in after Enoch.

Now Maria has made it to Enoch and is dragging him to the surface. Enoch despite being in his demon grim state doesn't lash out at Maria. Instead he clutches onto her terrified. "We can do this together, E!" Maria exclaims seconds after breaking the surface of the water. The duo are struggling, but the dragon is charging them. "I will do my best to get you in the air. You get on that things back and hopefully you can figure out how to kill it in your current state. Bite out its second eye if you feel like you can't do it in your current state. I am here to help you no matter what!" Maria explains before Enoch pushes off her chest making sure his claws don't do any damage to her. Enoch lands on the dragons back. Moving to its head Enoch bites down on the dragon's eye socket, then he rips its eye out.

The dragon is now blind, and ten times as pissed as a bunch of angry hornets that a child used their nest as a pinata. The dragon stops charging instead shooting a steady stream of white flames right in front of it. From what Enoch can see Maria is consumed in the flames. Enoch realizing, he has nothing to live for now lets the demon grim loose. The grim bites the top of the dragons head just ripping mouthfuls of flesh from its skull before spitting them out and biting of more chunks and repeating. Finally reaching the top of its bare skull the grim lets Enoch return back to his human state where he sends fireball after fireball at the exposed section of skull. During all this the dragon is flailing around in agony. Enoch finally obliterates the exposed section of skull before returning to grim state and going back to biting off chunks of dragon flesh and this time swallowing the dragon brains. He finally is physically inside the dragon's skull and he feels the dragon slam its head into the water. Water is now flooding into the cavity Enoch has made. Suddenly Enoch can't see the light from the hole but pure darkness. The dragon has gone belly up. It is dead. It is dead and apparently sinking with Enoch in its skull. Taking his last breath of available air Enoch tries to swim towards the hole. He doesn't make it.

Sometime later Enoch wakes up on the shore still very much so naked and in his demon grim state. Returning back to normal. "Oh, he is awake!" Cumulus exclaims getting Geoff's attention.

"Forget about me has anyone seen M!?" Enoch asks standing up and rushing to the water.

"She is over here, E! She dragged you in." Geoff yells trying to stop Enoch from diving in the water again.

Enoch rushes to Maria who is completely unburned. He collapses on top of her resting his head on her right breast sobbing because he can't feel her breathing. "I am alive, E!" Maria says running her left hand through Enoch's hair.

"I thought I saw you engulfed in the white flames! I chalked you up as dead! Figuring I lost the only reason I am still alive I let the demon loose on the dragon! How did you survive the flames!?" Enoch asks blathering.

"You unknowingly saved me when you kicked off me to get to the dragon. You pushed me down deep enough the flames couldn't reach me. I then saw the dragon splash down and start to roll over. When I could see the hole you made, I thought you might still be inside it so I rushed to it. When I found you losing consciousness, I knew I had to get us to shore. Then you woke up. I am whooped. Can we crash at a tavern

here before we set off on our way back to Alexander?"
Maria explains enjoying the cuddles with Enoch as he
lets out a snore like sound.

"Is he asleep? Sure." Geoff responds pulling out two
of the towels Alexander provided in their supplies bag
and covering the duo.

"For once I think so. He went grim at least twice in
rapid succession. Plus, he almost drowned twice. He is
actually snoring, I think. I guess you two can go find a
good tavern that has enough rooms for us. E, and I will
take a single room." Maria responds quietly.

Sometime later the duo stumble into the tavern
that was selected fully clothed. Enoch is struggling to
stay up right let alone walk. "What is up with him?" the
bartender asks looking at Enoch funny.

"He killed the dragon that we were sent here to
fight. It took everything he could give to kill it. Leaving
him struggling to so much as move." Maria responds as
Enoch nods off because she stopped walking.

"Dragon? We sent for a sea serpent to be killed. Not
a dragon." A patron says turning to face the duo.

"You said to throw some meat in to bait it to come
out correct?!" Enoch asks as his eyes start to glow.

"Yeah?" the patron responds slightly scared.

"A dragon attacked me when I did that. I killed a
dragon that responded to what you said for us to do."
Enoch says as the glow in his eye flickers ever so
slightly.

"Do his eyes normally glow like that?" The patron asks terrified.

"Only when someone challenges him when he has expended all energy doing something like killing a dragon." Maria responds annoyed as Enoch wanders back to her.

"Can we just find Geoff and Cumulus?" Enoch asks softly in Maria's ear.

"Where did the dwarf and Tabaxi go that paid for two rooms?" Maria asks aloud to the bartender.

"Upstairs and the two rooms farthest from the stairwell." The bartender responds.

"Thank you." Enoch says in perfect Draconian.

"What did you just say?" Maria asks quietly.

"I said thank you. Is your hearing going?" Enoch responds as they make it to the top of the stair.

"You didn't say it in a tongue anyone understood." Maria says as they make it to one of the rooms, they were told that has the door open.

"There you two are. You get the other room. Is he okay?" Cumulus asks pointing at Enoch.

"I am alright just very tired." Enoch responds in perfect Draconian.

"What did he just say?" Cumulus asks confused.

"He said 'I am alright just very tired.' in perfect draconian." Geoff responds sitting up.

"Wait you speak draconian?" Maria asks confused as Enoch wanders off into their room.

"Yes, I do. I am guessing he learned it when he was munching on the dragon's brain before it died from the destruction of its brain." Geoff responds chuckling at the drool stain on Maria's blouse.

"Yes, I know about his drool stain. I should probably head to bed with him. Don't want him to fall asleep hogging the bed to himself. Not fun dealing with him being a bed hog." Maria says before heading into her and Enoch's room.

Now they are laying on the bed both in their birthday suits. "Why did you have to drool on me while we walked to our room?" Maria asks caressing Enoch's hair.

"I didn't realize I drooled on you, honey. I am sorry." Enoch responds looking up at Maria from where he has his head resting on her left breast again.

"It's okay. Just going to need to wash my blouse before we set off tomorrow. Let's get some rest, E." Maria says as her eyes are getting heavy.

Chapter 14

The next day the group are setting out as they get near the center of town there is a crowd gathering. As the group get up to the crowd. "There they are! They Killed my pet!" A townsfolk yells pointing right at Enoch.

"What was your pet?" Enoch asks annoyed as smoke starts collecting around his fists.

"You know what you did!" The same townsfolk screams trying to get the crowd to follow suit.

"I only killed one thing yesterday! A dragon! Keeping dragons as pets is the dumbest thing I have ever heard of!" Enoch responds as the smoke around his fists turns into fire.

"I was the one who put out a hit on the dragon!" the townsfolk yells in response.

"Then I didn't kill your pet whatever it was!" Enoch responds as the flames turn blue before quickly going white.

"You killed my pet scorpion! I saw you climbing out of its corpse carrying a bag of its flesh!" the townsfolk screams still trying to incite the crowd. The crowd all let out a collective sigh.

"So does this guy always try and keep creatures that honestly shouldn't be kept as pets?" Enoch asks chuckling as the flames flicker between white and blue in time with his chuckles.

"YES!" The crowd yells.

"Then could you all cart him off before he truly angers me!" Enoch responds raising his right hand into view as the flames turn white again before he flips his hand, so his palm faces the sky causing the flames to hover above his palm almost forming a white ball of flames.

Sometime later the crew make it back to the port city which they started from as the first sun is setting. As Enoch and Maria enter the tavern. "We need to have a talk you two!" Alexander says standing at the door.

"Why?!" Enoch asks meekly.

"Cumulus sent me a letter last night." Alexander responds sighing as he leads the duo into the mission room.

"What about?" Maria asks squeezing Enoch's hand.

"They both don't want to work with either of you. Something about saying the inland sea is only salty because of spunk and urine." Alexander responds sighing once again.

"I explained that wasn't exclusively why. Fish urinate, defecate, fornicate in the water." Maria says meekly.

"Yeah they still don't want you working with them. I don't have work for you here if you can't get along with my longest standing team. Here is your pay. Good luck." Alexander responds sighing before getting up and leaving the room.

Now back on the deck of Enoch's ship. "What do we do now?!" Maria asks yelling at Enoch.

"I don't know." Enoch responds meekly.

"You just had to talk about your personal activities around people we didn't know. Then I had to pretend to be like you so hopefully they didn't think you were insane. Well that cost me a job. If I didn't have to shoulder your damages, I could still have a job! Yeah it wouldn't have been ideal me being the only one with a job while you try and find something to do while I worked but you just completely ruined our chances of working in this town. No, this country! Where do we go now, E!?" Maria yells pushing Enoch across the deck, but she doesn't stop when he hits the railing with his back, she keeps pushing till he falls overboard into the waters below.

A couple minutes have passed Enoch is on the deck with a towel wrapped around his shoulders as he sits and shivers. "You couldn't hold onto the railing?! Why did I have to be saved by such a pathetic were who can't even do anything by himself!? Hell why did I think he was anything different than the rest of the guys who act all tough till a girl opens their legs for him and then they become cowards who think just because they have scored they can quit being brave in their daily life. You are the most pathetic were I have ever had to deal with! I want to go back to South Jraconia!" Maria yells still monologuing.

"I can give you the ship. I don't want to live with a woman who treats me like shit. I gave up the most courageous part of me when I tried to revive your sister. I gave up the were's I could control. Now I am terrified of what will set off my demon grim state. I am terrified of them! I fought so hard last night when you saved me from drowning when I was in the demon grim state to not kill you for so much as touching me while I was in that state!" Enoch responds initially very confident before going completely meek.

"You were terrified?! I was terrified you were going to rip my throat out! You don't know what it is like fearing for my life every night since you went from just a grim state to a demon grim state!" Maria yells looking down at Enoch as he shivers. "Do you want to get into some warm dry clothes? I am going to get some dry clothes if you want to get changed come with me." Maria continues as her concern for Enoch returns.

Now below deck they are both naked as Enoch hovers a fireball above his hand in between the two. "Your magic has been very useful. I do have to admit that without it we would struggle to get warm after getting soaked. It is also useful for getting a fire started anywhere we go. You were once this charming man who I looked up to. That was up till we arrived here, and it all went down. I am sorry I blew up on you for how you changed to a coward. I would change if I went from being a were that I could confidently control to one that even terrifies me. I just wish I could have the old you back even for an hour. You made me feel safe and happy." Maria says monologuing.

"I miss not worrying what will set them off. If I knew their triggers, I would be more like I used to be. Back then I knew what their triggers were. Now I don't. Could we sleep naked cuddling tonight?" Enoch responds semi confidently around the end.

"I was thinking of asking you the same question. Maybe on the way to South Jraconia we could try to learn your new triggers." Maria says smiling at Enoch as she lets him see her full body that she had covered with a towel.

"Maria, could we maybe go into town once we are dry and find something to eat that isn't what we have on the ship? As is we need to buy supplies for our journey back to South Jraconia. Maybe we can dress like we used to before we had to hide our faces?" Enoch asks looking at Maria lovingly.

"I was thinking we could go to bed now but when you mentioned food my stomach gave me a sign that yeah I need to eat." Maria responds releasing the towel so she can scratch her head letting her bosom bounce while doing so.

"As much as I love watching your bosom bounce, M. I think we should get some dry clothes on and head into town, so we get to the places with food before they all close and we are stuck with Alexander's tavern. So why don't you let your hair down below grow? Most werecat women are famous for letting it grow in Koftan. Again, I only know because most weres refuse to wear clothes unless they decide to leave the tribe." Enoch says at first admiring the bounce before looking down Maria's body.

"The hair kept finding a way to like weave itself into my clothes so when I pulled down my pants it would pull them and that hurt really bad. Could you do one thing for me? One embrace the way we are?" Maria asks meekly as Enoch slides a hand around her back and kisses her before placing his free hand on Maria's right breast.

Now in a different pub in town the couple are sitting at a table across from each other with a lit candle between them. "What would you two like to order?" a human waiter asks looking down at the two who look very out of place.

"What is there to order? First time here." Enoch responds confidently.

"Here is the menu. Be quick it is my only copy." The waiter responds sighing as the couple look at the menu.

"This is too expensive, E." Maria whispers leaning in pretending to read the menu.

"Uh never mind we can't afford anything on the menu." Enoch says with the same confidence level he used earlier.

"You know where the door is. Good luck with life." The waiter responds backing up after grabbing the menu.

Now out on the streets of the town the couple are talking looking around. "I have a feeling the only thing we can afford is Alexander's tavern." Enoch says sighing in annoyance at how posh the port seems to be.

"I can't help but to listen to your conversation. You want a place to eat that is affordable but isn't that ex-ball star Alexander's tavern?" An older female Tabaxi asks looking at the couple.

"Do you know of a place that is affordable other than his place?" Enoch responds skeptically.

"Yes, right inside here. It is my restaurant. Bought it with money my daughter gave me. Tried to get a mercenary ring moved in but no one wants to compete with that were." The older Tabaxi says motioning towards the warm looking building she is standing in front of.

"You are Cumulus' mother?" Maria asks concerned.

"Yes, we don't talk anymore. She gave me the money I used to buy this place to get me to leave her alone. Come in I will make you whatever you want to eat. Even that were's one dish that everyone loves better than he does." The Tabaxi lady says trying to get the couple in the door.

"Hold on. We need to discuss this." Enoch responds before turning to Maria.

"Something not feel right to you as well? Feels like she is scamming us. Do you just want to suck it up and go to Alexander's?" Maria asks quietly as Enoch is holding her waist.

"Yeah that might be a better idea. Let's go. What do you want from Alexander's tavern?" Enoch responds playing with Maria's jet-black hair that falls down around her butt.

Now walking towards Alexander's tavern there is a guard posted at the door. "You two aren't allowed here!" the guard exclaims pointing right at the couple.

"Why not? This is the only affordable place to eat in this city for a shunned mercenary." Enoch responds not letting the annoyance in his voice show.

"Let them in! Just because we don't want to work with them doesn't mean they can't eat here." Geoff yells walking up to the guard from inside.

"Thank you, Geoff. I am sorry for what I said. I realize apologizing changes nothing, but it helps my conscience." Enoch says not letting his confidence waiver.

"Get in here before I change my mind. M, you look nice by the way." Geoff responds sighing at Enoch.

"Thanks for the complement but I am married to E." Maria says giggling as she grabs Enoch's hand.

Now inside at the bar. "I told the guard to not let you two in!" Alexander hollers before Geoff interrupts him,

"They need to eat just like you and me, this place is the cheapest place to eat that the food isn't sketchy. Even I wouldn't eat at the cheap places in this town. Let them eat here tonight then if they know what is smart, they will get the supplies they need and leave town tomorrow morning." Geoff responds sighing at Alexander.

"I would like the chef's specialty and a glass of water?" Enoch asks trying to remain confident.

"You don't want the water boyo. He'll take a bottle of mead. Water here is literally retrieved from the inland sea in a bucket. No cleaning is done to it." Geoff says before leaving to the back of the dining area.

"What will she be having?" Alexander asks annoyed.

"I would like some roasted beef with potatoes, carrots in the gravy made from the beef drippings. As for a drink I will have what Geoff suggested for, E." Maria responds before looking over at Enoch who is staring at her and she smiles at him.

"Well since it is a busy night could you guys find a table, so I have bar space open for my regulars?" Alexander asks as Geoff rushes up behind the couple.

"Don't he is going to take your money and forget about you. He does this trick when I let someone in that he bans from here. I forgot about this trick, but Cumulus reminded me. We may not want to work with you two, but you are living people like us, so we look out for you on his nasty habits." Geoff says a bit out of breath.

"I was opening an actual tab for them. I have only done that when even your kindness didn't extend to informing them on the water. You extended your kindness to the water so I knew my tricks wouldn't get past you." Alexander responds sighing in annoyance.

"I think we will stay seated here. I don't like when my feet touch the floor in taverns." Maria says grabbing Enoch's hand on the bar.

"We are staying seated here. Thank you, Geoff." Enoch chimes in glancing at Maria's hand on his.

"Not a problem, E." Geoff responds before he turns away and walks towards the back of the building.

"So, do you two want to know why he is being kind?" Alexander asks leaning in.

"Quit trying to spread lies. We just want our food so that we can get back to our ship then in the morning get the supplies we need to make the journey anywhere else in this world. We are done trying to fit the mold placed on us by people like you and your mercenaries. Last time I worked for an individual like you I lost everything I loved! Never again!" Enoch responds letting the demon grim wolf glow flash in his eyes.

"I was just going to tell you that they didn't want to kick you out of the team. I did! Weres while we aren't hated here that is because we are not all that common here. Well 5 happen to show up and then they fight one dies so two leave and the other two request me to employ them. Those two being upset with you just so happen to allow me to terminate you two without causing a stink of me being classed as Anti-were." Alexander says before walking into the kitchen.

"With how kind Geoff has been I was feeling like us being kicked out wasn't their request." Maria says softly as Geoff and Cumulus sit with Geoff by Enoch and Cumulus by Maria.

"Yeah no we didn't request you to be cast out. Just a complaint that you are a little to friendly way too soon." Cumulus responds bumping Maria.

"Well that and the ocean tiny bit was disgusting. I understand the other thing I initially took issue with. Can't call it by name as it isn't the most legal thing here. I will honestly miss the adventurous spirit the two of you share." Geoff says looking at the couple as Alexander comes out with the food for the couple.

"Where are our beverages?" Enoch asks annoyed with Alexander.

"I only have two hands." Alexander responds glaring at Geoff for letting the couple in.

A few hours have passed, and the couple are laying on the deck of the ship looking at the stars under a blanket as they both decided to cuddle in their birthday suits. "Hey, could we hang out before you two head to bed and then leave the country?" Geoff says knocking on the side of the boat.

"Crap! Go back down! We aren't exactly decent right now!" Maria yells squeezing Enoch closer.

"We have seen both of you naked before but ok." Geoff responds carefully turning around and walking back down the gangplank.

A few minutes later the four are sitting on the deck. "Why was there an issue with you guys being naked a few minutes ago?" Geoff asks confused.

"We weren't just naked. We were having some fun while naked." Enoch responds sighing.

"Oh." Cumulus says blushing.

"Fun while naked?" Geoff asks still confused.

"They were having sex!" Cumulus exclaims softly as she slaps the back of Geoff's head.

"How does a dwarf that is older than me not get what I meant by naked fun?" Enoch asks stumped at Geoff's ignorance.

"I am actually a virgin to be honest. I haven't bothered to find a relationship because I would rather be working with Cumulus by my side." Geoff responds slightly butt hurt.

"Have you ever considered a relationship with Cumulus?" Enoch asks as Maria snuggles with his shoulder.

"What she doesn't like me in that way?!" Geoff responds ignorantly.

"Yes, I do! Been trying to give you hints with offering to share a tent with you. When you do let us share a tent, I try to get you to share a sleeping bag, but you constantly refuse to share a sleeping bag." Cumulus says getting more and more upset.

"My family would definitely refuse to allow me back if I came back with someone other than a blood dwarf like myself. I would love to have relations with you, but my family status matters just a wee bit more." Geoff responds grabbing Cumulus' hand.

"Know what we want to head to bed so we can get an early start tomorrow." Enoch says getting up in a way that he is carrying Maria.

"Don't tell me you two were doing inappropriate things with us here!" Cumulus exclaims.

"No, she fell asleep." Enoch responds softly.

Chapter 15

Months later the couple are both mostly naked when they are coming into the port in the north of South Jraconia. "LAND HO!" Maria yells pointing at the land.

"Get dressed quick! I need to do so as well!" Enoch responds yelling and chuckling at Maria as she runs past him into the captain's quarters.

A few minutes later after Enoch has got the dock worker to help him moor the boat Maria comes out dressed the way Enoch had requested back in West Jraconia. "Go, E. I will get our rent taken care of if you haven't." Maria says patting Enoch on the back.

"Apparently Yennifer bought me this spot when she bought me this ship. I will be back shortly. You look nice, M." Enoch responds hugging Maria before he heads to get dressed.

Another few minutes have passed and Enoch comes out of their room and saunters up to Maria. "What's up, M?" Enoch asks placing a hand on Maria's shoulder.

"Apparently Yennifer wants to speak with us since we have returned, she is in a cave in a mountain range somewhere in the Mountainous Woods." Maria responds turning to face Enoch.

"So, she found them! I knew she would!" Enoch exclaims excitedly a little to close to Maria's ear.

Now down on the docks the couple have gotten all the supplies they needed and are collecting the revenue from transporting goods from West Jraconia to South Jraconia. "Why don't we just act as merchants?" Maria asks drooling over the amount of money sitting in front of them.

"Because I hate being on the water. Plus, I am thinking of changing ship. Get rid of the one in the inland sea and go for one in the world ocean. Maybe return to Koftan. I am starting to miss the climate of that place. Glad we figured out my triggers on this boat trip though. Most of this coin is for us to not need to work on our adventures through South Jraconia. Want to head back to the tribe here to see if the war has ended?" Enoch explains nudging Maria.

"Oh, the war has gotten worse! Non weres have joined in! I wish they would find whoever they are looking for and call the war off!" the recipient of the goods says looking up from his papers.

"I knew they wouldn't deliver the letter!" Enoch exclaims angrily.

"Oh, I did deliver it. They didn't believe it." Jennifer says from behind Enoch and Maria.

"Oh, hey Jenny. So, what brings you here? No one fitting your description has arrived yet." The dock worker responds waving at Jennifer.

"Yes, they have. They are right in front of you." Jennifer says putting her hand on the couple's shoulders.

"Please let us come along freely! I don't like letting the demons loose!" Enoch exclaims moving Jennifer's hand off his shoulder.

"You think I am dumb enough to challenge the demon and the psychopath?" Jennifer asks chuckling.

"I am guessing you are calling me the psychopath?!" Maria responds getting ready to pull her dagger.

"Leave the dagger in the sheath or you will prove why you have that nickname, M." Enoch says grabbing Maria's arm.

"Well is everything ok with our paperwork?" Maria asks trying to resist the urge to plunge her dagger in Jennifer's neck.

"Yeah. Go on ahead." The dock worker says chuckling.

Now outside of the port city. The trio are standing arguing. "I want to know what your outburst you had on the boat was about Yennifer?" Maria asks looking at Enoch trying to ignore Jennifer.

"Yennifer and I were planning to come here to South Jraconia to find her ancestral home. We had a theory that it may be in a cave in the mountains which Mountainous Woods is named after. Well I ended up not going on the journey with her and from what the dock worker said she found something there unless she met her untimely demise there. I am of course hoping for the former. As she is the first of my women, that I had relations with." Enoch explains smiling at Maria.

"Oh okay." Maria responds.

"I found it but they told me if I am connected to anyone from above that I belong with them. I was headed back to the house I bought on the docks to wait for you to return. Can I join your party?" Yennifer says sauntering up behind Jennifer.

"Well that only leaves one place I wanted to go. Meet up with Angus. But first get this war over with." Enoch responds offering a hug to Yennifer.

"Hey, E. Could I bother you for some affection? I am bound to you after all." Jennifer asks meekly.

"If we keep conversing here more people could die. Let's talk about all of our future when we get this stupid war over with. I am still kind of upset with you Jenny! Hunting me down and all!" Enoch responds as Yennifer let's go of him.

Now entering the warzone. "What the heck! I thought we didn't destroy buildings!?" Maria asks yelling.

"That was until the non weres joined in. Then they started burning were friendly places to the ground. It hurts to be back here." Jennifer responds fighting tears as she looks around at the others. Enoch holds an arm out to her. Jennifer grabs Enoch and he holds her while she cries her eyes out.

"Where is the front line, Jenny?" Enoch asks holding Jennifer with one arm.

"Last I knew it was the first row of trees of the forest. But there were reports of the non weres cutting trees down so they could move forward in the middle of the night." Jennifer responds looking up at Enoch's cold expression.

"I want this over now! I don't want to be the cause of anyone dying! I have witnessed one person die because of my actions and that was one too many!" Enoch exclaims as he feels a damp kiss on the cheek.

"I love you, Enoch." Jennifer whispers in Enoch's ear.

"Let's get headed toward the were tribe den. Jennifer lead the way." Enoch says not reacting to what Jennifer said to him.

Now at the den the group are trying to get the guards at the back entrance to let them in. "I want this war over! If you don't let me in, I will get in there even if I have to kill you to do it! I am why this war started and I am here to end it!" Enoch yells getting in the guard's face.

"If you would ditch the non were, I could let you in!" the guard responds yelling back.

"Let them in! She helped us to locate him when he left the country like what 4 months ago!" Zeke yells grabbing the guard before shoving them out of the way.

"Thank you, father." Enoch says looking at his father with a smile on his face for once.

Now in the main room of the den Enoch is standing with Maria to his left and Yennifer to his right. "So, do you promise to finalize your imprint with my daughter?" Jennifer's father asks glaring at Enoch.

"Honestly I just want to get this war over with. I could care less about were religious beliefs. I want you idiots to quit declaring wars because I don't want to live like you. Get M's mother in here NOW! I want this war over as soon as possible. I am not going to finalize anything with your daughter if it means I have to quit adventuring. I am an adventurer by nature. I hate being bound to one place. Finalizing with your daughter would bind me to one place. Yes, I have feelings for Jennifer, but my needs out weight my wants!" Enoch responds fighting his wolf grim to keep it from surfacing.

"I heard you I was on my way. So, my youngest daughter has actually been alive this whole time. Zeke wasn't lying. I am sorry for banishing you from Koftan, Zeke. Us declaring peace will stop our fighting but not this war, Enoch." Madison says walking into the den with her guards which includes Marley.

"Enoch..." Marley says quietly as she walks up to Enoch.

"Marley, can we talk in a little bit? I miss you. I know I only hung out with you for a day, but your imprint is strong." Enoch responds looking right in Marley's eyes.

"So, for the peace talks I want to assign a were to Enoch who will report back to the Koftan tribe with written letters!" Madison says standing in the center of the alpha chamber. "I already have my were picked out who will follow him. Marley go sit with Enoch and my youngest daughter! Now I would recommend your tribe to do the same of assigning someone to him. I would recommend someone who he has somehow imprinted on!" Madison continues as Marley follows orders.

"I can't assign the only were a part of this tribe he has imprinted on. She is slated to become Alpha when I retire, or he finalizes his imprint with her." Jennifer's father says from his throne glaring at Enoch.

"If you would let me adventure freely after I finalize with her, I would want to finalize with her!" Enoch responds standing up letting the werecat demon grim shine in his eyes.

"E no don't let that loose." Maria says panicking as she grabs the sleeve of Enoch's tunic.

"What is that wench on about, Enoch?" Jennifer asks giving Enoch a cold stare.

"I don't care what this news will result in, but I tried to revive Alice. To do so I gave up my were abilities. Well the gods of life and death have a sense of humor. They took my standard were powers and replaced them with a powerful version of both grim states. I call them Demon Grim states. Their eyes glow colors independent of each other. I had to relearn my triggers on the way from West Jraconia." Enoch explains before his eyes start glowing pure white. "Oh, and she isn't a wench. She didn't try and force herself on me unlike you did the first night that I knew you had imprinted on me. Yes, Jennifer forced herself on me after you left the pub, Sir. She forced herself on top of me and forced me inside of her." Enoch continues as the white from his eyes goes to his right hand and forms a ball of white flames.

"Enoch how could you break that promise!?" Jennifer screams tears flowing down her cheeks.

"You insulted the woman I have married." Enoch responds as the ball of flames turn into a black fire.

"So, she finalized it prematurely?!" Jennifer's father asks angrily.

"I am sorry father! Please don't exile me! Please ..." Jennifer pleads dropping to her knees.

"Your punishment is banished as far from Enoch as possible!" Jennifer's father responds angrily.

"Now don't make my life harder by limiting how far I can travel. Her worst possible punishment is she has to stay by my side, but she can't act on her urges or emotions." Enoch says looking at Jennifer directly as the fire turns purple.

"Well you seem like you wouldn't violate the punishment. Sounds fair. She will act as the person keeping tabs on Enoch and writing letters back to me. Go stand with his followers!" Jennifer's father responds looking at his daughter walking away.

"So, can we get the peace treaty signed?" Enoch asks letting the fire go out.

"Well we have our pawns in place, so I am ready to sign the treaty that we have been formulating just waiting for you to read it then agree to it." Madison responds glancing at Enoch and his group of rabbles.

Suddenly there is the sound of a massive tree falling when it slams into a fortification. "Enough with the pleasantries the mortals are attacking directly because you took our best general to act as your guard, Madison!" A wereboar soldier says as she transforms after running into the room.

Now in the thick of the battle Enoch, Maria, Yennifer, Jennifer as standing with their backs facing each other. "Should I go demon grim wolf?" Enoch asks turning his face to Maria.

"Uh when did the mortals get a flying beast?!" Jennifer asks scared.

"Dragons don't listen to anyone's orders unless they speak Draconian!" Enoch responds pulling his spear off his back. "M, cover me I will get that thing out of here!" Enoch continues as he uses his spear to vault into the air and lands on the dragons back.

The dragon decides it wants to get its passenger off its back, so it flies to the ocean and makes a dive for it as Enoch places a hand on the back of its head. "Why are you here?" Enoch asks using telekinesis.

"I have been following you since you killed my child in the port of West Draconia. Didn't realize you ascended to our level. Why do you kill our kind and disrespect our bodies? You don't bury our carcasses you just strip the meat you want and leave our prophecy stones." The dragon responds as it pulls up so they can talk.

"I didn't know about the stones first off and usually it is at most one person besides me fighting your kind. Your kind are massive which makes burial hard. I would love to know about the prophecy, but I only know how to speak your tongue from eating your child's brain." Enoch says moving so he is sitting atop the dragon's head.

"Well maybe find someone of the family line of Draconer they can read our text and point them to the stones we leave behind. If you don't mind, I am going to fly over your silly conflict and roll in flight. Good Luck." The dragon responds as it does what it said.

Enoch is falling through the air he points his spear down at the ground as he lands spear first in the top of some poor sod's head right in front of Maria and the other two. "What did I miss?" Enoch asks in Draconian.

"Not again! Thought you were going to kill it?!" Maria responds annoyed that her partner is speaking what she thinks is a made-up language to mess with her.

"Well when it tried to kill me by diving in the ocean, I decided to go the peace route of try using the knowledge from consuming its child's brain. Yeah, the water dragon back in West Jraconia was that dragon's child. Apparently, I have been just desecrating their corpses and not taking the most valuable part of their carcasses. They generate a stone with some prophecy written in their tongue in their bodies. I need to find some one of the Draconer family." Enoch explains getting back in formation as the non weres run because the dragon has turned around and is breathing fire down on the non weres. Enoch waves at the dragon as it turns to fly away.

"Well that made the battle a lot easier. Let's follow the mortals to find out why they suddenly started hating us!" Madison's best general yells motioning for the army to follow the fleeing opponents.

Now in the rubble of the port city the army are clumped together because they are concerned that the mortals have plotted to ambush them. "I am coming out with my hands up!" a voice yells from inside a barely touched building.

"Angus!" Enoch exclaims realizing who came out.

"I saw you on the back of that dragon. Do you believe me now that dragons are real boyo?" Angus responds looking at the army surrounding him.

"Do you promise to come with us! We want this war to be over!" Jennifer yells pointing a spear at Angus.

"My hands are in the air lassie! I am in surrender stance! Lead and I will follow!" Angus responds annoyed.

Now on their way back to the den Jennifer pulls Enoch back. "Why did you say you have feelings for me then suggest a punishment that doesn't let either of us act on our emotions?" Jennifer asks quietly.

"Do you follow your father's rules when you are miles from the den?" Enoch responds with a question at the same tone.

"Not all the time. But he expects me to write him reports on you." Jennifer says still quietly.

"Leave details out if you want to explore our emotions for each other. You are the head of this group get up front." Enoch responds before slapping Jennifer's bottom as if to tell her to move forward.

Jennifer doesn't respond verbally other than a small peep as she didn't expect Enoch to slap her bum.

Now at the den the soldiers have gone back to their posts and the tribal leaders have been called together.

Enoch is for some reason included in tribal leaders. "So, I have a question. Why am I included in this process I am not a tribal leader of any kind?" Enoch asks looking around.

"By assigning you two people to keep an eye on you and report back to us you have been made an Alpha of your own tribe. I have known of this tribe's existence since it was formed as I assigned your uncle to act as what Marley, Jennifer are for you. We have soldiers reporting that you told Jennifer to disobey her father's orders and she can have relations with you any time you are away from this den. She doesn't have the limitations you suggested. We chose members of our tribes that you have imprinted on because well we get sick of their moodiness while you are not around. They can have relations with you as much as you want. Now back to the matter at hand. So, we are trying ... Angus Draconer for crimes against the weres!" Madison explains coldly.

"Draconer? Uh let me take lead on this!" Enoch says walking towards the floor.

"Why are you going to let this criminal off without a punishment?!" Madison asks annoyed at Enoch's arrogance.

"Did you see the dragon over the battlefield? I was on it's back communicating with it. It mentioned the Draconer tribe can read the Draconian texts. Some huge prophecy on stones that form in the dragon's body." Enoch tries to explain but stops when he realizes everyone is snickering at him. "Would you all believe me if I spoke their tongue?" Enoch asks in Draconian looking around.

"Wait you speak the tongue!?" Angus responds as he goes white. "I can only read it!" Angus continues.

"Ok so you want us to punish him how exactly?" the head of the wereboar army asks annoyed.

"I would make him find the prophecy. The dragon didn't give me much other than it had to be someone of his bloodline that could discover the prophecy." Enoch responds as his confidence starts to waver.

"Let's call a break in the trial and we can discuss this. Only senior alphas need to attend the discussion." Jennifer's father says seeing that Enoch is starting to second guess himself. "Oh, and Jennifer will be attending the meeting!" Jennifer's father continues quickly.

Now outside Enoch is surrounded by Yennifer, Marley, and Maria. "Am I needed? I get the vibe I am not wanted here way too much." Yennifer asks looking around.

"I guess not, Yeny. Good luck." Enoch responds holding his arms open for Yennifer who just walks away.

"I wanted to ask you if it was ok if I joined you earlier, but you don't have a choice now." Marley says looking at Enoch.

"I would have told you to ask your alpha. Don't want to upset your tribe. Though I think I am upsetting all tribe leaders at this point." Enoch responds as Maria hugs him but he holds one arm open for Marley.

"I am sorry about this Enoch, but I guess I am taking my father's spot in this tribunal. Meeting is about to start again." Jennifer says meekly coming outside.

"Can I ask your honest opinion? Should I just give up and let the tribes decide the punishment?" Enoch asks turning to face Jennifer as he let's go of Maria and Marley.

"They are all against you. Though giving up will prove to them you are a weak alpha. Fight for what you believe. I only believe you because I have seen you do some pretty weird stuff. Come in. Leave your support out here. Bringing them will also prove you are too weak." Jennifer responds sighing because she has to be mean to Enoch for now.

Now everyone is back in their seat except Enoch and Madison. "Why do you want us to not properly punish this mortal to find some supposed prophecy?!" Madison asks angrily without getting in Enoch's face.

"Has anyone here even seen a dragon?" Enoch asks looking around. Only one hand goes up and it is Jennifer's. "Anyone other than one of my imprints?" Enoch continues looking around. No more hands go up. "Ok fine I will question the one person I didn't want to for fear people will think I have plotted with her. Jennifer of Xile tribe, when did you see the dragon?" Enoch asks turning to face Jennifer.

"Well other than today I have witnessed you being attacked by them from afar before. Even when you used magic to kill one with Maria by your side. I realize I now sound crazy saying I have witnessed two impossibilities with you present but a winged flying lizard breathing fire doesn't sound too farfetched when you consider we can turn into animals. Unless I get a reasonable argument against me siding with you on dragon's existence I am going to quit talking for now." Jennifer explains looking around before looking at the spot her father said he would stand which he isn't there did she do something he didn't like.

Jennifer's father walks in from the hallway to Jennifer's right. "I have seen dragons before. Maybe not the one today. I put my daughter in my place hoping she hadn't seen more than the one today. I tried to rig this against Enoch. Dragons are real." Jennifer's father says dropping to his knees in front of Enoch. "Forgive me!" Jennifer's father asks looking at the floor.

"Are we going to believe these three people that dragons are real?" The wereboar tribe leader asks annoyed.

"Well it is an even 3 and 3 split. So, I say we ask the prisoner if he thinks they are real!" Madison responds sighing as she grabs Angus' gag.

"Yes, they exist. Untie me and I can show you some scars caused by them!" Angus screams terrified.

"Wait I could show some scars I have!" Enoch chimes in unbuttoning both his shirt and cloak and letting them hit the ground. "That is from the dragon my spear came from. Yes, my spear is dragon bone!" Enoch continues slowly turning so everyone can see his scars.

"Oh, those are just from a monster and he is making excuses!" The wereboar leader yells.

"Take the spear and just set any part of it like the handle to my bare back." Enoch responds fed up with the wereboar leader.

The wereboar leader does as Enoch said and the scars light up as Enoch screams in agony. "Enough! Get it away from my-my b-back!" Enoch screams in agony as the wereboar ignores him causing Enoch to go full demon grim wereboar with glowing white eyes.

"Great you just made him transform! I haven't dealt with him in wereboar state before! How did he do that he doesn't have any wereboar in him!" Jennifer yells rushing to Enoch before she cuts her hand and holds it in front of his face. Enoch licks the blood of Jennifer's hand before turning back to the normal state.

"What was I? All I know is my hearing sucks in that state?!" Enoch exclaims very loudly.

"He c-can go wereboar? Grim wereboar? How?" The wereboar leader asks terrified.

"My guess is the gods of life and death love to pull pranks on those who ask a favor and aren't extremely specific." Enoch responds getting dressed again. "Now I know why your soldiers don't listen once they go were state. They can't hear at all." Enoch continues turning to face the wereboar leader.

"So, what is the vote on dragons being real?" Madison asks looking around as all hands including the wereboar leader go in the air.

"Well you win, Enoch." The Wereboar leader says holding a hand up to Enoch.

"So, Angus is going to be trying to figure out the prophecy. To make sure he does I will be following him. Obviously, my tiny tribe will be following me." Enoch responds grabbing the wereboar leader's hand and pulling him to his feet.

"Let's break for the night and continue this tomorrow." Madison says yawning and stretching.

"My bed should be able to hold the four of us, Enoch." Jennifer says walking up to Enoch.

The four are now in bed and it is kind of obvious someone is upset. Maria is in Enoch's arms. "What's up, M? You seem upset?" Enoch asks whispering in Maria's ear.

"It's nothing!" Maria responds huffing.

"Obviously not! I know what you huffing means. You're upset. What is the source of this issue though?" Enoch asks as Maria rolls over to face him.

"You have become what you hated, and you seem like you are enjoying it!" Maria responds trying to remain quiet.

"I seem like I am enjoying having a tribe? No, I enjoy having all the living were women I have made a mark on around me. If I would have known coming here to end the war would have resulted in my being declared an alpha, I would have told Jennifer no on coming back to this den! If I could get the decision that was made without me reversed I would! I hate the idea of having my every move reported back to the tribes. That is why I disappear from the tribes so often." Enoch explains as he feels a tap on his back.

"You have to do it tonight, but you can get the decision nullified. They will probably hold off on the results of your action tonight till tomorrow morning, but you can get the decision nullified." Jennifer says meekly behind Enoch.

"Who do I go to talk to?" Enoch asks as Jennifer hugs him from behind.

"I will miss you. My father should still be in the alpha chamber." Jennifer responds sobbing.

"I need to get up. Marley, could you lift your head off my leg. M if you want our life back you need to sit up so I can have my arm. I am going out there alone." Enoch says wiggling the limbs he mentions.

Now out in the alpha chamber. "Something wrong new alpha?" Jennifer's father asks looking at Enoch.

"That is the problem. I only returned to end this war not to be declared an alpha against my will. I don't want this. I just wanted to be able to roam freely. I hate the tribe life. Now here I am I have become what I hate. I am a member of a tribe. I don't want this. If I could go back to roaming this mortal coil with my wife I would. Yes, M and I have gotten legally married before we set off from the northern port city before we went to West Jraconia. Your daughter said I can get the decision cancelled by expressing I don't want to be a tribe alpha. Well consider this me stating I don't want to be a tribe alpha. I am headed back to bed if you can't finalize that tonight." Enoch explains as his eyes glow blue in the dimly lit room.

"Noted. We will deal with this first thing tomorrow morning. Sleep as well as you can for now." Jennifer's father responds leaning forward in his chair.

"How'd it go?" Maria asks sitting on the edge of the stone bed as Enoch enters the room.

"Don't really know he only said that we will deal with it first thing tomorrow morning and to sleep as well as I can for now." Enoch responds walking up to Maria.

"That's not good. You are probably being exiled from all tribes completely. Like kill on sight if you cross paths with a tribe member level exiled." Jennifer says sitting up.

"Well nothing I can do right now but sleep." Enoch responds yawning as Maria stands up on the edge of the bed and hugs him, so her head is on his shoulder.

Chapter 16

It is the next morning and Enoch is screaming as he is tied up and a bag is thrown over his head. "WHAT ARE YOU DOING?!" Enoch screams as the ropes around his wrists start to tear from him trying to break his bonds.

"Knock him out!" An unfamiliar voice says before a searing pain as something hits him in the head.

Sometime later Enoch awakes he is on his knees and his hands are bound with chains of mithril behind him while the bag is still on his head. "Enoch of Koftan! You are accused of having thoughts against our way of life! What do you say!" A semi familiar voice yells when the bag is taken off Enoch's head.

"Guilty!" Enoch responds honestly.

"You aren't even going to ask what the thoughts against our way of life are?" Madison asks as Enoch's vision normalizes.

"No. Why would I? I told Jennifer's father that I don't want to be a tribe alpha. I was informed his response means I am probably going to be marked for death." Enoch responds looking right at Madison as his eyes glow red.

"Worse. You are being marked for life by your two imprints that still are recognized as living by the tribes. They will become slaves to their respective tribes" the wereboar leader says dragging Jennifer and Marley into the room.

"Where is M?!" Enoch asks as his eyes go from red to blue.

"I am perfectly safe despite one of the pigs who grabbed you pushed me off the bed and stomped me several attempts under the excuse of it was an accident." Maria responds from behind Enoch.

"Hush it whore!" Madison screams fighting tears.

"You don't call my wife a whore!!!" Enoch yells fighting against the chains as one link snaps.

"Relax Enoch or they may just execute you if they can't contain you!" Jennifer exclaims as she is forced to stand in front of him.

"For them to mark you they will summon their preferred claws and scratch your face. You aren't allowed to just go were and undo the damage or we will make you kill on sight. Jennifer you are up first." Madison explains looking at Jennifer.

"Can I go last?" Jennifer asks trying to stay confident.

"Just do it, Jenny." Enoch says quietly.

"Fine step aside so Marley can mark him!" Madison responds as she couldn't hear Enoch.

Marley steps forward and slashes in a diagonal across Enoch's face right across his left eyelid ripping into his eyeball. "Gyah!" Enoch makes a loud noise in agony.

"Now Jennifer do as you are told!" Jennifer's father yells from his seat.

"I am sorry, Enoch." Jennifer says raising her werecat grim claws hesitantly. "I can't do it!" Jennifer exclaims taking a step back as Enoch tries to catch her as she stumbles.

"If you refuse to do it you will suffer the same punishment as Enoch!" Madison states annoyed.

"I can't. He has admitted he loves me!" Jennifer responds standing up from Enoch's hold.

"Then I must finish what you couldn't do!" Zeke exclaims as he saunters up to his bloodied son.

Zeke summons his wolf claws and slashes in the opposite way that Marley did but misses Enoch's one eye. Enoch just groans from the pain. "I am sorry father." Enoch says in pain quiet enough hopefully only Zeke and Jennifer heard him.

"Get him and the exiled daughter of mine out of here! Don't you two linger!" Madison yells pissed off.

Now at the one remaining tavern in town. "What is the reason the war started doing here? Where is Angus?!" A civilian at their table asks yelling.

"Can't you see he has been exiled?!" A familiar voice responds from behind the bar.

"Can I get a bucket of body temp water? I need to clean up." Enoch asks as Maria helps him onto a stool with his one good eye closed because of the blood that ran down into it.

Now Enoch is all cleaned up except his slashed eye. "How are you going to get that to not be an open wound?" Maria asks as Enoch makes his one good eye glow red.

"Like that hopefully. How does it look?" Enoch responds turning to face Maria.

"The eye is straight white. You are going to be scarred up pretty bad." Maria says motioning for Enoch to look in the mirror behind the bar.

"I have no depth perception now so I can't see much in that mirror. Where is the owner of that familiar voice I heard when we entered, and they defended me?" Enoch asks looking up and down the bar not accounting for his lack of left eye use.

"I am next to you now, Enoch!" Yennifer responds tapping Enoch's shoulder.

"Sorry you are on my left side. Yeny! I figured you would have left by now!" Enoch exclaims turning to face Yennifer.

"They needed a barkeep and I need money. They technically don't allow weres but more and more with scars like your wounds are walking around saying they can't return to the tribe, so I let those be patrons. They have coin and this place runs on coin. I should get behind the bar. There is another were as it looks with fresh wounds on their face entering just now!" Yennifer explains before getting behind the bar and taking care of the bucket.

"It looks to be ... Jennifer." Maria says with a slight bit of panic at the end.

Enoch gets up and heads to the door to get Jennifer. "Hey. Can you see me at all? Open your eyes if you can." Enoch says grabbing Jennifer's shoulders

"I can't see out of my right eye. They slashed it. As for the left I can't see out of it because of the blood running down into it. Is that you, E?" Jennifer responds scared.

"I've got you, Jenny. I will guide you to where I was just sitting." Enoch says grabbing Jennifer's hand.

They have now got Jennifer cleaned up all but her slashed eye. "So how did you get your eye to not be bloody?" Jennifer asks looking at Enoch's face.

"Hold on! I am going to need to take a step over as our bad eyes are currently lined up so for me to see I need to take a step over." Enoch responds as he summons some magic to the palm of his right hand and sets it over Jennifer's Right eye and prays, he is healing her eye so that it is at least intact.

"I can't see out of it are you sure you healed it?" Jennifer asks scared.

"You know that if I completely healed it and you bumped into a tribe member that you would be killed on the spot! I just made it, so it wasn't an open wound." Enoch responds patting Jennifer's leg.

"So, is she joining our adventuring party?" Maria asks looking at the two as they giggle at each other.

"That is up to you, M." Enoch responds as Jennifer hugs him.

"Well she is exiled like the two of us. At least we think she is." Maria says sighing. "So, if she is exiled, I would say we excommunicated need to stick together." Maria continues rolling her eyes at the two impaired hugging.

"Jenny could you scoot over a stool so I can sit at the bar?" Enoch asks patting Maria's back.

Now the group are in their rented room as Enoch stumbles over the bag Maria set down in view of his now blind eye. "M, we have to talk about this. Maybe you should stay on my right side. I know you prefer my left, but I am blind in my left eye now." Enoch says as he catches his balance.

"I promise not to do that again I was just seeing if you are faking being blind considering you made your eyes glow to heal yours. You made it so Jennifer's look like it was cut versus your pure white eye." Maria responds picking her bag up.

"So why are we here now? Isn't it still daytime?" Jennifer asks confused as she looks around looking for Enoch.

"I thought E would catch me on my joke. I wanted to get our room setup then I planned to head back down to try and find us some employment. E, your headed into the bathroom you realize, that right?" Maria explains before looking at Enoch.

"Good I haven't gotten to use the bathroom since last night. Considering I didn't wakeup of my own accord." Enoch responds as he goes to sit on the toilet and Maria comes into the bathroom.

"I need you to look at something. I realize if it is bad, I can't get revenge but knowing how bad it is would be nice." Maria says stripping so she is naked and the bruises from being stomped on can be seen.

"Well I could heal you if you wanted or you could transform and heal it on your own." Enoch responds touching around Maria's bruises.

"I know I could transform but I would like to feel you cast magic on me. You did it for Jennifer and I felt kind of jealous." Maria says meekly as Enoch is carefully touching her side.

Enoch doesn't say anything just closes his eyes and focuses energy to the palm of his hand and hovers it over Maria's bruised body and as the bruise starts disappearing, he collapses and stops healing her. "Are you okay?!" Maria asks dropping to catch Enoch.

"Sorry just a little over drawn today. I was using magic to stop me from bleeding out when we were trying to find a place to call home for the day. Then I healed Jennifer's eye with what magic I figured was safe to use then I thought screw it you are my actual wife so I should try and help. I need a good meal is all." Enoch responds as he attempts to stand up.

"So, are you two actually married like he keeps saying?" Jennifer asks peaking around the door frame.

Maria doesn't speak just shows Jennifer her left hand and her ring. Enoch once stood up holds out his left hand even though he can't see it all that well considering he is front on with Maria, so he is reaching past her to holdout his hand.

"So, we technically can't legally do anything?" Jennifer asks with a hint of sadness in her voice.

"We can so long as we don't do it out in the town square. What happens in the bedroom is none of the public's business." Maria responds before Enoch can say anything.

"Why did you respond?" Jennifer asks looking at Maria funny.

"I've wanted to have relations with you for a seemingly long time. Plus, you and I are both E's so if he wants the two of us at once we kind of have to do it for him." Maria responds smiling before going werecat and quickly back to normal.

"You are bi?" Enoch asks looking at Maria funny. "You apparently never touched your assigned female back in Koftan." Enoch continues as Maria walks up to him.

"Wouldn't you like to know my exact sexuality? If you all are ready, I am going downstairs to try and find us a job. I want to get out of this hole as soon as possible. I am guessing Koftan is now forever off our list considering it is probably crawling with tribe members because of the war." Maria responds initially touching Enoch's lips before heading to the door.

"She seems weird now." Jennifer says as she walks next to Enoch and stops.

"I think she is processing that her own mother called her a whore or processing that her mother sees her as dead." Enoch responds looking at Jennifer so he can see her with his left eye being useless and all.

"Enoch, I know I lied at the den but please tell me if I got myself exiled for nothing?" Jennifer asks looking at Enoch fighting back tears.

"I caught you because I care. I need time to process my emotions. You knew about them making me an alpha, didn't you?" Enoch responds touching Jennifer's shoulder.

"Yes and no. I knew about them having Marley act as a spy for them following you. I didn't know it was because they were going to make you an alpha. I didn't know the knowledge you let slip would make my own father make me follow you around." Jennifer says as a tear falls from her left eye but not the right one.

"Let's join, M." Enoch responds before leaning in as to kiss Jennifer.

Now downstairs the trio are sitting at the bar enjoying their separate plates of food when a belligerent drunk shoves Maria's plate shoving the other two in a way, they go sailing off the bar onto the floor. "WHAT ARE THESE WERE'S DOING HERE!" the local swill bowl screams before shoving Maria.

Enoch turns to face the swill bowl revealing his eyes are glowing blue. "If I were you, swill bowl I would get your arse out of town. Before I reveal why I am here and not allowed back in the tribe!" Enoch responds as his voice starts getting extremely gravelly.

"E, you can't transform till the wounds heal completely but I can!" Maria chimes in letting her fangs show.

Suddenly Angus walks in looking a little worse for wear. "Angus!" The room of mortal's yell raising their glasses.

"Where are the weres that got my sentence reduced from death to letting me live! There they are! Quit hassling the people who helped me end that fecking war!" Angus exclaims grabbing the drunkard from behind and tossing him to the floor. "Fecking swill bowl!" Angus continues.

"That swill bowl threw our food on the floor that was the last of my silver! I ought to take it out of his hide!" Enoch chimes in letting fire rise from his right hand as his eyes are still glowing.

"Please don't we just got the war over with. While everyone agrees he is a swill bowl we don't dare touch him more than getting him to quit attacking people who everyone except him likes. His father is the mayor. Although we are not totally sure if his father is still among the living to be honest." Angus responds explaining why killing the swill bowl is a bad idea.

"Can the three of us work for you?" Maria asks looking at Angus.

"Depends has the wounded girl been actually exiled or did they send her to be a spy?!" Angus responds looking at Jennifer.

"They didn't say anything other than my father apologized when he slashed my face. Marley snickered. Madison told me to get out of the den. I stumbled my way here sniffing for the familiar scent of E and M." Jennifer explains staring off as a tear rolls down her cheek from her good eye.

"Yes, the dishonored daughter has been exiled. As have Enoch and Maria. I am here to tell them that while they aren't on the kill on sight list but that they should avoid all known hotbeds of were activities for at least six months as we are struggling to get in touch with some groups of weres." Marley says coming in before leaving when she is done speaking.

"Let's go kill that were!" A group of non weres scream.

"No, the war is over! Plus, she is connected to the head of the Koftan tribe killing her would undo what these three patriots have done for us! Don't make their sacrifice be in vain!" Angus exclaims rushing to the door as Yennifer blocks the door.

"The war has ended why start a new one so soon? We should focus on rebuilding what we lost in the war!" Yennifer responds standing in front of the door.

Now in the backroom of the tavern the trio are eating fresh plates of food paid for by Yennifer. "Enoch, so what did that dragon say of the prophecies?" Angus asks looking at the two half blind weres attempting to eat with their reduced vision in a semi dark room.

"Not much other than we have to kill them to get the stones the prophecy is on. Kind of an odd thing for them to know about unless that dragon is an elder dragon." Enoch responds unable to locate Angus with his vision blurring from a mix of exhaustion and fighting slipping into demon grim state.

"Is everything ok with Enoch?" Angus asks looking at Maria.

"I am exhausted and struggling to not go into my demon were states from being exhausted." Enoch responds as he finishes his plate of food.

"So, what are your demon were states?" Angus asks confused.

"When Alice died, I made a plea to the gods of life and death. I offered my ability to go were. They took it and revived Alice. I insisted Alice go were. She went grim werecat with glowing eyes and tried to eat my arm. M killed Alice to save me and while I was rolling around on the deck of my ship in agony a glowing light came out of Alice's mouth apparently and I inhaled it and instantly went grim were with glowing eyes. I call the glowing eyed grim demon were state. It is the only were states I have access to. I had to relearn my triggers for the demon wolf and demon cat states. Yesterday I learned of the demon boar state. There is another one I haven't identified yet. It only shows up in moments of intense anger worse than the demon wolf state. My eyes glow red in for that one." Enoch explains before chugging the mead in front of his right eye.

"Oy that was my mead!" Jennifer yells annoyed.

"Where is mine?" Enoch asks looking around. "Here it is!" Enoch exclaims grabbing his glass which was fuller than Jennifer's and passing it to her.

"So, are you two seriously blind in those eyes?" Angus asks looking between Enoch and Jennifer.

"I can't see out of my left. I only know M is on that side of me because of my were detection senses." Enoch responds as he leans back in his chair.

"I am blind in my right can't see if anything is that way of me. Which is why I am on E's right side." Jennifer says looking at Enoch as he leans back like she is longing for something.

"J if you want something can it wait till, we aren't in something akin to a job interview?" Enoch asks leaning into whisper in Jennifer's ear.

"Well I would like everyone mentally on the top of their game if we are talking about important matters like employment. Let's meet up tomorrow morning?" Angus says looking around the table at the three disheveled weres.

"Can the two of us finish eating?" Maria asks meekly.

"Take your time. Although it is just you who isn't done." Angus responds watching the interactions between the two who are finished eating.

"E quit touching her that way in public!" Maria quietly exclaims as Enoch is touching Jennifer's shoulders.

"He isn't touching me inappropriately he noticed that one of the people who marked me got my shoulder as well." Jennifer responds as Enoch stands up, so Maria has a clear view of Jennifer's shoulder.

Now out in the main part of the tavern the trio are sitting in the back where the lighting is darker. A familiar dwarf saunters up to the table the trio are sat at. "Mind if I join you three?" Yennifer asks as there is a snore from Enoch.

"Sit down if you want, Yeny." Enoch responds looking up at her.

"I thought you were asleep from the sound you made!" Yennifer exclaims as she sits down.

"No, when he is exhausted and fighting going demon grim state, he makes noises that sounds like snoring, but they aren't it is more like the demon grim growling to get out." Maria explains kind of jealous of how Jennifer is asleep on Enoch's right shoulder.

"M if you want to cuddle with me like J is go ahead. I am not going to stop you. Actually, I would quite enjoy if you would cuddle with me. I want both of my fellow exiled female weres to cuddle with me." Enoch says moving his left arm for Maria to cuddle with him.

"Wish I could cuddle with you, Enoch." Yennifer says meekly.

"Sorry about the past but how I feel about you hasn't really changed. Except I am grateful you were my first time." Enoch responds glancing at Yennifer as a snore like sound is heard but this time it is Jennifer on his shoulder as Enoch heard it as well.

"Oh, ok. She is out." Yennifer says somewhat saddened.

"Yeah we may be headed for our room shortly. M, you still have the key I gave you?" Enoch responds wiggling his left shoulder which Maria is starting to fall asleep on.

"I put it in your pocket when I scooted over here to cuddle with you. Can I please cuddle with you for a little bit before we head to bed?" Maria asks sleepily.

"You two could cuddle with me in bed you do realize that?" Enoch responds kissing the top of Maria's head as he lets out a snore sound. "And we don't have to wear these clothes that non weres force us to wear." Enoch continues as Jennifer lifts her head.

"M I have to side with E on this. I hate having to wear clothing." Jennifer says sitting up and groggily looking around.

Now back up in the room the trio are all getting ready for bed when there is a knock at the bedroom door. "I will get it! As I can answer the door shirtless." Enoch says opening the door just a crack.

"Hey, I am sorry for what I did. I wish I could have not done it, but they were threatening to kill me as my master is dead so why should I exist. Will you forgive me?" Marley explains meekly looking at Enoch's straight white eye.

"Marley go home! I am done with the tribes. My blind left eye is proof I am done. You caused me to have this blind eye. Why would I forgive you for messing up my vision? Get away from me. I don't want to declare war against the tribes. It is not a battle I could win. However, my demon grim states hate you enough that they don't care the consequences." Enoch responds as his eyes glow blood red.

"I will be going then." Marley says sorrowfully.

Now back in the room with the door locked the trio are all naked when suddenly Enoch's were senses start going nuts. Suddenly the door flies open with Zeke in the lead and Yennifer cowering behind him. "Where is that slave?!" Zeke demands growling.

"You mean Marley?" Enoch asks turning to face his father still naked.

"Yes, the slave!?" Zeke demands getting angrier.

"Don't know sent her away a couple of minutes ago. I would like to not have the tribe constantly in my life so why would I let her hide here with me. Plus because of her I can't see out of my left eye. You at least left me vision in my right eye." Enoch responds yawning with a small snore like sound.

"What was that sound?!" Zeke asks still growling.

"Being marked took a lot out of me. My demon grim are fighting to get free and when exhausted it sounds like a snore when one of them growls." Enoch tries to explain as his vision is going fuzzy.

"I guess she isn't here." Zeke responds before turning away and leaving.

"Yeny, did you unlock the door? If so, could you close it and relock it, please?" Enoch asks looking where he thinks Yennifer is standing.

"Sure thing, Enoch. Get some sleep you look like you are about to fall over." Yennifer responds doing as she was asked.

The trio are lying in bed with Maria behind Enoch and Jennifer in his arms. "I would like to do something before we fall asleep if you don't mind E?" Jennifer says rolling to face Enoch.

"May I ask what you want to do Jenny?" Enoch asks looking in Jennifer's left eye with his right.

"No sexual acts tonight!" Maria softly exclaims.

"Is making out with E considered sexual?" Jennifer asks meekly.

"I wouldn't say it is unless you are planning to use making out as an excuse to slide me into you." Enoch responds pulling Jennifer in closer.

"No, I may climb on top, but it would be just to get a better angle on you." Jennifer says meekly.

A little while later just as the two are finishing making out. "Could you go back to in front of E please? Your knee is in my stomach." Maria asks slapping Jennifer's leg.

"Yeah and I can't sleep with this much weight on my chest. Well it is more your bosom is pressing into my chest squishing air out of my lungs." Enoch says pushing on Jennifer's left side.

"Ok fine I will lay in front of you. Can you hold me again?" Jennifer asks meekly.

"Planned on it, Jenny. I was enjoying that till it got harder to breath from your bosom pressing into me. May I ask when your birthday is?" Enoch responds as he rolls onto his left side.

"It is coming up in the next month. I will be thirty next month. I was hoping I would have had my true first time by now to be honest." Jennifer says partially zoned out.

"Maybe I can get that done before you turn thirty years old. M when is your birthday again?" Enoch asks touching Maria's thigh with his right hand.

"It is in two months. I will be twenty years of age. I haven't revealed that information to you yet. Not even on our wedding day did I let that information slip. Kind of didn't think you would go through with it. You know with you disappearing for a decade after we just met and all." Maria responds meekly before hugging Enoch from behind and sobbing on his shoulder enjoying both his touch and his smell.

"I hope to be in your life till we both die." Enoch says wiggling the fingers on his right hand.

"E if I moved your hand someplace would you leave it where I put it?" Maria asks meekly.

"As long as it isn't painful to leave it there sure." Enoch responds as Maria moves his right hand on to her personal place.

Chapter 17

As the sun starts to rise Enoch awakes, he is on his back and the two girls are asleep with their heads on each shoulder. His right hand is still between Maria's legs, but it is resting on her thigh and his left hand is on Jennifer's back as she snores in his ear. "You are finally awake?" Maria asks quietly as she lifts herself to kiss Enoch on the cheek.

"What's up, M?" Enoch responds turning his head to look at her.

"I thought maybe freedom from the tribe would feel differently. Here I am sharing my husband with his predecessor and I feel like I have been ignored on my wants. Why did you agree to bring her with us?" Maria explains before looking up to meet Enoch's gaze.

"I asked you if it was okay with you. You said if she was exiled like us, we needed to stick together. Why are you just now taking issue with it? I have made promises to her I can't break again." Enoch responds looking down at Maria as Jennifer reaches across Enoch's chest and puts a hand on Maria's hand.

"If you don't want me around M just say something. I will find a way in this world on my own. You aren't the only one cast out of your tribe by your only parent." Jennifer says opening her eyes revealing they are red from crying herself to sleep last night.

"E, I found out yesterday that my mother sees me as dead. All I really remember is you losing vision in your one eye and going to bed with your hand on my private place." Maria responds as she turns Enoch's hand, so he is cupping her down there.

"So, can we talk about Jenny being a part of our group?" Enoch asks wiggling the fingers on his right-hand making Maria squirm.

"Sure, but I am very ... in need of attention down there." Maria responds enjoying as Enoch continues moving his fingers down there.

"We need to get moving and see if we can work." Enoch says slowing his fingers.

"Can you please focus on me for five minutes?" Maria asks grabbing Enoch's arm as if to stop him from pulling away.

"I was going to finish what I started with you here then we need to get a move on with finding a job. Jenny can you wait on what we talked about last night?" Enoch responds as Jennifer gets up sobbing.

"You just don't want to do as you said you would, do you?!" Jennifer asks getting upset.

"Jenny, that isn't what he said. Unlike you or I he can't reach climax so soon after having just done so. I will hold him to whatever he said last night if you will let me have some fun with him right now." Maria responds climbing on top of Enoch.

"I promised to do this with her before she turns thirty years old next month." Enoch explains.

Now a duo of the trio is downstairs. Jennifer has been down here for a little bit while the other two were having their fun. "What would you like to order miss?" the bartender asks looking at Jennifer.

"I don't have any money. I can't order anything till my roommates get down here." Jennifer responds upset.

"Go ahead and order, J. I am down here while M gets cleaned up." Enoch says sitting next to Jennifer.

"I don't honestly know what I want, E. Why didn't you think of me instead of her?" Jennifer responds quietly looking at Enoch revealing she is crying.

"If you had expressed interest in some fun this morning before M did, I would have done it with you instead. It is kind of first come first serve on that kind of thing." Enoch says grabbing Jennifer's left hand with his right.

"I am new when it comes to relationships. I wasn't allowed contact with anyone other than my father for fear of being imprinted on. He wanted to use me as a bargaining chip. No one realized you imprinted on me when you were a newborn. No one really thought that kind of thing could happen let alone that I could imprint on you when you were a newborn." Jennifer responds leaning on Enoch's shoulder.

"Honestly I am glad I marked all the weres I marked. I miss Alice dearly. I even am glad I marked Marley despite she is the one that I marked who in the end had no problem marking me as an enemy of all tribes." Enoch says kissing Jennifer's forehead.

"What are you two talking about?" Maria asks sitting on the other side of Enoch.

"She was upset that I did it with you and not her this morning. I explained it is kind of first come first serve considering the limitations of the male body. Then she mentioned how we marked each other when I was born, and I was talking about how I am thankful that I marked all the weres I did even Marley." Enoch explains as Maria rests her head on Enoch's left shoulder.

"What would you three like to order?" the bartender asks annoyed.

"Got any suggestions for breakfast?" Enoch responds as he hears a snore from Jennifer.

"Our breakfast plate is pretty popular. Fried bread, 2 sunny side up eggs, a scoop of beans, blood sausage, mashed potatoes, kippered herring, sautéed mushrooms, rasher of bacon, banger of sausage. If you want, we can add a broiled tomato with local goat cheese melted on top. Can't forget our black coffee. We also offer white coffee if black is too strong for you." The bartender explains looking at Enoch.

"Blood sausage? Hrph!" Jennifer says waking up at the mention of blood in food.

"Sounds like a slice of home. Is the person in charge of the menu from Koftan? I will take it by the way with a broiled tomato with the cheese and a black coffee." Enoch responds drooling a little.

"Yes, I am! I am the owner. By the way I am not anti were. Just so happens most of my patrons are." the bartender says writing down Enoch's order. "How about you miss?" she asks turning to Maria.

"I will have the same thing he is having. We are both from Koftan." Maria responds lifting her head.

"How about you miss?" the bartender asks looking at Jennifer.

"Remove the blood sausage and I will take the breakfast plate without the tomato and a white coffee." Jennifer responds meekly while yawning.

A few minutes later the trio have their plates of food when angus saunters down the stairs. "How was your sleep tonight, Angus?" the owner asks standing across from Angus as he sits next to Maria.

"Better than if I tried to sleep in my house. Considering it is still smoldering from the swill bowls in the war burning it down because I associated with Enoch here before the war." Angus responds looking down the line as Jennifer is trying to not watch the other two eating the blood sausage. "What is the problem miss?" Angus asks looking at Jennifer.

"Blood sausage is disgusting. Blood is something you shouldn't eat as a non were." Jennifer responds not looking towards whoever is asking questions.

"Well the two sitting next to you are weres." Angus says chuckling.

"They aren't in a were state." Jennifer responds gagging.

"So, I like the three of you as potential employees but ..." Angus says before Maria interrupts.

"You are declining because we are weres aren't you!?" Maria asks angrily.

"No not at all. I can't afford to pay anyone right now. All my money was in my house that got burnt down. If I could afford to pay you I would." Angus responds annoyed.

"Well what would the mission be if we offered to work for free for the first mission?" Enoch asks taking a sip of his coffee.

"E, we can't really live off working for free?!" Maria responds angrily.

"M, remember the money we got from the transport job we did? I still have all but the coins I spent last night so I have more than enough to live off of for at least one job." Enoch says annoyed with Maria.

"I thought we were putting that towards another ship?" Maria asks still angry.

"One job isn't going to make it so we can't afford a ship. Plus, if someone is willing to pay for this job, I think forfeiting our pay to help Angus for one job isn't bad. He is taking a risk employing three of our kind in a town that hates our kind." Enoch responds sighing at Maria.

"If Angus can find a job, I will pay for it if you give all profit to Angus." The owner says looking right at Enoch as she slides Angus his usual order of food.

"I have finished my food can I go somewhere that people aren't consuming blood?" Jennifer asks meekly looking at Enoch from the side.

"Go take a bath, Jenny. When you are done, we should be done eating. If I had known I wouldn't have ordered it. Jenny, I don't intentionally do things to upset you. I am not that kind of person." Enoch responds offering Jennifer a hug.

"I love you." Jennifer whispers in Enoch's ear.

"Love you, too." Enoch responds in Jennifer's ear.

"So, what is the relationship between the three of you?" the owner asks confused after Jennifer has headed upstairs.

"So, you know we are weres correct?" Enoch responds looking at the owner.

"Yes, I could figure from your conversation earlier." The owner says still looking at Enoch funny.

"So, Jennifer and I are a bit unique. We are both half werewolf and werecat. We were both born to be a peace treaty if you will. Well the requirements required the child from the werewolf and werecat pairing to be a son. So, Jennifer and her parents were cast out and exiled here to South Jraconia. Apparently, they expected a girl to be born from the pairing of my parents, so they were sent here while pregnant with me. I was born. I am a male obviously. Well a side note Jennifer was there when I was born, she held me and newborn me imprinted on her. Even more weird she imprinted on me right then and there. Fast forward to when I was 16 years old, I am running through the forest known to house the Koftan were tribes and I find a werecat attacking a young girl. I step in threaten to kill the werecat if she doesn't leave the young girl alone. Well that young girl informs me her sister would leave us alone. I set out patching the young girl up. I imprinted on that young girl. I also imprinted on her sister when I held my knife to her throat. Well the one I patched up was young M here. Fast forward a decade and I find out M is still alive after her family informed me; she died a year prior. I get upset and tell her I want nothing to do with her. A little bit later I get upset and tell her older sister and Jennifer I want nothing to do with the tribes and then set off on a journey of self-discovery. Eleven months later I end up in OxenDeValley in a tavern where I bump into M for the last time. I say the last time because we haven't been separated from each other since. We actually got married legally by non weres in West Jraconia. We get cast out from there after a job and Alice got killed. We return to the port on the Inland sea of Jraconia Jennifer bumps into us begs us to end the war. Stuff goes down where all three of us were cast out of the tribes completely. Jennifer and I getting marked losing vision in one of our eyes each. Well here we are more or less." Enoch explains between bites of food and sips of coffee.

"Wow that is the quickest I have heard someone sum up their life story. I am guessing you left out my newest bartender from your story. She said she knows you." The owner responds a little surprised.

"She was who I was the reason I was in the forest when I encountered M. We were taking a small break from adventuring before a big job. I set off on a decade of self-reflection when she told me she wanted nothing to do with me after she witnessed me patching up M." Enoch explains as he slides his empty plate and cup forward.

"Wow you eat quicker than I do!" Maria says looking at Enoch's empty plates.

"I needed to recoup some energy after our morning activities." Enoch responds turning to face Maria.

Some time has passed and everyone at the bar of the group is done eating when Jennifer comes down and sits down on Enoch's right side. "So, what kind of job do you have for us, Angus?" Enoch asks sliding Jennifer on her stool closer to him.

"Well there is a job where a dragon is terrorizing a farmer over towards the mountainous woods." Angus responds not paying attention to Enoch as he is looking through the stack of job scrolls in front of him.

"Well anything else?" Jennifer asks meekly.

"All I have is jobs where we have to slay dragons." Angus responds sighing at Jennifer's cowardice.

"We will go with the one terrorizing the farmer near the mountainous woods." Enoch says as he puts his arm around Jennifer's back.

"Which one? There are quite a few in that area complaining of dragons." Angus responds sighing.

"Uh pick one maybe we take down one dragon we may complete multiple jobs." Enoch says as Jennifer taps his leg.

"Why did you scoot me in so close?" Jennifer asks looking up at Enoch.

"Thought you might want to cuddle with me." Enoch responds looking right at Jennifer.

"Meh I am content with just being near you right now. I may have taken care of my horniness while I was in the tub. That is why I took so long to get back down here." Jennifer says kind of meekly.

"Well if you want fun time before we go to bed tonight then I am open to it." Enoch responds looking at Jennifer before turning his head to look the other direction. "We should probably set out if we want to make a decent time on getting there." Enoch says looking down at Angus.

Now out on the road the group are headed through the shivering mountains as a group of green skin can be spotted from the distance. "Hold up! Green skins here are very savage and very hostile. In other areas they are slave owners. Here they are practically cave men." Angus says stopping the group as Enoch rushes past transforming into a werefox with glowing purple eyes.

Enoch sneaking in his all white furred demon grim werefox state is getting close to the green skins. He vaults into the air above the one carrying a horn and lands on top of it sinking his teeth in its throat, so it doesn't make a noise before he rips its throat out. He moves on to the next green skin repeating the process till he has just one green skin goblin left to kill. Enoch for this one returns to his non were state and then goes demon werewolf quickly and bites the green skin general's throat out but due to the size of his maw he rips the green skin's head off and spits it out before returning to his non were state with his scars still very much so intact. Sauntering up to the group. "That felt amazing. Don't recommend trying to eat them though.

Tastes awful and it is tougher than a leather boot. Don't ask how I know how tough a leather boot is." Enoch says sauntering up to Jennifer as she is barfing in the snow.

"Why is she getting sick so much?" Angus asks worried that Jennifer is a liability more than a useful member.

"I haven't heard of anyone who swallows the throats of things they bite in were state. That is about as gross as blood sausage." Jennifer responds wiping her chin on a cloth Enoch held out for her.

"Well you must live with a bunch of snobby weres." Enoch responds refusing to take Jennifer's sick rag back.

"No, E you are the first I have heard of a were swallowing the throat of a humanoid kill." Maria says agreeing with Jennifer on this one being an Enoch thing.

"Well in my defense my parents didn't bother teaching me how a were deals with the throats of what they kill. So, I just have always swallowed them. Including the throats of other weres. Might also explain why I used to eat a lot of workhorse meat. I just saw it as another type of meat that is almost always cheaper than anything else in most markets around the world that I have been to." Enoch responds rubbing his chin.

"Workhorse meat?" Jennifer asks terrified.

"You don't want to know, J." Maria says quickly before Enoch can talk.

"Some call it long pork. They also call the people that eat it cannibals." Enoch responds trying not to go into too much detail on this one as his stomach is starting to roll before he barfs up the throats of the green skins in the snow.

"Yeah, green skin flesh makes everything I have witnessed try to eat it get sick. Only seen a gnome eat it successfully." Angus says laughing at Enoch barfing up the green skin bits he ate.

"Gnomes are real?" Maria asks shocked at the news she just heard.

"Yes, ma'am. As real as you and me. Let's get a move on. I don't want to try and set camp up in these frigid mountains." Angus responds nodding.

The group are just getting outside of the mountains when there is a roar behind them. A shadow bear has followed the group for some distance. "So, which of you wants to kill this thing?" Angus asks hoping he gets to see another were state.

Enoch transforms into a demon grim werebear state towering over the shadow bear with glowing red eyes. Enoch roars hoping the actual bear is too stupid to run. The bear starts to run away as Enoch gives chase on all fours. He is faster than the bear. When he catches up, he grabs it by the leg in his giant maw and starts spinning before letting go throwing the bear against the rocks at the mouth of a cave spine first as a loud crack echoes around both the cave and the mountains.

Enoch lunges grabbing the bear by the throat throwing it back towards the group as he rips its throat out and swallows the bit of flesh in his maw before bolting towards the group. As he gets close to the group he returns to his human state and trips over a stone and tumbles up next to the bear corpse. "So, bear meat for dinner?" Enoch asks standing up and brushing the snow off.

"Do you think everyone loves obscure meats?" Jennifer asks looking at Enoch like he is mentally insane.

"Seeing the other two are drooling I would say it isn't too far off to say they would like to try it." Enoch responds looking at the other two fighting drooling.

"I don't like eating weird meats. I barely like eating meat in general." Jennifer says crossing her arms over her chest.

"I can't cut meat out. It is what is giving me energy to do all this demon grim state transformations. Plus, it gives me the energy for some fun time on top of all the transforming." Enoch responds as he starts carving the bear.

"Avoid it's paws they contain poison pouches." Angus says chiming in.

"Thank you for that warning. Never actually fought one of these let alone carved one." Enoch responds as he is carving. "M, grab the bag I tend to put meat in, please." Enoch continues as he is holding a huge chunk of meat from the bear's shoulder.

Sometime later the bear is nothing but skeleton except for its paws and head which Enoch decided to leave alone as he saw a purplish liquid drip from the bears fangs. Now the group are setting up the camp. "J, do you want to have some fun tonight? I ask as I think a separate tent for that would be wise, so we don't disturb M." Enoch asks looking at Jennifer as she is struggling with hammering in the stake to hold the tent in place.

"I just want to get this stake in the ground at the moment!" Jennifer yells fighting tears.

"You aren't hitting the stake sweetie. You need to focus your one good eye on the stake not put it in your blind spot." Enoch responds rushing to help Jennifer.

"You think I don't know what I am doing, E!?" Jennifer asks still yelling.

"It isn't that I don't have faith in you, Jenny. It is I watched you miss the stake several swings in a row." Enoch responds offering Jennifer some assistance as together they get the stake in place.

"I think I would like a tent just for us." Jennifer says softly as she looks at the ground.

"Ok, sweetie. If you could maybe help M with starting the fire, I will get the tents for M, you and I." Enoch responds before kissing Jennifer on the cheek.

Now all tents are setup and the group are frying bear meat and something for Jennifer to eat. "So why does the lass with one eye not want to try the bear meat?" Angus asks looking at Jennifer funny.

"If I could survive without eating flesh of animals I would but being a were I need to eat animal flesh every day to be able to transform." Jennifer responds annoyed at Angus as Enoch plates up her food and hands it to her.

"She is a weird one however I do still care about her. Just got to get used to her little quirks." Enoch says plating up Maria's food for her before moving onto plating up Angus's food. "Now for my food." Enoch continues as he tosses a mix of what he made for Jennifer with a small amount of bear meat.

"You are chancing eating the same thing as her?" Angus asks giving Enoch a funny look.

"She is who I am sharing a tent with tonight so I should give what she likes to eat a try even if I have to add a small amount of the bear meat so my body can recoup the energy I have spent with the three transformations." Enoch responds keeping his eye on Jennifer's plate and what he is cooking.

"Enoch, could I try some of the bear meat?" Jennifer asks quietly leaning in so she can whisper in Enoch's ear.

"Figured you would want some hence why I added extra in what is on the stone currently." Enoch responds whispering for only Jennifer to hear him.

A little time has passed, and Enoch plates up his food. "Can we share the plate?" Jennifer asks quietly looking at Enoch.

"I need to recoup my strength if you want to have fun tonight, but you can try as you asked a couple minutes ago." Enoch responds looking at Jennifer who looks like she is struggling to even hold her own fork up. "Is something wrong, Jenny?" Enoch asks concerned.

"I just started feeling weak a couple of minutes ago." Jennifer responds meekly.

"Let me try what you asked for and I will hand you the plate." Enoch says looking at Jennifer with a look of worry.

Dinner has finished Jennifer has seemed to regain some strength. The duo are in the tent now both are nude while cuddling. "Are you sure you can do this tonight?" Enoch asks concerned for Jennifer.

"I want to. I don't care if I can't physically do it." Jennifer responds looking at Enoch with her one eye.

"You seem more upset than physically weak." Enoch says softly as he gets to Jennifer.

"I once swore that I would someday be completely reliant on plants for my nutrients, but I couldn't figure a way to pull it off. Heck what I had you cook me originally is vegetarian, but my body was screaming that I needed meat. Which is probably why I was so weak, and you had to give up the plate of food you made for yourself. I am sorry about that." Jennifer responds looking down trying to avoid Enoch's eye as he puts his hand under her chin and lifts it up so he can look her in the eye.

"I am not upset with you. I would rather give up my food than have you collapse because you aren't eating what you need. Jennifer you are just as important to me as M is." Enoch says holding Jennifer's chin so she can't look down.

"So, do you want to do it in non were state or in were state?" Jennifer asks looking at Enoch like she is hoping he just goes with her changing the subject.

"I don't trust any of my were states with having fun. We aren't done discussing your dietary needs. Just know I will bring that up at a later time." Enoch responds as he grips Jennifer's bum with his left hand that she has been laying on.

"Would you two quiet down!?" Angus yells annoyed.

The duo decide it is best to have fun without speaking so they go at it and fall asleep when they have finished.

Chapter 18

The next morning the duo wake up before sunrise and decide they should probably take baths since they went to sleep immediately after the festivities last night.

Out by the nearest body of water the two are bathing while talking about seemingly unimportant things. "So how about fish?" Enoch asks as he washes himself.

"I don't mind eating fish if that is what you are asking. Though my preference is Salmon." Jennifer responds before turning to face Enoch in hopes she can get another round in before they officially start their day.

"I don't want to chance a second day doing it first thing in the morning. Though if tonight you express interest before M does I will gladly do it with you again. You arch your back way differently than she does. I enjoy it with both of you but for your first time you really focused on me not all that much on yourself." Enoch says moving in closer to Jennifer.

"Well maybe if I focus on you, you will make sure I get to reach climax as well." Jennifer responds meekly as Enoch embraces her.

"I would focus on you getting to reach climax anyway. You are just as important as I am in the act. Without you I am left having a toss, without me you are left fingering yourself." Enoch says leaning into kiss Jennifer.

A little while later the duo are at the campsite setting up the fire to cook breakfast as Maria wakes up and stumbles out of her tent and about falls into Enoch's lap. "I didn't sleep good without you, E." Maria says groggily looking up at Enoch from his lap. "Wait your hair is wet! Did you bathe without me?!" Maria continues sad.

"Sorry, yes. I went to sleep immediately after having fun with Jenny last night, so I had to clean up this morning." Enoch responds looking down at Maria.

"She is so loud when she reaches climax!" Angus says angrily as he leaves his tent.

"I am sorry. It was my first-time last night. I can't help that I was loud." Jennifer responds meekly.

"Oy! Quit giving her guff because she is different. I don't like working with Jraconian's because your kind are so harsh to my kind. I think this may be the only job we do with you if you don't quit being mean to us.

I may even request our pay for this job." Enoch chimes in as his eyes glow red and his voice turns more into a growl like a bear.

"Get your attack dog in check!" Angus says looking at Maria.

"Sorry sir you are on your own from this point on. If you can't quit insulting our kind you don't need our help with killing dragons." Maria responds sitting up in Enoch's lap.

"You all agreed to help! You can't back out!" Angus screams before kicking over the stone with their breakfast on it.

"YOU ARE ON YOUR OWN! YOU DEMANDED ALL THE PAY YOU CAN EARN IT!" Enoch screams back fighting the urge to maul this racist bigot. "Ladies we are packing our stuff up and leaving this idiot to deal with his mistakes himself." Enoch says quietly.

The trio left the racist Angus Draconer 'Dragon Slayer' as they went towards OxenDeValley. Arriving in OxenDeValley. "Halt! You can't enter there are reports of dragons attacking a nearby farmer!" A guard exclaims stopping the trio.

"Let them die! If Angus Draconer 'Dragon Slayer' who they requested can't kill the dragons then that is their fault! That racist dolt doesn't need the help of weres as he sees my kind as inferior!" Enoch responds letting his right hand ignite in purple flames and holds it ready to throw it at the guard.

"Let them in. If they are telling the truth, the farmers are either dead or will be by the time the guy they mentioned gets there. Plus, the farmers are weres as well." The guard captain says pushing the guard of the gate aside.

"Did you say the farmers are weres as well?" Enoch asks letting the fire go out.

"Yes, a farm owned and operated by members of the tribe from the port on the world ocean." The captain responds watching Enoch.

"We can't really interfere with the tribes. But if he finds out he was hired to help our kind he may just bail on them." Jennifer says quietly.

"We will be back!" Enoch exclaims looking at the captain. "Weres have to stick together." Enoch says quietly to the other two.

Now at the farms before Angus even shows up the trio are conversing with a farmer while waiting for a dragon to attack. "So, you two are exiled from the tribe yet you came to help?" the farmer asks looking at Enoch and Jennifer funny.

"Weres need to stick together in this world. Some one here hired Angus Draconer who is hardcore racist against our kind." Enoch responds looking right at the farmer with his right eye.

"Oh well the dragon should show up as the second sun is directly overhead." The farmer says nodding.

As a Dragon comes flying in the trio have set up to defend when Angus comes running towards the farm chasing the dragon. "Turn back citizen!" Enoch yells as he sends a purple fireball at the dragon hitting it with a huge flash of light. The fireball doesn't cleave off the wing it hit but it ignites the thin fleshy membrane allowing the dragon flight causing it to crash down in front of Enoch. The dragon roars in agony of impact. To the everyone but Enoch it just sounds like a roar. "Why!?" the dragon asks in agony looking right at Enoch.

Enoch walks up to the dragon blocking any attack possible from the girls. "Why are you attacking these farmers?" Enoch responds placing his hand on the dragon's head.

"I was headed back to breeding ground when I discovered these little creatures have made it their home. I was hoping flying over would scare them off, but they remained, and you showed up again. You at one-point rode on my back. Please don't kill me." The dragon responds roaring to everyone else.

"Will your wing heal? If not, I am sorry, I have to kill you. If so, please leave this place and don't return." Enoch says crouching down and lifting the dragon's head.

"No, you burnt the flesh away. I can't regrow that skin." The dragon responds lifting its head. "Just cut my throat at the base of my jaw, then reach your arm in and pull the stone out. It may be attached to my esophagus." The dragon continues before Enoch follows the instructions the dragon gave.

Now the trio are processing the dragon when Angus walks up to them. "Here!" Enoch exclaims throwing Angus the stone. "I can't read it." Enoch continues as he goes back to carving the dragon.

"Go collect your pay and leave us be." Jennifer says not even looking away from the dragon as she assists Enoch.

"Why is miss refuse to eat meat touching the dragon flesh?!" Angus asks shocked.

"Bugger off, swill bowl!" Enoch responds anger showing in his tone.

"Go back to the city you call home! We only did this for the were farmers because we weres need to stick together." Maria says as she pops her head up and slides the dragon's heart to the bag Jennifer picked up.

Angus has been gone for a long while as the group finishes carving the dragon and now the farmers are waiting for them to finish as the trio turn to face them. "So, since the suns are setting, we figured as we don't have any money after that bigot demanded his pay despite, he didn't even help, you three could crash at one of our houses for the night. Maybe the new girl who has a three-bedroom house would let the three of you take 2 of the rooms for a night." The head of the farmers co-op says semi confidently.

"We should be headed to OxenDeValley. If another dragon starts bothering you send for Enoch, Maria, Jennifer next time we will gladly help. While all three of us have been exiled from all of the tribes we don't care if they don't want us helping their farmers survive with native Jraconians being racist against our kind we need to stick together." Maria responds offering to shake the head farmers hands while Jennifer and Enoch are washing their hands of the blood.

"Thanks for the offer though." Enoch chimes in taking the canteen from Jennifer to allow her to wash the blood off her hands.

Now back at the gate to OxenDeValley. "Dragon is dead can we come in now?" Enoch asks looking at the current guard.

"Yes, just don't head to the high markets right now. There is a protest against your kind there. We are trying to get it under control, but they are outnumbering our men. We are afraid to use like half of our guards as they are your kind. That war in Trawlers Wharf has polarized opinions in cities all over the country. I may not be a were, but I have fought both against your kind and by their side. I prefer you guys on my side." The guard responds as the gate opens just enough to let the trio in.

"I would offer assistance, but we need to find someone to buy the meat." Enoch says adjusting the sack on his back.

"Sadly, you can't right now. The only butcher in the city to take it is in the high markets. Unless we can use you demon grim boy?" the guard captain responds.

"How do you know about my secret?" Enoch asks on edge.

"Because I am the head of the cities were division. We could use you son!" Zeke responds stepping from the shadows.

"I thought you stuck to the den?!" Jennifer exclaims stepping back scared.

"I needed a way to make money and they needed a guard captain who is a were." Zeke responds sighing. "Can you help, son?" Zeke continues looking at Enoch.

"What do you need? Bear? Fox? Boar? Wolf? Cat?" Enoch asks sighing in annoyance.

"Bear? Fox? When did you gain those?" Zeke responds shocked.

"Yesterday. Bear I am like 12 feet tall and can take down a shadow bear on my own." Enoch says still annoyed.

"Let's head up there and look at what you think you need. I hope bear isn't needed as I fear the mess it may make. I know my grim was uncontrollable." Zeke responds motioning for Enoch to follow him.

"We come with him. As his mates we stand together. Can we leave the bags of dragon meat and organs somewhere?" Jennifer asks trying to remain confident.

"Bring it with as the butcher will want it now. Maria take the meat to the butcher. You don't look like an obvious were unlike E and J do." Zeke responds as they get to the top of the hill and he points at the door to their right with a butcher's sign next to the door.

Now looking out over the rioters as they violently protest. "Uh a bear may be the best option along with J's grim cat." Enoch says quietly as the three are huddling.

"I haven't gone grim since I tried to go vegetarian. Don't really have the strength to." Jennifer responds meekly.

"That is why I am trying to find meats you will eat. I need you to imagine these scoundrels have hurt the person you love most." Enoch says sighing.

Now as Enoch goes demon grim bear, Jennifer goes grim cat and Zeke goes wolf. Enoch rushes into the crowd after letting out a roar that broke every piece of glass in the plaza followed by Jennifer keeping close to Enoch as the crowd starts to scatter all but one courageous swill bowl brandishing a sword tipped with the guts of Belladonna berries. Enoch turns to this swill bowl as Zeke grabs him by the sword brandishing arm and snaps it off causing the sword to clatter to the ground and the swill bowl pulls out a dagger with the remaining arm and stabs it into Zeke's side repetitively before Enoch picks up the swill bowl head first as he squeezes crushing his skull in his giant paw. "Father!

Are you okay!?" Enoch yells as he returns to non were state and rushes to his fathers' side.

"Belladonna is our biggest weakness. Yes, it is semi poisonous to them, but it is the bane of our existence. I have lived a long 57 years. It is about time I pass the torch to you. Keep your girls safe." Zeke responds as he exhales his last breath in Enoch's arms.

"Let's go meet up with Maria." Enoch says coldly as he sets his father down and closes his eyes.

Now in the butchers shop all the butchers are weighing meat on all 3 of their scales when Enoch and Jennifer enter. "How is it going?" Enoch asks coldly.

"Uh they are still weighing it. Why are you covered in blood?" Maria responds pointing at Enoch's shirt.

"A swill bowl murdered my father. That is my father's blood. He died in my arms. I just want to get this done and get to the tavern so I can get cleaned up and get some sleep." Enoch explains with a blank emotionless expression.

"I can follow you to the tavern so I know where we are staying, and you can stay there, and I return here so I can lead M to where we are staying." Jennifer says placing her hand on Enoch's shoulder as the head of the guard rushes in.

"Enoch! Your father gave me something for you if you ever came here and he had passed away! Here!" The guard captain exclaims handing Enoch an envelope.

Enoch opens it and reads the letter before pulling out the deed to a house and the key.

"Dear Enoch,

I am sorry I had to mark you. I regret not being a father for you in your youth. I know this won't really make either up to you, but I feel you at least deserve this and could put it to better use than I can.

Love,

Zeke"

"Do you know where he lived?" Enoch asks quickly as the guard is standing there.

"Yes, I would recommend getting the other key from his corpse. Bring one of your girls with you." The guard responds nodding.

"J come with us. M, I trust you with this." Enoch says following the guard captain.

Now outside of his new house Enoch is fighting crying after the guard captain leaves the duo standing there. "You need to let your emotions flow sometime, E." Jennifer says opening her arms to Enoch as he then embraces her and just starts crying on her shoulder.

"He was a shitty father, but I already miss him. The way I treat you and M is because of him. I saw how he was abusive to my mother, so I vowed to never treat a woman like that. I will admit I have broken that vow once or twice, but I instantly regret it when I do. I just hope I can keep my emotions in check now that I don't have a guardian angel in the tribes. He admitted in a bit of the letter I didn't read aloud that he has been protecting me with the tribes. What we did today with those farmers may come crashing down on our heads." Enoch explains between sobs on Jennifer's shoulder.

"Keep it coming, E." Jennifer responds quietly stroking Enoch's head.

"He one time was so drunk that when I came home late, he threatened to do what his father did when he was late getting home. Which was casting out the son who was late and saying he couldn't return till the father had heard stories of something great the son had done since being exiled. I cried for months and refused to leave the house. The first time I left the house after that I encountered Yennifer and started myself down the path I am on now. I only became a mercenary to allow myself to have adventures in hope my father would hear of them and be proud of me. Now while I doubt, he hadn't heard of my adventures he is dead and can't hear of them anymore, so I won't find out if he was proud of the things I have done. I chose to end the war in hopes he would be proud of me. Then I stood up for my beliefs because I didn't want to grow up like him so I think he may have been ashamed of me for that. I just wish I could know if he was proud of me even just a little. J, thank you. You should probably get back to M." Enoch says crying at first before lifting his head wiping his nose on his arm and leaning in to kiss Jennifer.

"E you are not done releasing your feelings, but you are right on the bit I should return to M. Don't hurt yourself, please. I need you." Jennifer responds before she departs from Enoch.

"I need you too." Enoch says quickly in hopes Jennifer hears him. She does as she freezes in her step before she keeps walking.

As Enoch enters the house, he finds a letter on the table across from the door.

"Dear Enoch,

I realize I could have included this with the letter I gave my boss for you. However, I figured you would want to be alone when you read this. I am so proud of you. You have made such an impact on this world. The sea dragon in West Jraconia, The dragons on your way to OxenDeValley the first time. I was a member of the guard on that visit of yours, but I was instructed by the tribe to just watch you and not to interact. I am even proud of you for standing up for your beliefs even though it got you marked by the tribe. I have written the letter so many times because you keep doing things, I am so proud of. Obviously if you are reading this then I am dead. I hope you didn't have to witness me die but if you did, I am sorry if it hurts watching your old man die. I watched the last breath leave my father's lungs myself. Though I killed him as way to take his position, but they decided to give it to my older brother because they feared I would be too brutal. In the armory is a weapon just for you. It was given to me by my father just before I killed him with it. I have held on it just for my first-born son. Well here you are reading this letter. I was hoping to give it to you when you finalized your imprint the first time, but I wasn't around when that happened. Probably for the best if you are anything like me when I first held the blade.

Sincerely,

Zeke"

It has been a little while as Maria and Jennifer enter to find Enoch curled up in a ball on the floor clutching the sheathed sword his father left for him with the letter on the floor next to him. Jennifer picks up the letter and reads it. "He was proud of you, E. Do you want to talk some more? You didn't get cleaned up, did you?" Jennifer asks crouching next to Enoch.

"Can you sit on the floor and I just rest my head in your lap till I feel ready to talk?" Enoch responds sobbing.

"Of course, E." Jennifer says doing as asked.

"E I am here for you as well." Maria says chiming in looking down at her husband clutching a sword crying.

Some time has passed as Maria returns from taking a bath. "Has he opened up yet?" Maria asks sitting next to Jennifer.

"Not yet. Nor has he stopped crying. I just wish I knew how I could help him. He has done so much for me. Giving up his dream of making his father proud because some guy was insulting me." Jennifer responds looking down at Enoch.

"I didn't give up that job just for you. He was being racist before I left to find myself and found, M. I just wish my father would have expressed he was proud of me in person someday. I would have gladly tried to repair our relationship earlier if he had just expressed that he was proud of me. Maybe the first war wouldn't have happened if he had expressed that he was proud of me when I returned after patching up M before I left for almost a decade to figure out who I was. I regret all the bad things I ever said to him. If I could bring him back without any side effects I would. Did either of you bump into the guard captain again? Maybe ask when his burial would be?" Enoch says before sitting up laying the sword down in front of him.

"He came back in before J came back saying the memorial would probably be tomorrow around twelve in the afternoon. Told me that if I wanted you to love me even more to let you know. I could care less if telling you this makes me love you more. If my mother died in front of me, I would expect you to tell me when her memorial would be. Don't care she cast me out. She is still my mother so I would want to attend her memorial." Maria responds lunging to hug Enoch as he hugs her back.

"He didn't just die in front of me. He died in my arms. I need to bathe. Jenny, want to join me? M I realize you took one but if you want to join you can. Nothing inappropriate will be happening." Enoch says as he gets up.

Now in the bathroom Enoch is in the tub as both girls come in and climb in on either side of him. "Wow, M! I didn't actually look at all of your scars. May I ask what they are from?" Jennifer asks as Enoch puts his left arm around her.

"From E's actions. The one on my back you had done to me when I chased after him when he said he wished he wasn't a were. Others are from various things he has done that somehow end up injuring me. No new ones since we have been together. So why am I on the right side of E?" Maria responds as Enoch rests his head on her shoulder.

"J read my mind what I wanted. I want to have some time where I can see you and talk to you. Though if you decide to say sit on my lap, I will gladly allow it." Enoch says softly in Maria's left ear.

Maria stands up and climbs on Enoch's lap facing him so that he can see her face as he talks to her. "So, will this do? I just noticed how much bigger J's bosom is to mine." Maria responds from Enoch's lap.

"I like both of you two's bosoms. Yours is perfect for your body. As is Jenny's. Now how do you feel about living here? We aren't too far from the Misty district. Which could be a little sketchy as we are weres and we know how racist they all seem to be." Enoch says resting his right hand on Maria's left hip.

"It is a nice house, but I don't want to spend all my time here. I want to get back on the road and making money. Yes, I realize we are practically set for life, but we need to do something in our daily lives." Maria responds shrugging her shoulders bouncing her ample bosom.

"Can we just get clean and maybe head to bed?" Jennifer asks yawning.

Now in the bedroom off the bathroom they were just in Enoch is drying off as Maria comes up behind him and leans forward so her bosom is on Enoch's back. "Can we have fun tonight?" Maria asks reaching around Enoch to play with him.

"I want to head to bed, M." Enoch responds getting ready to attempt to stand up with Maria pressing her bosom into his back.

"Why can't we have fun? I convinced Jenny to join into a threesome." Maria says with a hint of disappointment in her voice.

"Maybe tomorrow after the memorial for my father. I just want to sleep so I can process what happened today." Enoch responds standing up and turning to face Maria as Jennifer comes out of the bathroom with a silk robe on. "Where did you get that robe?" Enoch asks looking at Jennifer funny.

"Bought it before we set off to fight the dragon. This is what I asked for a platinum for. Also, the food I bought that you made for me." Jennifer responds walking up to be in view of Enoch's right eye.

"I want to sleep the way we did last time we all slept in a bed together. You two on each side of me laying on my chest." Enoch says holding his arms out to the girls.

"Which side do you want me on?" Maria asks hugging Enoch as Jennifer joins in on the hug.

"My right when we are on the bed. Same as the other night." Enoch responds kissing both the girls on the cheek.

Chapter 19

The next morning Enoch awakes as the first sun starts shining through the windows on either side of the bed. Both girls have climbed so they are resting their whole bodies on his. "Oh, you are awake. How did you sleep, E?" Maria asks softly looking up at Enoch's face.

"Good considering you two decided to lay directly on top of me." Enoch responds chuckling.

"You asked us to lay on you at some point." Jennifer says looking up at Enoch's face as he smirks because he just goosed both girls' bottoms.

"You pervert!" Maria exclaims jokingly slapping Enoch's chest.

"You enjoyed that, and you know it, M. How about you, J?" Enoch responds chuckling.

"I did really enjoy it." Jennifer says meekly hiding her face blushing.

"Don't be embarrassed that you enjoyed me goosing your bottom. It means that you enjoy my advances." Enoch responds kissing the top of Jennifer's head.

Now at the location they were told the guard captain greets the trio. "Thank you miss for telling Enoch." The guard captain says looking at Maria.

"I would expect him to do the same for me if my mother passed away and I was close enough to attend the memorial." Maria responds saluting.

"So, I have some questions for Enoch." The captain says turning to face Enoch.

"What do you want from me chief?" Enoch responds looking at the captain with his right eye.

"Your father was a vital member of my team. What the non were members reported is that you were in the lead of the riot dispersal force. Is that true?" The captain asks giving Enoch the you up to the challenge task.

"I already don't like where this could be going. I cannot join your guard forces. I am an adventurer. I don't like the idea of settling down. Having a house doesn't mean I am settling down. Heck that isn't even my first house. That would be back in my hometown in Koftan." Enoch responds shooting down the captain's idea.

"So, you wouldn't be interested in doing what you did last night for a living?" the captain asks looking at Enoch with a bit of disappointment.

"God no! I hated the worry that I could be killed by a racist. The risk of dying by a dragon or shadow bear excites me but the risk of dying as my father did terrifies me. Doesn't help I didn't just witness him die I held him in my arms as he died. I realize now I could have saved him and risked my own life I saw the guy before I ran into the crowd I could have went towards him instead of where I did but no I had to go for the center of the crowd. I am a crappy son for not going for what could have left my father alive." Enoch responds as tears start welling up in his eyes.

"Enough making my mate hate himself for his decisions." Jennifer chimes in putting her arms around Enoch and walking him away from the captain. "E you did the best you could. You are only one person after all. It wasn't your fault. Even if you went for the guy maybe you would have saved your father, but you might have been the one to die instead." Jennifer continues trying to comfort Enoch.

"Why does my life matter? I was conceived to act as a peace treaty that didn't even last twenty years." Enoch responds looking Jennifer right in the eye.

"Your life matters to me, E!" Jennifer exclaims trying to force back tears.

"One person isn't enough to balance out the fact that all I have done is disappoint everyone I associate with!" Enoch responds as Maria slaps him across the face.

"So, you think I don't care about you? I have risked and lost everything for you!" Maria screams as tears streak down her face.

"Son, you matter more to this world than you will ever know. Your exploits are told like hero stories and they will continue to be. Your father knew his death was coming which is why he left you what he did. He wanted you to become a legendary hero. You are close keep going." The captain chimes in before sauntering away.

"Why do I matter? All I have done is fight to survive in this world?" Enoch asks looking between the two in front of him

"You saved me from death many times." Maria responds shoving Jennifer over so she can hug Enoch.

"M you have saved me from death just as many times as I have you. If you hadn't been in the places you were, I would have let the monsters kill me if I was alone. Slaying dragons without disposing of them properly haunts you. Their spirits linger and haunt you till you dispose of their body respectfully." Enoch says deadpanned.

"Everyone I would like to get started!" The captain hollers looking around at the people who have gathered. "To show members of the family of the departed whom we are honoring today I would like all non weres who are here to pay their respects to Zeke raise their hands." The captain continues looking around as about ninety percent of the one hundred plus people raise their hands. "Ok so I will say the standard lines we say when we lose a guard then I will bring up Zeke's only son to say his speech I hope he has prepared." The captain says before clearing his throat.

"Brother, you will be missed. You have touched many lives outside of the family you have with the guard and your own family. We hope to meet you again in the afterlife. We hope you are comfortable without pain wherever you are. With that I bid you farewell, brother." The captain says fighting back tears.

Enoch has stepped up to the podium. "Father well you were an abysmal father in my youth. Always drunk, verbally abusive, sometimes physically. I will admit I wasn't easy to take care of. Constantly disappearing to do jobs to make money as a child. Getting home late if I did come home on the same day. Fighting with you every step of the way. Defending mother when you got so drunk you started getting abusive. But when I disappeared from sixteen years old till twenty-five going on twenty-six to find out you had supposedly died in a war over my disappearance where you ended up killing my mother in battle. In the time I was gone you quit drinking and cleaned up your act. I wish you had done that when I was still there. I may have never gone off to make a name for myself in hopes I could make you proud of me. I only just recently got to know you even a little. Every short encounter I learned more and more about who you were as a person. I just wish I could have learned that you were proud of me before you died in my arms. Now all I have to remember you by is what you have left behind for me. No positive childhood memories, no real positive adulthood memories. Heck I have one scar on my face to remember you by when you had to cast me out of the tribes. I wish you well wherever you may be father. I will miss you dearly." Enoch says tears streaming down his face from both eyes the whole time.

Now at the reception of the memorial Enoch and the girls are sat at the bar. Enoch is still crying as his tears hit the wooden bar. "Your father was a great man, kid." A non were says putting a hand on Enoch's shoulder.

"Thank you I guess." Enoch responds not even moving.

"He was also very proud of you. He told stories of your exploits he had heard of as often as he could. Whenever new tales of something you did started to circulate, he would celebrate often by throwing a party." The non were continues with his hand still on Enoch's shoulder.

"I need time to process his passing, please." Enoch responds sobbing even harder.

"Good luck. Make him proud." The gentleman says before turning back to the festivities.

"When can we go home?" Enoch asks looking at the girl to his right which is Jennifer.

"That is up to you. This is for your father after all. I would like to see an honest smile out of you before we leave though. You have revealed just how emotionally unstable you are to me. Which makes me want to help you feel good." Jennifer responds scooting over so she can hug Enoch from the side.

"So how emotionally unstable is E?" Maria asks looking at Jennifer as she is hugging Enoch.

"When I went back to the butcher to act as your escort to the house, I feared we would have found him dead in a puddle of his own blood honestly. I was so thankful he didn't off himself." Jennifer responds looking Maria dead in the eye.

"I couldn't do that. I have two wonderful women who I love dearly. I honestly stay alive for you two more than to make stories for others to tell." Enoch says kissing the top of Jennifer's head before Maria hugs him from the opposite side.

"Young man! You have plenty of reasons to live. Whenever you decide you are tired of adventuring you are welcome to come join the OxenDeValley guard." The captain chimes in from behind Enoch.

"I am sorry, but I doubt that will ever happen." Enoch responds sighing.

Now the bar is clearing out and Enoch isn't sobbing but he hasn't smiled yet, so Jennifer won't let them leave. "Why does me smiling mean so much to you, J?" Enoch asks looking right at Jennifer.

"Other than when we were in that tavern room with Yennifer and Alice I don't think I have seen you happy at all." Jennifer responds looking right at Enoch as he chuckles.

"I have been happy plenty with and without you since then. Hell, up till my father's death I was extremely happy with the way my life was going. I have Maria the first were I remembered marking, I have you which while you are my actual first were that I marked I didn't remember about that till after marking Maria. I just don't like smiling. My teeth are a dead giveaway I am a were." Enoch explains moving his right hand onto Jennifer's left thigh.

"Prove to me that you are happy." Jennifer responds demandingly as Enoch is playing with a seam of her skirt.

"Why are you playing with her skirt?" Maria asks looking at Enoch funny.

"I want to prove it in a way that can't be done here. Let us go back to the house and I will prove it to you that I am happy. I don't like having fun time if I am not in a good mood." Enoch responds moving his right hand onto Jennifer's personal place over her skirt.

"Sex doesn't prove anything other than the two involved are horny." Maria chimes in looking at Enoch from the side.

"I hate smiling. Can we find another way for me to prove I am happy?" Enoch asks looking at Maria directly with his tear stained eyes.

"Turn to face away from the bar and let me climb on your lap and let me take the lead with something and if I deem you as happy we can go back to the house and do your plan." Jennifer responds moving Enoch's hand off of her personal place.

Enoch does as he wasinstructed as Jennifer climbs on his lap and starts making out with him.

A little time has passed, and Jennifer has climbed off Enoch's lap a is collecting her belongings she brought with her. "Get up if you want to head home." Jennifer says tapping Enoch's leg noting that his pants are a bit tighter.

"How is you snogging him proof he is happy?" Maria asks confused.

"Look at his face right now. He is in a daze smiling like a goof." Jennifer responds as she is ready and waiting for Enoch to get out of the daze.

"She knows that making out if I am actually happy, I will smile like a fool when she stops kissing me. Yes, it would have worked with you as well." Enoch says as he stops smiling and zones back in before adjusting his trousers.

"So, he is a simple guy who thinks with his trouser snake?" Maria asks disappointed.

"Yes and no. With the women I love and adore yes, I am a simple man. Not so much with women I have no feelings for." Enoch responds offering Maria a hug. "Want to have a three some with Jenny and I?" Enoch asks whispering in Maria's ear as she hugs him.

Some time has passed Enoch is out cold as the two girls come in from cleaning up. "I am hungry." Jennifer says meekly in Enoch's right ear.

"He is out cold like he can hear you." Maria chimes in crossing her arms across her chest.

"Do you not know how to cook, Jenny?" Enoch asks taking a deep breath in as Jennifer has put her freshly washed hair up to his nose.

"No, I wasn't allowed near fire so I couldn't hurt myself or something like that. My father used that excuse anyway. So, you like what my hair smells like?" Jenny responds as Enoch gets seated and she sits next to him.

"What did you use to wash it?" Enoch asks looking at Jennifer on his left.

"That soap you said that doesn't leave much scent." Jennifer responds smiling as Enoch picks up some of her hair to give it a sniff.

"So that is your natural scent?" Enoch asks looking up at Jennifer.

"I guess so. Do you like it or something?" Jennifer responds chuckling.

"It reminds me of ... when you revealed the memories of you imprinting on me when immediately after I reacted to the flood of memories you mounted me 'accidentally' impaling yourself on me." Enoch says before hugging Jennifer.

Now in the kitchen of the house Enoch is cooking. "M, where is the money from the butcher?" Enoch asks looking behind him.

"Oh, uh Where did I put it?" Maria responds struggling to remember.

"You told me to grab it. I put it in Enoch's bag full of coin purses." Jennifer says drooling over the smell of the food cooking.

"I was asking because I would like to know how much we all made off a job we were slated to make nothing off of. Kind of hoping it was more than what Angus made in total." Enoch responds chuckling at Jennifer drooling to his right.

"Well over one thousand platinum coins." Jennifer says glancing at Enoch.

"Jenny, why do you feel the need to bother E while he is cooking?" Maria asks letting her annoyance show.

"She isn't bothering me. That would imply I don't like having one of you by my side. I love having either of you next to me. I am both upset that her father didn't let her learn the basics of just about everything and happy he didn't. I have a buddy for just about everything. I love having someone by my side at all times." Enoch responds smiling at Jennifer.

"She is older than you, yet she acts like a child! How do you like that?!" Maria asks showing that she is upset.

"Well yes it could be seen as childish how she acts I don't see it that way because the way she is watching me maybe someday she could do what I am doing on her own. I see that she is actually trying to learn from what I am doing." Enoch responds as he starts plating up the food for everyone before he gives Jennifer's shoulders a squeeze and kissing her on the top of her head.

The group is done eating and Maria is working on doing dishes. "So do we want to go see about getting a job today?" Enoch asks as Jennifer is resting her head on his shoulder.

"Well considering it is only about four in the afternoon and still very much so light out. I say why not?" Maria responds as she finishes with dishes.

"How about you, J?" Enoch asks shrugging his shoulder to get Jennifer's attention.

"You lead I will follow." Jennifer responds yawning.

"Why are you tired, J? You haven't done much of anything besides getting laid and bathed?" Maria asks showing she is severely upset.

"M what is your problem?" Enoch responds annoyed with Maria's attitude.

"Why are you letting her slack off?! When I call her out you defend her laziness?! If I was being lazy like she is, you would have a problem with it?!" Maria yells tears streaming down her face.

"M come here. Now." Enoch says calmly.

"Why should I you are just going to tell me to relax? We don't have a source of income anymore because you sided with her over me and making money?!" Maria responds screaming.

"Maria of Koftan come here! Now!" Enoch exclaims looking at Maria directly.

"Fine!" Maria responds stomping her way over to Enoch.

"Why have you been so easily upset since I got exiled?" Enoch asks in a calm tone.

"I don't know what you mean?!" Maria responds crossing her arms over her chest.

"Since both Jenny and I got marked and exiled you have been a bit mean to both her and I. I am doing things slower so that we don't bump into the forces that may not know about the deal I was given when I was exiled. I am taking it slow to save our lives more or less." Enoch explains grabbing Maria's arm with his right hand.

"I want to get as far from them as possible. Yet you mosey like your life isn't in danger." Maria responds letting Enoch get her left hand.

"My life has always been in danger. I ran from my home because I hate how tribes work so if they caught me, I could be killed for my view on tribes. Now it is just as dangerous however you are aware of how dangerous it is, so you are worrying about it. I don't react that way because the only major change is now, I only have one eye and two partners to live with." Enoch says calmly as he lifts Maria's left hand up to his face and kisses it.

"So, you are saying nothing has changed despite listing two major changes. You are no longer just looking after yourself and you only have one eye to look after us." Jennifer responds looking up at Enoch all serious like.

"Well I figure you two are daughters of alphas so you should be able to defend yourselves for the most part. As for the loss of vision I am learning to live with it much like you are Jenny." Enoch says looking right at Jennifer.

"So, you got me on the defense one but how long do you think it will take you to get used to the halved vision?" Maria asks looking up at Enoch.

"I don't know on that. Let's get headed out." Enoch responds shrugging.

Now in the biggest tavern in OxenDeValley the trio are in the back room when the head of the mercenary ring comes in from the door leading to the outside.

"What would you three like?" the individual asks looking at the trio.

"Well a job as a group of mercenaries would be nice." Enoch responds lighting the candle in front of him with a small flame from the tip of his finger.

"Well first I must know your names?" the individual asks looking at the trio from the candlelight.

"My name is Enoch, to my right is Jennifer, left is Maria why does that matter?" Enoch responds concerned as Maria punches his shoulder.

"I have a job specifically for a trio matching your description, but I asked if they had names for the three the employer described, and he gave the same names you just said. Something about meeting him outside the city gates as they won't let him in blah blah blah. Sorry he was rambling a bit, so I tuned him out a bit. Oh, he apologized about being racist or something." The individual explains sighing.

"Any other jobs? We don't want to work for Angus." Enoch responds nervously.

"Not right now. The dragon you slain yesterday has been scaring away all potential jobs. Unless you want to act as merchants for a while." the individual says sighing.

"Let me talk to my girls." Enoch responds sighing.

Now outside the bar the trio is conversing with Enoch leaning against the building. "So, we can either do the most boring job on Jraconer or we can fight through dealing with Angus? Personally, I would rather deal with the racist bigot than work as a merchant. I enjoy danger more than money. Plus, the jobs tend to pay better the more dangerous they are." Enoch says looking between the two girls though keeping an eye on Maria is difficult with her pacing.

"I have worked merchant jobs as well. They don't pay well but they don't involve a racist who insults the easy target that is Jennifer." Maria responds pacing around the street.

"Well I need Jennifer's input on this one." Enoch says sighing.

"I think I can stand up for myself." Jennifer responds trying to be confident.

"As much as I hate chancing it on racists, I hate being a merchant even more. So, I say we go with Angus." Enoch says reluctantly as he sighs.

"So, do we want to head back in?" Maria asks looking at Enoch.

Now back inside the room they were in earlier. "So, what do you say?" the individual asks looking right at Enoch.

"We will take the Angus job." Enoch responds reluctantly.

"It will pay fifty platinum a person. Meet him outside the city after the second sun sets tonight." The individual says sliding three pouches across the tables at each of the trio.

"Why so late in the day?" Enoch asks looking cautiously at the person who slid them coin.

"Again, the guards won't let him in." the individual responds. "If they seem him near the wall during the day if they don't kill him, he will get in only he will be headed for a jail cell. Apparently, someone said he is racist against weres that the guard actually cares their opinion." The individual continues annoyed.

"Well we will be headed there, I guess. So has the first sun set yet?" Enoch asks a hint of meekness in his voice.

"The second should be setting in about an hour." The individual responds looking at Enoch funny.

Now outside the wall at the place specified in a paper in Enoch's coin pouch. "I thought you wouldn't come!" Angus exclaims softly.

"Only decent paying job." Enoch responds sighing.

"What is the job?" Jennifer asks confidently.

"I need help finding more dragons. Help killing them would be nice as well, but I don't expect such generosity." Angus explains as his tone wavers.

"Just cut the racist remarks and you will get the generosity. Only reason I killed the dragon at the last job is because I singed it's flight membrane and it couldn't fly." Enoch responds sighing as a guard is patrolling and Angus hides his face.

"Is everything okay Enoch? Is this gentleman bothering you?" the guard asks stopping.

"No, sir. We are just having a conversation working out the details of something." Enoch responds bowing his head.

"Ok just give a holler if he is. Angus!" The guard says before going back to patrolling.

"How do they know you by name?" Angus asks shocked.

"Father was a member of the guard till yesterday. He died in my arms after being stabbed multiple times by an anti-were rioter." Enoch responds coldly looking Angus dead in the face.

"Oh, so how is Jennifer? Is she still hurt from my remarks?" Angus asks meekly.

"Just leave her be ..." Enoch responds before Jennifer interrupts him.

"Quit talking for me, Enoch! I am still pissed off at you, but a job is a job. Money is money no matter who it comes from." Jennifer says confidently.

"So, when do we head out?" Enoch asks shocked at Jennifer's confidence.

"Tonight! I can't be seen near the wall during the day." Angus responds shaking.

Now a little way away from OxenDeValley the group are setting up camp as they see what looks like fire raining down in the distance in a straight beam of fire. "That is one I know of where it resides during the day. They don't let me near them at all." Angus says sighing as the trio across from him stare at the dragon burning the land.

"Aren't we near that farming village from yester-day?" Enoch asks in attack mode.

"Yes, the dragon is attacking said village." Angus responds as Enoch and the girls bolt towards the village.

Now near the village the trio are setting up as Enoch sends a ball of yellow fire at the dragon. The fireball strikes the dragons back causing it to quit breathing fire and turn around to face Enoch. Enoch is standing there with his right hand out and no weapons on his person. The dragon gets close to the ground and puts its head in the palm of Enoch's hand. "Why are you at-tacking this village?" Enoch asks aloud in perfect Dra-conian.

"Remember E, we are getting paid to end them not give them a chance to leave!" Jennifer yells confidently.

"I refuse to leave!" The dragon responds roaring.

"Let me guess? Ancestral breeding grounds?" Enoch asks still in perfect Draconian.

"That and my mother was murdered here! I see her skeleton!" The dragon responds roaring before flying up above the trio and resuming breathing fire on the crops.

"Well I don't know how to kill this one!" Enoch yells rejoining the girls in the line they have formed.

"Why not?!" Angus yells rushing up to the trio.

"If your presence unsettles them more than they already are I am sorry you need to stay away!" Enoch screams not even turning to face Angus as a beam of fire comes right towards him.

"I have an idea!" Maria exclaims chiming in.

"Out with it, M!" Enoch responds looking right at Maria with his right eye.

"J, is the strongest between her and I so if she would stand right in front of you about twenty feet ahead of you, then you run at her she grabs your foot and catapults you in the air. All the while we time it so you end up landing on the dragons back. Then while you are up there you decide how you want to take the thing down. Slit its throat or cut a wing off you decide. Sound plausible?" Maria explains looking right at Enoch as he dodges several fireballs from the dragon.

"Sounds ... exciting!" Enoch responds pumped up.

"I only suggest you do it as you have killed the most dragons of anyone here. What did the one yesterday make? 20 dragons killed?" Maria says looking at how excited Enoch is and laughing at him.

They have timed it and Enoch is in the air flipping before landing on the dragons back. Enoch grabs on the dragon's neck as it rolls trying to dislodge him. Enoch goes with the route of take off its right wing and ride the dragon down to the ground. He just hacked it's wing off and the dragon shrieks as the spiral reverses and the descent to the ground starts at a breakneck speed. The impact kicks up a cloud of soot as Enoch and the dragon crash land in the burnt remains of what used to be a wheat field. Enoch climbs off the dragons back and lifts its head before slitting its throat and shoving his right arm in the slit. Pulling out the prophecy stone and walking away from the corpse. "Here Angus. Now we need to return to OxenDeValley for a few hours. Might go to bed while we are there and meet you in the morning. We are making most of our money from the meat of the dragons I kill." Enoch says tossing the stone at Angus. "I want to know what you have translated so far come morning. I may be able to speak it but reading it is your specialty." Enoch continues as he motions for the girls to come help with the dragon.

Several hours later they are carving by a torch that Angus is holding when they finish carving. "Uh so do we want to open the stomach that looks like it ate a humanoid like creature?" Maria asks looking at Enoch.

"Go ahead. I am going to be tying off the bags of meat while you figure out if you are correct in that it ate a humanoid creature." Enoch responds gagging a little.

"Why did he gag? Didn't he used to eat workhorse meat?" Angus asks confused.

"Keywords used to. Now the thought of it turns my stomach." Enoch responds before barfing on the ground.

"I am on Enoch's side on that. You okay, E?" Jennifer chimes in walking to Enoch's side.

"Yeah. I am going to start heading back to the camp and tear down our stuff and head to town." Enoch responds before throwing as many of the bags of dragon meat over his back.

"Can I join you, E?" Jennifer asks confidently.

"Anything you need to take with you or help with here?" Enoch responds glancing at Jennifer as she runs up beside him.

"She could help me with this?" Maria asks looking at Jennifer.

"As disgusting as it is J go help M. Show confidence." Enoch says softly facing Jennifer. "Only way to not seem weak is to power through it. I realize I am doing the opposite, but I have a history with consuming workhorse and the thought now makes me barf as I proved back there." Enoch continues looking at Jennifer still.

Enoch is back in town at the butcher who opened just to process this large amount of meat. "I can't offer as high of a price as I did last time as I still have some left from what you had your girls bring in. I only paid so much as we had a shortage." The butcher says weighing the meat.

"Understandable." Enoch responds as Jennifer comes in the building looking kind of green. "Oh, what's up J?" Enoch continues.

"It was someone I knew." Jennifer responds before throwing the door open and heading outside to barf.

"What happened to her?" the butcher asks confused.

"The dragon you are weighing the meat from had something large in its stomach. It apparently was a were she knew." Enoch responds looking at the door from the corner of his right eye as Jennifer comes back in looking much less green.

"I feel better. So how much we at so far?" Jennifer chimes in standing next to Enoch.

"Still tallying. It is just me tonight. No one else wanted to come in." the butcher responds moving around behind the counter.

"Where is, M?" Enoch asks turning to face Jennifer.

"She may have been targeted for some bullying." Jennifer responds meekly.

"Why did you leave?" Enoch asks panicking.

"She wreaks of the stomach of a dragon." Jennifer says meekly.

"Can you give her the coin if you finish before I get back?" Enoch asks rushing to the door.

"Sure thing, Enoch." The butcher responds.

Now catching up to Maria who is sobbing slowly walking her way to OxenDeValley. "Come here, M!" Enoch exclaims holding his arms open for Maria as she hugs him and buries her face in his chest.

"Do we have to work with him, Enoch?!" Maria asks between sobs as Enoch strokes her hair.

"Yes, we signed onto a job without a listed end date." Enoch responds trying to comfort Maria.

"Well he picked on me because I am the smallest and youngest of the three of us. How could you love me? I am the size of a child? I don't even have actual breasts. All three of those are things he said trying to break me. Well it worked." Maria says looking up at Enoch who is looking down at her.

"I love you because your personality fits with mine so well. You are young yes, but you are what 19 years old. As someone who has seen you when you were younger than 10 years old you are much bigger in every department than you were then. Your bosom is what a size b or c. Compared to J's D or DD I would say while yes, they are small, they are perfect for your body. Plus, you can cuddle close behind me without concern of either hurting you from them getting squished or hurting my back from pressing them into my back." Enoch responds lowering his head to kiss Maria on the lips. "J said you smelled but I don't smell anything." Enoch continues looking at Maria while his eyes glow yellow.

"I found a river and stripped and went for a swim. When I got out, I pulled my change of clothes I carry with me everywhere and put them on. Can we get to town?" Maria responds meekly.

"Sure, thing sweetie." Enoch says kissing Maria's forehead.

Now back in the butcher shop Enoch and Maria are holding each other while Enoch is talking with Jennifer and the butcher with the occasional moment where Maria decides to speak. "So why is she so upset?" the butcher asks talking about Maria.

"Angus Draconer the racist prick harassed her after I left to get the meat here." Enoch says bluntly.

"Well it looks like you have three hundred pounds of meat. That is six hundred platinum for the whole transaction." The butcher says not paying attention to what Enoch had said.

Now back at the house Enoch is exhausted as are the girls. Carrying Maria up to the bed as she is out cold in his arms. "J, sleep behind me tonight." Enoch says yawning as he sets Maria down and she looks at him doe eyed. "You are sleeping in front of me tonight." Enoch continues looking right at Maria as she scurries up to the pillows before covering herself up.

Chapter 20

The first sun is coming up as Enoch awakes to Maria facing him out cold with her face against his chest and Jennifer snoring in his right ear. Not loud obnoxious snoring but gentle cute snoring. "Hey, E. Your heartbeat and breathing change woke me up. Can I sleep in front of you from now on?" Maria asks sweetly looking up at Enoch.

"Did you sleep well?" Enoch responds softly giving Maria a gentle loving squeeze.

"I was out like a light once you climbed in bed with me. Other than waking up and rolling over to face you I slept great." Maria says softly enjoying being pressed against Enoch as he hugs her.

"I think J wouldn't mind. She is still making cute noises in my ear. She seems to know a way to cuddle close without hurting her bosom or my back." Enoch responds as he hears what sounds like the end of the snoring and Jennifer waking up.

"I did enjoy having someone in front of me. I commonly want to do what M did, but my large bosom may make it hard for the two of us to breath." Jennifer says softly in Enoch's ear.

"We need to get a move on." Enoch responds moving to lay on his back which the girls get the hint and lay on his chest.

"Why can't we relax today?" Maria asks looking down at Enoch's standing soldier.

"Because we are still under Angus's employ, so we have to at least do what he wants till he signs off on us working for him. I don't want to do it as much as you two, but I am a were of my word." Enoch responds sighing as both girls are pondering something. "Leave my member alone today please. One of you is going into heat." Enoch continues kissing one girls head before kissing the other one's head.

"That would be me." Maria says meekly as she raises her hand.

"Why does it have to be the one I was thinking of sneaking off with randomly today." Enoch responds sighing looking down at Maria as she blushes.

"Just because she is going into heat doesn't mean you can't have fun with her. That is only an issue once she is in heat." Jennifer chimes in as she stands up and Enoch gets a view of her personal place which has some blood on it.

"Your place is bleeding, J. Is everything okay?" Enoch asks poking Jennifer there as she is slowly standing up.

"Your senses haven't synced up with my clock yet. You deflowered me while I was at the stage M is in now. Did you just poke my bleeding place?!" Jennifer responds annoyed.

"I've never really seen period blood or anything." Enoch says at first sniffing the blood on his finger before putting it in his mouth.

"Don't tell me he just stuck my period blood in his mouth?!" Jennifer asks not turning around so she doesn't slap Enoch.

"He did... Well I have wondered the same thing but my own would be weird. No, I am not going to follow suit as the smell deters me from anything that has period blood on it." Maria responds sighing at Enoch's expression.

"You have to remember I am a male were with the ability to become just about any were. Maybe one of them likes period blood." Enoch says as Maria gets up as well.

Now outside the wall the trio are at the place they agreed with Angus to meet at as his loudmouth is heard approaching. "There you three furries are!" Angus exclaims sauntering up to the trio.

"Furries?!" Enoch responds his anger showing massively.

"He isn't worth the legal ramifications of killing him!" Maria exclaims grabbing one of Enoch's arms as Jennifer grabs the other.

"What did I say wrong?!" Angus asks shocked.

"You called us animal fuckers! We only have relations with humanoids!" Enoch responds as Maria quickly let's go of his right hand as it ignited in his anger causing him to whip around. "Are you okay, Sweetie?" Enoch asks facing Maria as he summons healing energy to his right and holding out his left to Maria.

Maria holds out her hands and Enoch sets about healing the burns with his magic. "Thank you, E." Maria says meekly as Enoch finishes healing her hands.

"Don't say anything about her being weak. You are on thin ice. You weren't supposed to harass any of us. You made her cry when I left. Now you called us 'furries'!" Enoch says facing Angus as his eye starts glowing red.

"It's not my fault your kind are so thin skinned!" Angus responds before Enoch grabs him by the throat squeezing enough to make Angus's eyes bug out of their sockets.

"We aren't thinned skin you racist! Your kind just think putting down people who are different is okay when that is the complete opposite of okay! You racist bigots are hated wherever you go. Your kind are only tolerated because money is money and your kind for some reason have a lot of it despite everyone, I have met refuses to hire your kind because your kind scare off customers!" Enoch exclaims squeezing till Angus is about to pass out before throwing him to the ground with a bruised trachea to match the skin on his throat.

"We aren't done with our agreement!" Angus responds struggling to get the words out.

"You keep being racist and yes we are!" Enoch exclaims making sure Maria is okay ignoring Angus struggling to get to his feet.

Now at the site of where Enoch killed the last dragon. "So, the stone from this particular dragon was about properly putting the dragon's spirit to rest." Angus says struggling to speak.

"Come here. Your voice the way it is will definitely piss me off." Enoch says summoning healing energy to his hand.

"What are you going to do now?!" Angus responds scared while struggling to speak.

"I am going to fix what I did to your throat. You struggling to talk is pissing me off." Enoch explains impatiently as Angus steps closer and Enoch puts his right hand to Angus's throat to heal his trachea. "Is that better?" Enoch asks annoyed.

"Ok now you will need enough highly flammable fluid to dowse the bones if you aren't doing this immediately after cleaning the flesh off. If you were smart you will have collected the dragon's blood and you can use that as their blood is highly flammable. Then you will need to ignite it while reciting this chant. I hope you have enough fluid for both skeletons in the area." Angus explains looking up at Enoch showing him the stone.

"I can't read that although that looks if you will familiar to something I learned when I ate the brain of that underwater dragon back in West Draconia. I mean West Jraconia. Sorry I sometimes default to the Draconian way of pronouncing the countries here." Enoch responds pulling the barrels of blood he extracted over the past few days slaying the two dragons. "Let's do the older dragon first then we set this one alight and I will do the process for it at that time." Enoch continues before sauntering off to the first dragon skeleton that the local farmers children have taken to using as a jungle gym.

They are just finishing with the second ceremony and the kids are sad that their toys have collapsed from being burnt. "So, the stone from the last mission was something of a map telling us where the potential prophecy dragons are located. I don't know how a stone that forms in a dragon could account for their brethren flying?" Angus says looking at the stone funny.

"No that is where they were the exact moment, I killed the dragon. So somewhere around there is where they are currently located as they could sense when this one died. All beasts connected to the draconian brainwave could. It was like a massive fire going out." Enoch says coldly.

"How would you know how it felt?" Angus asks wearily.

"I am connected to the dragons. Are you not?" Enoch responds surprised.

"No, I just know how to read the language." Angus says meekly.

"So where is the closest one on the map?" Jennifer asks looking at Enoch who is stretching from carrying the heavy barrels.

"It is in North Jraconia." Angus responds looking at the stone with a bewildered expression on his face.

"Let's get headed to the port city. Unless you know of a place that will fly us there." Enoch says lifting the bags.

"We don't have the money to fly there." Angus responds meekly.

"You might not but I have enough coin to fly to anywhere on Jraconer." Enoch says sighing. "Transport jobs and dragon meat during a shortage are worth quite a bit of money." Enoch continues trying to sound modest about the fact he has over 10,000 platinum in a locked container somewhere.

"It is up to you." Angus responds sheepishly.

"No offense but the less time I have to spend crammed in close quarters with you the better. So, do you know of a place for us to fly to North Jraconia?" Enoch asks sighing.

"Back on the coast where it may be difficult for you three to go." Angus responds deflated.

"Let's go. So long as we don't upset the tribe members, we should be safe." Enoch says pointing to the direction of Trawler's Wharf.

Now at Trawler's Wharf the group are conversing with the air service flyer. "So, let me weigh everyone's bags and we should be able to set off for Draconer's Grove in North Jraconia." The flight attendee says.

"Uh my bag may weigh too much." Enoch responds raising his hand.

"Well let us weigh yours first then." The attendee says as Enoch tries to hand his bag over causing the attendee to fall straight to the ground from the weight.

"What is in your bag?" Angus asks trying to help the attendee of the ground.

"All supplies needed to survive in the wilderness of any country on Jraconer." Enoch responds picking the bag up and setting it on the scale which reads 72 stone.

"Uh we may have to do two trips as long as that is the only super heavy bag." The attendee says trying to pop her arm back into joint.

"What all can fly with my bag?" Enoch asks sheepishly.

"I would prefer just myself to be honest. But if one of the girls is light enough, I can carry her with it if you are afraid of losing contents of your house in a bag." The attendee responds.

"M, could you step on the scale?" Enoch asks moving his bag off the scale before Maria steps up on the scale which reads 8 stone. "J, do you know your weight?" Enoch continues sheepishly.

"More than M." Jennifer responds glaring at Enoch.

"Well I guess if M doesn't mind going with my bag, I would like her on the second trip." Enoch says sheepishly.

"Well then if you want to say your farewells now and maybe some butt kissing then I will give you a few minutes to do that while I load my bird." The attendee responds before turning away.

"I am sorry I embarrassed you, M. I just know I weigh more than you and I don't trust flying with my bag with all of our coin in it. Yes, I am having you stick with the money. That is most of the weight along with my choice cooking stone." Enoch says pulling Maria into a bear hug.

"You didn't just embarrass me. You let my weight known to everyone in visual range and earshot of those near the people who may have read it aloud. You may have put my life in danger E!" Maria responds angrily but enjoying Enoch's embrace.

"So, I have some good news!" The attendee says loudly coming back to the group.

"May I ask what that is?" Enoch asks holding Maria close.

"My boss overheard the weight limit issue and is letting you use the cargo bird for both its intended purpose and to ferry your crew over on its back as none of you should equal the maximum capacity combined with your cargo." The attendee explains chuckling at Maria being both super angry and comfortable at the same time.

"Can we dangle, E from the bottom with his bag!?" Maria asks angrily.

"We could put him in the container where we put the cargo." The attendee responds chuckling at Maria's question.

"Why ...!?" Enoch asks before Jennifer knocks him out and the group load him in the container.

Now unloading the container, they just splash presumably water on Enoch to wake him once they've emptied everything but him and his bag from the container. "What the?! Why did you knock me out!?" Enoch demands attempting to get up.

"You were an absolute ass to M and your apology sounded half assed at best." Jennifer responds coldly.

"You weren't alone. They demanded I stay in there with you!" Angus says annoyed.

"Sorry your history with my girls I understand them demanding that." Enoch responds throwing his bag on his shoulder thumping Angus who thought it was smart to stand next to Enoch against the wall of the container almost knocking him out. "So, did they pay you before the flight or do I need to pay you now?" Enoch asks sauntering out of the container.

"We paid. Dang you carry a lot of coin." Jennifer responds.

Now the group are at a local pub and they are figuring out which way they need to go from here to make it to the last known location of the dragons. "So, the compass says we need to go west." Enoch says glancing at his compass that he has pointed north.

"Do you even know how to read a compass?!" Angus asks looking at Enoch like he is an idiot.

"He is reading it correctly. I learned that look to the inland sea to know north and well we are north of the inland sea and he has north lined up with the pointer in his compass." Maria responds defending Enoch.

"Well it doesn't look right to me." Angus says sighing.

"That's because you suck at maps, Cousin." The Jraconian bartender chimes in deep belly laughing.

"Oh, crap I forgot this place would be crawling with my relatives." Angus says putting his face in his hands as a young-looking girl skips her way to the group before sitting to the right of Angus.

"What brings you here mister Dragon Slayer?" the young girl asks making fun of Angus.

"Don't you lie and take credit for my slaying of dragons, Angus!" Enoch chimes in placing his dagger between the third lumbar and fourth lumbar of Angus's spine.

"Woah you haven't slain a dragon cousin! Shocking!" the girl exclaims mocking her cousin.

"No, I haven't but I am helping decipher the stones they leave behind. Can you remove your dagger from my spine please?" Angus responds sheepishly.

"Please tell me your family at least knows dragons are real?" Enoch asks sighing as he sheaths his dagger.

"Oh, they are real boyo. Just don't know of a mortal capable of killing them." The girl responds confidently.

"I have killed ... at least 10. Pain in the bullocks it is but it is possible. My spear is made of dragon bones. I would take my shirt off to show some scars, but it feels a wee bit chilly for this southerner here." Enoch says still focusing on writing down the map in a tongue he can easily read without having to think too much about it.

"What are you? I mean your race?" The girl asks looking at Enoch shocked.

"Were. May I ask your age and potentially your name, Miss?" Enoch responds not looking at the girl.

"I am turning 21 in about a week and I go by Aed! What is your name boyo?" Aed asks looking at Enoch.

"Name is Enoch. I refuse to look at you due to a curse of the were and looking at women." Enoch responds as he finishes drawing the map in a tongue he knows.

"Curse?" Aed asks moving to try and get Enoch to look at her.

"So male weres have this ability to look at a female and mark them as their own. Well I have enough marked women to live with." Enoch explains as Aed grabs him and spins him around to face her making him see her fiery orange locks with beautiful blue eyes and pale white skin dotted with freckles.

"I doubt you will have an effect on me. Your kind haven't imprinted a Jraconian once in recorded history." Aed responds chuckling as she holds Enoch's head so he can't avoid looking at her any way other than closing his eyes.

"E would you just look at her so she will leave you be. She isn't bad looking if you became the first to mark a Jraconian to begin with." Maria says shoving Enoch's shoulder.

Enoch opens his eyes and is taken aback at how pretty Aed is and how much her name fits her hair. "Wow what is your relation to Angus here?" Enoch asks looking at Aed as she decides to mess with Enoch and sits on his lap.

"He is my older cousin. So, what do you think big guy? Am I prettier than the two ladies who are watching my every move?" Aed responds trying to seduce Enoch.

"No. You aren't even my type. Too clingy." Enoch says colder than the hills of North Jraconia.

"Wow the first guy to not jump at a chance to even touch me!" Aed responds as Enoch pushes her off his lap onto the floor.

"What can I say I like my women semi-independent and well my kind." Enoch says pulling Maria onto his lap as she lets out a squeak from being jostled unexpectedly.

"What do you mean by kind? These two don't look alike at all?" Aed responds offended.

"I mean they are both weres like myself." Enoch says as Maria crosses arms across her chest as she was enjoying standing up.

"So, we have three weres in our little hole in the wall?" The bartender asks behind Enoch.

"Please tell me you all aren't racist against our kind like Angus?!" Jennifer responds readying her hand on her sword hilt.

"No, he is the odd ball of the family. Although my brother behind the bar would like to offer you three drinks." Aed says chuckling as she grabs her flagon of ale.

"I don't drink anymore. Too much drink leads to guessing who I ate the night before. I used to eat workhorse meat and the next morning make sure I didn't know the poor sod." Enoch responds refusing the ale.

"Come on just try the mead." Aed says grabbing the mug from behind Enoch and handing it to him.

"Could you keep your breasts out of my face?!" Maria responds kicking Aed's shin.

"I forgot you were there was hoping to try and seduce Enoch with my bosom." Aed says being honest.

"What would you say you feel towards, Enoch?" Jennifer asks looking at Aed funny.

"I took his calling me unattractive as a challenge." Aed responds looking at Jennifer funny.

"Hey how much is a room here for three people?" Jennifer asks turning to face the bartender.

"25 gold coins. Why?" the bartender responds.

"Well the first sun is setting, and it is about a day walk to the last known location of the dragon we are here in North Jraconia for so I figure E, M, and myself would need a room." Jennifer explains sipping her mead.

"I will cover it just give her a key and tell her the room." Enoch chimes in enjoying having Maria on his lap.

"I will go with her." Maria says getting off Enoch's lap making him sad.

Now it is just Enoch and Aed and Angus. "Now that I have you to myself answer honestly am I prettier than the two weres?" Aed asks sitting next to Enoch.

"No. You have to realize I am legally married by non were standards to M. J is my counterpart. I am half werewolf half werecat. As is she. No, we aren't related." Enoch responds bluntly as he sips the mead.

"Where is your ring?" Aed asks looking at Enoch's left hand.

"I left it in the bag at my feet for the flight here as I didn't trust it not to fall off my finger while we were flying." Enoch responds pulling his ring out of the 72 stone bag.

"So why does your bag weigh 72 stone?" Angus asks looking at Enoch funny.

"You have seen my cooking stone! Plus, I don't trust the Kobold with my money. Neither should you." Enoch responds synching his bag shut.

"So, what is with the scars on your face and the white eye?" Aed asks looking at Enoch's face funny.

"Got marked for going against the tribe leaders wishes. Banished more or less. The scars and permanently blinded left eye are to make it easy for the tribes to tell I am no longer welcome in their dens. J is marked similarly for refusing to mark me as she was one of my imprints. M was declared dead a couple years back because my father found her severely wounded during the first war caused by me adventuring and he took her to his brother's tribe to be healed without sending word to the Koftan tribe that she was alive." Enoch explains finishing his mead.

"Do you want me to cut the crap, Enoch?" Aed asks sighing glancing over at Enoch.

"Sure, maybe if you are honest with me, I can go upstairs with my girls and get some sleep." Enoch responds yawning.

"You look like a boy I saw when my family went on something of a world tour of areas where your kind are supposedly heavily focused when I was a little girl. I bumped into a kind child who you look like the grown-up version of and I have been infatuated with weres ever since. I saw your face and that flame came back." Aed says turning to face Enoch.

"So, when was this?" Enoch asks turning to face Aed with a look showing how little he cares for the bs story.

"I was about six years of age." Aed responds unable to sit still with Enoch focusing on her.

"Well I don't feel anything. Though your hair reminds me of a girl who dropped a toy in my village when I was about 11 or 12. I was working to keep myself alive and train a dwarf girl who I imprinted on just before I turned 11 years old." Enoch says as cold as ever.

"Can we do something I did to thank you for returning my doll?" Aed asks meekly before holding her arms open.

"You want me to hug you despite you have been trying to seduce me. Why would I oblige you on this?" Enoch responds looking at Aed in front of him with her arms wide open as she starts to sob from him being so cold.

"Enoch, please if she remembers it correctly you and her could be the first were Jraconian coupling that isn't complete bs." Angus says pushing Enoch from behind.

"Fine." Enoch responds hugging Aed as her hair covers his nose and he instinctively inhales and gets a whiff of hazelnut and cinnamon with a hint of burning hickory before a flash of a repressed memory.

"You alright, Enoch?!" Aed asks as Enoch falls back on the stool behind him.

"I don't like what just happened but apparently I have a repressed memory of you. When you hugged me all I could smell was hazelnut and cinnamon with a hint of burning hickory. I don't want another woman in my life." Enoch responds looking up at Aed with his one eye. "Last time I had three I cared about my favorite one at the time died. I don't want to lose either of M or J." Enoch continues putting his head in his hands.

"Can I spend the night with you to see if it is true or complete bs as you thought the story was?" Aed asks trying to appear cute as both Maria and Jennifer come up behind her.

"So, what's the verdict E? Do we have a fourth member on our own?" Jennifer asks walking up to the duo as Enoch gives Aed a glare.

"Apparently she imprinted on me when she was young and I for some reason suppressed the memory of that. I don't want to lose either woman I truly love like the last time I had three I cared about. M, would you mind sleeping behind me for a night with J at my feet in her preferred were state?" Enoch responds sighing as he looks at the three standing in front of him.

"We already discussed that, and we have no problem doing a trial run if Aed could either imprint on you now or reveal you two had already imprinted on each other." Jennifer says giggling.

"Aed, is your hair dreaded or just in braids?" Enoch asks standing up lifting his heavy bag at the same time.

"Just in braids why?" Aed responds.

"Could you take them out? I would prefer something softer as you will be in front of me." Enoch explains walking away from the bar.

"I get to join you tonight! Yay!" Aed exclaims excitedly as she rushes to be at Enoch's side.

"We aren't having any inappropriate contact tonight outside of I like to sleep naked." Enoch responds turning his head to look right at Aed with an exhausted expression.

Now in the room Enoch is laid in bed as Maria crawls up behind him and Aed stands nude but confused how to go about climbing in the bed. "Come on just lay in front of me. I will be putting my arms around you." Enoch says annoyed at Aed just standing there.

"It is I am worried you may try and 'impale' me." Aed responds meekly.

"I said no inappropriate contact so don't worry I just want to sleep and when the three of us weres leave in the morning for the dragon leave you here. Not saying leaving you here is permanent just trying to lessen the chance of losing one of the other two because how the gods of life and death like to be fickle." Enoch explains sighing as Jennifer does what he wanted and pushes Aed onto the bed. "Thank you, J." Enoch continues as Aed climbs into his arms.

"You are so warm!" Aed exclaims softly.

"Are all of your kind so cold?" Enoch asks whispering in Aed's right ear.

"Don't know haven't cuddled with anyone of my kind. Hoping maybe I would see you again y'know. Though I am kind of known for needing a lot of blankets and firewood come winter. So, are you going to touch me inappropriately at all?" Aed responds enjoying being held.

"Not consciously. Unless I say I want to have fun I avoid feeling my girls up. Well except, M. As she is my wife, I try to make sure she feels pleasure when she needs it." Enoch responds as Aed grabs his right hand and puts it on her right breast.

"I just want your hand there is all." Aed says meekly as Jennifer goes werecat and curls up on Enoch's feet.

Chapter 21

The next morning Enoch awakes to Aed asleep facing him and Maria sobbing behind him with a worried Jennifer behind her. "What is going on you two?" Enoch asks rolling to face Maria and Jennifer.

"She just started crying and won't talk to me." Jennifer responds looking at Enoch.

"M what is going on?" Enoch asks touching Maria's face.

"I thought I was okay with being behind you and you cuddling with the new girl, but I miss sleeping in your arms." Maria responds meekly.

"I just put her in front of me tonight to see if my feelings for her would grow with her in my arms." Enoch says touching Maria's face before kissing her on the lips.

"Did they?" Aed asks sheepishly scooting so her bosom is pressed against Enoch's back.

"Can we talk about it later, Aed?" Enoch responds not trying to look behind him.

"Did your feelings grow for her?" Maria asks looking Enoch in the eye.

"A little. She did what you do in my arms when you get a little cold. Y'know when you scoot back as if to share my body and when your back gets warm enough you roll to face me then you bury your face in my chest. She didn't do the burying her face part, but she did the rest." Enoch responds sheepishly.

There is a knocking at the door. "You three awake?" Angus asks through the door.

"We are all awake, cousin!" Aed responds annoyed.

"I forgot you went to bed with him. What will your parents think of you and a were?" Angus asks through the door.

"We didn't have relations, Angus!" Enoch responds annoyed.

"Still what will her parents think?" Angus asks not knowing Aed is rushing to the door still nude.

Aed opens the door. "They unlike you don't care if we breed with people outside of our kind! Quit trying to keep people away from me! I am free to have relations with whoever I want!" Aed exclaims pushing Angus away.

"Aed you are still naked get back in here! Now!" Enoch yells from the bed.

Everyone has gotten bathed and dressed. Aed has been down in the restaurant for a while when the trio come down.

"So, I heard you actually snuggled my little sister?" the bartender asks looking at Enoch.

"Yes, nothing inappropriate happened between her and I." Enoch responds yawning as he sits at the bar. "Where is that girl anyways?" Enoch asks looking around.

"She wanted to cook you breakfast. Here is the coffee she asked Jennifer what you liked with your breakfast." The bartender responds chuckling. "I don't care you do anything inappropriate to her. Just don't hurt her and abandon her." The bartender continues giving Enoch a dead cold look.

"I am leaving her here for this mission. When we get back and figure out where to next if she truly wants to live with me, she should have as much as she can carry on her back packed. I honestly enjoy the energy that little redhead lets off. Don't get me wrong I love M and J but Aed let's off a completely different energy signal than they do." Enoch says as Aed comes out with his plate of food.

"Here it is what J said you like for breakfast! Hope you like it!" Aed exclaims setting the food in front of Enoch.

"Do you know why I order so much for breakfast?" Enoch asks looking up at Aed as the girls to his left are drooling.

"Why? I couldn't even eat that much?" Aed responds looking at Enoch funny.

"Take this to a table with four seats bringing along 3 more sets of utensils and you will see." Enoch says getting up and walking to a table with four seats with the duo in tail.

Now everyone is seated with a plate of food in front of them in various states of eaten. "So, you don't just order it all for yourself. That makes sense, I guess. Not my normal taste in food but it is filling." Aed says nodding looking at Enoch to her left.

"Aed, I have a question for you." Enoch responds glancing at Aed as she is eating.

"Fire away!" Aed says excitedly.

"Do you want to leave this town with us after we get back from slaying this dragon?" Enoch asks putting his arm around the back of Aed's chair.

"I would but I couldn't part with all my stuff. I overheard you and my brother talking." Aed responds sighing.

"It wouldn't be permanent on parting with your stuff. Just till we could get you settled into my lifestyle. I didn't include that as I wanted to leave some surprises for the conversation, I wanted to have with you." Enoch explains enjoying the vibes coming off of Aed.

"So, you want her to come with us on adventures?" Jennifer asks looking at Enoch befuddled.

"If she wants to come with us the offer is open as well as that would be fair to her. I was talking if she wanted to maintain the house while we are out making money. Though we need to get finished working for her cousin first." Enoch responds as he feels a change in Aed.

"I think I need to reveal something to you three." Aed says looking around the table. "Lean in you three." Aed continues.

"What is it, Aed?" Enoch asks leaning in to listen to Aed.

"Angus isn't actually my cousin. He was to be my husband till I revealed I didn't want anything to do with him or my own kind. I revealed I thought that a were in my youth imprinted on me so while his parents are mad at me mine understood and cancelled the marriage. He was hoping last night that I was wrong when he pushed Enoch to hug me. Because if I was wrong, I would have to marry him no matter what. Well I am so glad I was right. I get to see what tribe life is like." Aed explains looking right at Enoch.

"No, you don't I have been banished from all tribes." Enoch responds sighing.

"In a way E we do have a tribe right here." Jennifer chimes in chuckling at how Aed is looking at Enoch.

"You don't want true tribe life." Maria says looking at Aed coldly.

"Why not?" Aed asks shocked.

"Since you are not a were all you would get is screwed then when the baby is born more than likely you will die in childbirth if you survive then you will get impregnated by your mate as soon as possible. If you don't die from that baby being born you will forever spend life as a birthing mother to your mate till you die in childbirth." Maria explains coldly as she stairs Aed dead in the face.

"As dark as it may sound M is being honest." Enoch says looking at Aed.

"When will we be leaving you three? Aed!" Angus asks chiming in.

"Give us five more minutes." Enoch responds sighing at Angus. "Can I ask you a question Aed?" Enoch continues as Angus walks away huffing.

"What is it, Enoch?" Aed responds turning on her chair to face Enoch completely.

"Is the fact that you wanted a were over Angus the reason he hates weres?" Enoch asks looking down at Aed as she is wearing a rather short dress.

"More than likely yes. Now that he knows it is you, he may be meaner than he was. Enjoying what you see?" Aed responds revealing she knows Enoch is looking at her.

"I have enjoyed seeing you whether you were fully clothed or completely naked." Enoch says smiling at how his response made Aed blush.

"So, I have to ask. Is she prettier than us?" Jennifer asks watching Enoch and Aed's interactions.

"No. I don't compare different races against each other. She is a very pretty Jraconian. Just like you are a beautiful half breed and Maria is a beautiful full breed werecat." Enoch responds not breaking a sweat.

"What if you compared us just once?" Aed asks getting in on the fun.

"It is a tie. I love the black hair blue eyes combo that M has going on just as much as I love the blonde hair green eyes combo of J. Red hair and blue is equal to those two. I don't include bosom judgements as M would win instantly with hers being the perfect size for her body. Let's get a move on to find that dragon M and J." Enoch says yawning before moving to stand up.

"Could you kiss me before you go?" Aed asks sheepishly before Enoch hugs her and kisses her on the lips.

"Check in the coin purse on your hip for something you may want to keep on your person." Enoch whispers in Aed's ear before turning around and sauntering away. Aed looks in her coin purse to find something akin to an oath ring.

Now on their way to the last known location of the dragon they are hoping to give a clue to the prophecy. A distant flapping sound can be heard on the wind. "I think we may have found it. Or it has found us. Dragons can detect when a flame is out of place." Enoch says readying his spear.

As the Dragon lands in front of Enoch he tries the peace trick but as he gets closer the dragon breaths fire at him. Enoch of course uses his magic to avoid the fire making contact with his flesh. However, Enoch's clothes burn off revealing his scarred body as he crouches down to vault into the air so he can get on the dragon's back. The dragon takes off before Enoch can land on it. Enoch hits the ground hard cracking it. "I could use some help! This one may just best me!" Enoch screams looking around at the three others just standing dumbfounded like they don't know how to fight a dragon. "M and J help me now!" Enoch screams again as he dodges more fireballs. Enoch is dodging constant barrages of fireballs when Maria decides to join in using a bow she keeps on her person when they are not in a town. She hits a couple arrows through the dragon's flight membrane causing it some pain and it to make some noise before it lands to catch its breath giving Enoch the chance to vault onto its back. Placing his hand on the back of the dragon's skull. "Why do you not want us to figure out your prophecy?" Enoch asks in perfect Draconian.

"Because it isn't like we are just born to provide the prophecy! We are born to live just like you are, dauði!" The dragon responds with a mighty roar in agony as more arrows hit its hide.

"Cut the attack!" Enoch hollers before he drops and slits the dragon's throat spraying blood and fire everywhere. Now on the ground Enoch reaches in the dragon's throat and pulls out a stone. Throwing the stone to Angus. "Can we just burn it with its flesh still on the bone?" Enoch asks exhausted.

"You don't want to attempt selling the meat here?" Jennifer asks surprised.

"I am exhausted, and I will level with you. I only brought one change of clothes so if we carved it after I finish getting dressed, I would be waltzing back into town covered in blood." Enoch responds as he pulls his change of clothes out of his surprisingly fireproof bag.

"We need the money, E. Don't put your clothes on yet simple as that." Maria chimes in sighing at Enoch.

Sometime later they have filled all bags they use for meat with dragon flesh and have finished with the ceremony for properly disposing of a dragon corpse. "So, uh this isn't the one we need. This isn't the first one sadly." Angus says meekly.

"Of course, it wasn't I took a glance at it before tossing it to you. With each one I kill and properly dispose of they seem to impart the ability to read their texts." Enoch responds as he heads to the river nearby. "Whoever hasn't bathed yet after helping carve the dragon lets get bathed." Enoch says aloud hoping one of the girls would come with him.

Enoch is in the river as Maria comes to join him. "I have bathed but you seemed like you wanted someone to join you. We both bathed while you performed the ceremony." Maria says climbing in now that she is nude. "So, what did you want to talk about, or did you want to y'know?" Maria asks meekly.

"While y'know would be nice I actually wanted to ask you if I made a mistake finding out I imprinted on Aed?" Enoch responds looking at Maria with genuine concern in his face.

"Well neither Jenny nor I died like you had feared. I don't really know what to tell you. It is up to your interpretation whether awakening repressed memories was a mistake or not." Maria says looking at Enoch like she cares but doesn't know what to say.

"I just feel like having her is going to change what I have come to enjoy. Two warm bodies in bed with me. You in front with J behind me. I have never really liked sleeping with a were curled up on my feet." Enoch responds opening his arms as he has made his way to Maria in the river.

"Please don't get my hair wet." Maria says meekly.

"Didn't plan on it, sweetie. Do I have any blood on me still?" Enoch asks after letting go of Maria and doing a little spin.

"Not that I can see. So, can we get a move on?" Maria responds both enjoying what she is seeing and getting cold, so she wants to get out of the water.

"After you answer one more question. Do you think Aed will mix with the three of us well?" Enoch asks looking at Maria lovingly.

"Honestly with how you are worrying about it. No, you worrying will cause you to find flaws with her so she will always feel like she is walking on egg shells. Now I get not all of your imprints will get the absolute trust I did when we bumped into each other in Oxen-DeValley while you were on the run. Or how Jenny gave you absolute trust when she was marked and exiled for refusing to mark you. But she does deserve your trust that she will try and fit in with out ruffling our fur so to speak. She is the first of her kind to be imprinted by our kind. Give her some faith and everything should turn out as the gods intend. I love you, E. Let us get moving." Maria responds as Enoch starts nodding.

"That is why I wanted you to come with me. You would be able to give me an honest opinion. I love you too, M. Thank you." Enoch says making his way to the shore.

Now reentering the village of Draconer's Grove the group are sauntering into the restaurant with an inn attached that the trio called home the night before. "Hey Aed's brother do you know of a place that will buy dragon meat? I have a whole ton of it that I need to sell

and well being new here I have no clue where to sell it."
Enoch says sitting at the bar.

"Give my crew some time to deal with the dinner
rush and we will gladly deal with it. Aed is preparing
you your favorite meal post hunt. My name is Aibne by
the way." Aibne responds nodding at Enoch.

A few moments have passed and Aed has come out
with a bowl of squirrel and rabbit stew. "I hope you like
it. I struggled to get my hands on the meats for it." Aed
says trying to be confident.

"Have you ever had it sweetie?" Enoch asks looking
at Aed with love in his eyes.

"No never heard of people eating squirrels or rabbits
to be honest." Aed responds sheepishly.

"Grab yourself a spoon and I will share with you if
you come sit next to me. I find this is a meal that can
help two who may have differences come to understand each other." Enoch says slapping the chair to his
right.

Aed has joined Enoch as the duo are sitting to his
left trying to order some of the stew. "I left the ladle
next to the pot. This is amazing!" Aed says after taking
a spoonful of the stew with a chunk of rabbit.

"Do you see why I love it? Now it has been brought
to my attention that I may be approaching well bringing you into my inner circle completely the wrong way.
I am trying to correct that now. Which is why I had you
grab a spoon to share the bowl of stew. Now this stew

is a meal I may order a lot of however I never share it. I am letting you share with me so maybe you feel welcome in the group. Aed, I am sorry that we got off on the wrong foot. I have no excuse for treating you the way I did. Will you let me try and make it up to you?" Enoch explains watching Aed with his right eye.

"I was wary of how you were treating me at first, but Jennifer and I had a conversation about many things to do with you. Among those were your food preference, your eccentricities, etcetera. So is the stew up to your standards?" Aed responds glancing at Enoch.

"I must ask if this is your first time making this stew. This is a hard dish to master. Well okay hard to make it to my standards." Enoch says chuckling looking at Aed.

"I haven't really dabbled in cooking at all. That has always been Aibne's thing. But Jennifer says that you would love to have someone who can cook your favorite foods in the group. I asked Aibne for assistance and he said that for me to learn what I want to learn the best assistance he could give was to let me use his kitchen and resources. Something about not having a love for cooking but wishing to please someone rather than to satiate my own hunger to cook." Aed responds showing confusion at the end.

"Aibne is a wise man. Doing something you enjoy because you enjoy it is the best thing one can do. However, doing something you maybe are ok with to try and please someone else is like having a toss in the wind that is blowing towards you. It may get you what you want but it will also make a mess. If you don't like cooking, you shouldn't do it just for me. I don't want to make you do something you don't enjoy." Enoch explains looking over at Aed as Angus sits on the other side of her.

"So, you kind of kept the translated map, Enoch. Could you pull it out so I can figure out where we need to go next?" Angus asks butting in.

"Let me finish eating. I wrote it in were." Enoch responds sighing.

"Why would you do that?!" Angus asks annoyed.

"I wrote it in a tongue I understand that way you can't just kick the three weres out." Enoch responds getting increasingly annoyed.

"Angus, leave the true dragon slayer alone." Aed says upset with the interruption.

Enoch has since finished the bowl of stew with Aed's help. He is looking at the map while Aed is sitting next to him nursing a beer. "So, what is this a map of?" Aed asks looking at the slip of paper befuddled.

"Where the dragons were when I killed the eldest titan dragon. I sadly had to slit its throat to end its suffering. All suffering it was feeling was caused by me. I sent a purple fireball at it causing its wings to burn. It crashed down on the earthen soil unable to even defend itself against my rage that I felt because it was attacking my kinfolk who cast me out. I had no issues with that dragon other than the belief all were should stick together even if they have been cast out." Enoch explains as a tear hits the bar in front of him.

"I am sorry if I made you cry, Enoch!" Aed responds trying to comfort Enoch.

"You didn't make me cry. I am crying because every time up until now I have slain a dragon because of my kin. Whether it was because I was angry at my kinfolk or to protect them now I do it because I promised to find some prophecy only individuals of the Draconer tribe could read on stones formed inside of dragons. I didn't promise this to Angus but to the dragon I burnt its wing membranes off." Enoch says sounding as honest as he can.

"How is it going figuring out where the next dragon was at the one that came from when it died?" Angus asks being an annoying little twat.

"If you would leave me alone for more than five minutes, I could figure this out! No Aed isn't bugging me. Her voice unlike yours doesn't make me want to strangle its source!" Enoch responds anger showing severely.

"Sheesh! Just a little impatient I want to get out of this country as soon as I can." Angus says before turning the other way.

"Angus get out! You are pissing off the gentleman who has help put dragon back on the menu. Not only that he has made my little sister happy. You upsetting him upsets my sister." Aibne says motioning for Angus to leave.

"Hold on! There were quite a few here in North Jraconia! We will be here a few days more! There is one to the east, then one to the north!" Enoch says excitedly.

"Yay! I have longer to pack my stuff up and to sell my house!" Aed exclaims.

"You aren't selling your house. Just packing what you want to take back to South Jraconia. Though knowledge of you owning a house would have been nice last night." Enoch responds looking at Aed with a look that could only be described as dumbfounded.

"My bed we would be lucky to fit just you and me. So, M and J wouldn't be able to join us. So, are you renting a room tonight?" Aed asks meekly.

"Well I guess I have to as I can't leave two of my three girls without a place to sleep. What does the meat come up to?" Enoch responds before looking at Aibne.

"About two thousand platinum. Thankfully I make that in about a day with dragon on the menu." Aibne says chuckling.

"Here is the price for last night's room and the room for tonight." Enoch responds handing Aibne the proper amount of coin.

Chapter 22

The next morning the group are on their way to the dragon to the east in the mountains separating East Jraconia from North Jraconia. The dragon could be sleeping in the mountains as they have a lot of caves for them to hide in. As they get near a forest a roar is heard. Sounds like a bear. "Enoch, can you deal with that?" Angus asks more than just a hint of fear in his voice.

"Wow, Angus scared of a bear, are we?" Aed asks as she tags along.

"I love her commentary of Angus being a coward!" Maria exclaims giggling.

"Well until it shows itself, I can't very well turn Demonic grim bear to fight it." Enoch responds hiding a giggle as the bear throws a tree their direction before charging. Once the bear gets to the clearing it turns into the human state. "Oh, a fellow werebear!" Enoch exclaims excitedly.

"Wait you are just a werewolf and werecat mix?" Aed asks confused.

"It is very complicated to explain." Enoch responds sighing signaling for the were to come to them.

The were has now joined them to converse. "So, you three are weres? How about these two?" the werebear asks looking Angus and Aed over.

"No, they are Jraconian. M, J, and I have been exiled from the tribes down south. I don't remember there being any werebears present for the exiling ceremony." Enoch responds bowing to the werebear.

"We as a tribe were exiled a long time ago. I doubt they remember that our kind exist. Same goes for our brother tribe of Werefoxes. Would you like to come back to our den for the night then set out for the dragon that has been terrorizing our brother tribe?" the werebear asks looking at the group.

"Isn't it the morning still?" Enoch asks confused.

"You are new here this far north. We only experience light from the twin suns for about 4 hours a day. Nighttime is extremely dangerous to be out and about up here. We had a tribe split off from us that attacks our members if they are out at night. We are only 2 hours north from here. The foxes are 4 hours east from here." The werebear explains trying to not sound condescending.

"I think we will soldier on. I have slain dragons. The rest of the weres with me have slain monsters bigger than a werebear." Enoch responds confidently.

"Ok proceed at your own peril." The werebear says before turning back into a bear and running off.

Now on the edge of the mountains the crew hear the telltale sound indicating a giant shadow scorpion is near. Hearing the sound makes Enoch's ears perk up. "Ooh FOOD!" Enoch exclaims excitedly as the beast bursts from the ground beneath his feet throwing him into the air. Enoch in excitement turns into his demonic grim bear state crashing down on top of the scorpion causing it to sprawl out flat on the ground. Enoch knowing it isn't dead as its shell didn't even crack. Enoch climbs off the scorpion's back and grabs it by the tip of its tail and starts spinning causing it to lift off the ground before the joint holding its tail on disconnects sending the scorpion flying into the nearest mountain side. Enoch drops the tail and chases the scorpion and when he reaches the beast it has risen to its six legs. It acts like it is going to stab him with its that tail he ripped off. Enoch then catches one of its pincers as it realizes it lost its tail and does the same thing except when the arm detaches he keeps a hold of it and chases the scorpion and impales its head with the claw killing it before he bites through the shell into its claw allowing him to return to his normal state. "That was fun!!!!" Enoch screams excitedly as the rest of the group finally join him. "Anyone have a giant maul?" Enoch asks as the group get up to him.

"Maul?" Aed asks confused.

"Big hammer!" Enoch responds still high on endorphins.

"Why?" Angus asks scared.

"I love the taste of fried scorpion meat." Enoch responds chuckling.

"I have a hammer we used to break the skulls of dragons to get some brains from the dragon you sold to Aibne. Will that do?" Jennifer asks looking at Enoch funny.

"It should Dragon skulls are stronger than scorpion carapace." Enoch responds taking the hammer before slamming it down on the head of the scorpion carcass shattering the shell.

Now a while later after Enoch has obtained all the meat the group is setting up a campsite. While Enoch is starting the fire Aed is following him around. "Could you give me a little space, Aed? I don't want to set you on fire when I do this." Enoch says readying a ball of fire in his hand.

"So why did you invite me along instead of having me pack my stuff?" Aed asks stepping back as the fire explodes into life.

"Aed, leave me alone!" Enoch responds annoyance showing in his voice while he is setting up the cooking area.

A little time has passed and Aed's sobs can be heard from Enoch's tent. "Why did you make her cry?" Jennifer asks annoyed with Enoch.

"I am trying to focus myself for what is coming what is wrong with that?!" Enoch responds anger showing in his tone while staying focused on flipping the meat.

"You are being very mean to the girls who only wish to make you happy! Maybe if you told us what is going on, we could maybe help you with dealing with it!" Jennifer yells before stomping as she heads into the tent.

Enoch sighs and decides to hold off cooking while he deals with his issues. Heading into the tent he finds Maria trying to comfort a sobbing Aed while Jennifer sits away from them moping. "So, do you three want to know what I have been working through in my head?" Enoch asks sitting a little distance from all three in the tent.

"It would be nice to know why you were mean to Aed and Jennifer?" Maria responds showing that she is very upset.

"Hang on I need to get a stone from Angus. My paper map doesn't have what I need to explain. Angus! Can I get the stone map?!" Enoch hollers sticking his head out of the tent before ducking as the stone comes flying at his face.

"Why is that needed?" Aed asks meekly.

"I need all those interested to come here so I can be certain I am pointing at the correct spot on the stone." Enoch responds sighing as Aed leads the crawl to him.

Now that the girls are situated around Enoch. "So, you see these symbols around the dragon we are headed towards. Notice they aren't on the paper map I made. I didn't know what they meant when I made the paper map, so I left them out. Big mistake there. This one is warning that this dragon is very dangerous. No context in that symbol as to why it is dangerous. This second symbol doesn't explain the danger, but it notes this is where we should have started here for the prophecy. The third symbol is the danger. If I try to kill this dragon the way I have been killing all the others I will end up dead. Its skin is coated in a poison that soaks into those who are foolish enough to touch it. So, unless I can find a way to kill it without touching it then I am going to die days after touching it. As I don't have access to the poison right now, I can't say if the antidote is known yet. I am trying to figure out if this prophecy is worth dying for. As we know nothing of the prophecy either I have no justification for it being worth my life. I have three amazing women who I love dearly, so I can't say I would give up my life for such an unknown. But I can't kill a dragon or even get the stone without touching it. Unless we do the ceremony with the stone inside, I have no way of staying alive and doing what we are getting paid to do. I want to live. I don't want to die because some prophecy requires someone who knows how to kill dragons to sacrifice them self for the good of people they will never get to meet. I don't want to die for Angus!" Enoch explains crying at the end.

"What about using magic to kill it like you did with the one that put the giant scar on your back?" Maria asks looking up at Enoch's eyes as she laid on him during his speech.

"I don't know if I can do that with a dragon that isn't wounded like that one was. I had prior contact with that dragon. Not so much on this one. Plus, as time is going on my spear is losing its magic. So, my power decreases the more I use it. I can't just take bones from a dragon I have performed the ceremony on. That dissipates the magic." Enoch explains as Aed adjusts how she is seated next to him.

"How about we help fight it?" Jennifer asks sheepishly.

"You can't touch the dragon, or you will die! I don't want to lose any of you as much as I don't want to die." Enoch responds tears still streaming down his face.

"I know how to use a bow." Jennifer responds sticking her tongue out.

"Do you have one?" Enoch asks sighing before kissing the top of Jennifer's head.

"Yes, I hide it in your bag!" Jennifer responds hunkering down cuddling with Enoch.

"So that is the thing that digs into my back. How about you Maria?" Enoch says picking on Jennifer.

"I am good at throwing spears." Maria responds sheepishly.

"If you have one that isn't my bone spear then go ahead. Aed, come here." Enoch says opening his arms to Aed.

"What are you going to do to me?" Aed asks meekly.

"You look jealous of these two. I want to hold you for a minute then I have to go about cooking." Enoch responds as Aed climbs in his lap.

A few moments later Enoch is cooking and Aed is by his side while the two girls are making sure they aren't rusty with their weapons. "So why are they fiddling with their weapons they never use?" Angus asks sitting around the fire.

"Because none of us can directly touch this dragon unless you want to die." Enoch responds sighing at the ignorance of Angus.

"Oh, is that what the symbols next to the dragon mean?" Angus asks sheepishly.

"Two of them yes." Enoch responds now loading Angus's plate.

"What is the third one?" Angus asks taking the food from Enoch.

"Telling us to start here." Enoch responds sheepishly. "In my defense I couldn't read them at the start. Reading them was your thing not mine when we started." Enoch continues as he throws more meat on for Aed's plate of food.

"What exactly do the two danger symbols say?" Angus asks looking at Enoch.

"That this dragon is dangerous for the first one. The second one is that it is a very bad idea to make skin contact with the dragon or it's bodily fluids. We will not be carving this one. Don't care that we said we would be bringing more meat back to Aibne. I personally didn't say that, so I don't feel bad not bringing meat back. I knew the danger which is why I didn't say anything. I of course didn't know the danger till I had Aibne make me a dish out of the dragon brain I provided from the last dragon. This could be the end of the road for me." Enoch explains plating up Aed, Maria, and Jennifer's food. "Girls come eat!" Enoch hollers giggling watching Maria and Jennifer using their weapons.

"So why don't you use a ranged weapon?" Angus asks looking at Enoch with concern.

"I don't actually have any of my own. I am more up close and personal. My farthest-reaching weapon allows me to get a max of three meters away. But that leaves very little surface to make contact with. I prefer to allow my maul as much contact as possible. Though I could maybe use the hammer's reverse side to decapitate the dragon." Enoch responds plating up his food as Aed nudges him. "What is it sweetie?" Enoch asks looking at Aed.

"You never mentioned you had weapons other than your spear when we were in the tent. Why hide that fact?" Aed responds looking up at Enoch.

"I haven't really been hiding that I have other weapons. The massive box in my bag is full of them. I just don't like using them as they are the majority of the weight in my bag. Plus, some are worth more than your brother's restaurant." Enoch says looking at Aed lovingly. "M even knows about the majority of them. She was there when I purchased most of them or commissioned them. Though the maul she wasn't around for as I did that one night while her and Jennifer were asleep, and I couldn't get to sleep." Enoch continues chuckling.

"So, when you called out for the maul you were hoping one of us had snooped in your bag. Which I will admit I have, and I have just never opened the massive box." Jennifer responds leaning forward and looking at Enoch.

"Yes, I was hoping someone had looked in the box I have been slowly filling with enough weapons to supply a group twice our size." Enoch says smiling at the girls.

Chapter 23

Now the next morning and the group have made it to the cave marked on the map. They have setup a distance away so that the crate of weapons can be opened safely without worrying of waking the dragon early. "So, I am going to need one of you to hang on the maul. When I call for you to toss it to me well you throw it to me. Careful it is about ninety percent of the weight in my bag." Enoch says pulling the maul out of the box as the axe edge glints in the morning sun.

"That is your maul. That thing is absolutely massive. How can you lift it?" Angus responds in shock.

"I carry it in a bag that weighs 72 stone and this maul weighs less than that and you are shocked that I can lift it! So back on the task at hand. I will sneak in to make certain the dragon is asleep and if so, I will throw this axe on my hip at it. If my accuracy is decent enough it will hit its mark of the dragon. Then I will rush out demanding this be tossed to me. If the dragon is home and awake, then it will probably notice me which means I run and demand this be tossed to me. Does everyone follow me so far?" Enoch asks looking around at the four of his teammates surrounding his crate of weapons.

"What if you don't hit the dragon?" Aed asks looking at Enoch with grave concern.

"Then the noise of it hitting whatever it does will probably wake the dragon and I run and demand this to be tossed to me. Any other questions?" Enoch responds looking around the group once again.

"Not really other than how do you expect us to lift that?" Maria asks looking at Enoch funny.

"I know J can. She has lifted my bag without breaking a sweat." Enoch responds looking right at Jennifer.

"So, I have to toss you that maul axe combo thing?" Jennifer asks with as serious of a tone as possible.

"Yes. Now once I have this, I will need everyone who knows how to use ranged weapons and magic to start attacking while I work to turn around and start fighting the dragon. I will aim for the head with a hammer blow to get it on the ground long enough for me to switch to the axe side and bring it down on the dragon's neck. I pray to the gods that it doesn't spray me with anything when I do that. I can't use this with heavy armor. Then we will start the ceremony for burning the dragon." Enoch explains looking at the group. "Does everyone understand what I expect from them?" Enoch asks looking right at Aed as she raises her hand.

"What do I do?" Aed asks meekly.

"You haven't expressed any ability to use a ranged weapon. So, I honestly don't know of anything for you to do." Enoch responds. "Let's get into position!" Enoch continues handing Jennifer the maul.

Now at the entrance to the cave Enoch is mentally prepping himself to throw the axe. He enters the cave and feels a gust of warm breath pushing against him to leave the cave. He looks right at the dragon before hurling his axe right at the dragon's head. The axe hits and sticks in the dragon's head right between the eyes. Enoch turns around and starts booking it out of the cave. "Maul Now!" Enoch hollers looking right at Jennifer. He catches the maul. "Positions now!" Enoch hollers as he tries to turn around. The dragon finally catches up to him and lets out a roar.

"Who dares disturb my slumber?!" The dragon demands with the roar.

Enoch launches himself into the air as he slams the maul on the dragon's head maul side down. They both land with a loud thump and the ground quakes from the impact. With the impact there is a extremely loud crack like a skull giving way beneath the axe. Enoch doesn't chance it and flips the maul, so the axe side is down while moving into position and bringing the blade of the axe down on the dragon's neck. A small spray of fluid comes from the veins of the dragon's neck. "Time for the ceremony!" Enoch hollers tossing the maul aside.

"We didn't have to do anything!" Angus hollers.

"The hope was that you wouldn't have to. You all were back up just in case the dragon decided it wanted to attack instead of roar. Who has the fire-starting kit?!" Enoch responds looking around.

The group have burnt the flesh away and Enoch has grabbed the stone with a leather covered hand to be safe before dowsing it in water to both cool it down and rinse off any potential poisons. "Here Angus. Is that J, M, and my deal done?" Enoch asks handing Angus the stone after he finishes dowsing it in water.

"Yes, it technically is. You were being paid to help find the beginning of the prophecy. Unless you want to help even more with my mission." Angus responds sighing.

"I would prefer to get Aed moved to South Jraconia and only do local jobs from there. I have had enough adventuring in my life for a good long while." Enoch says looking at his girls to see if they react.

"I agree with you on this one, E." Jennifer responds as Enoch looks at her.

"Same here. I miss the easy jobs maybe we can get Aed trained and we have a team of four between us, so we just have to find an employer to find the missions and pay us." Maria says looking at Enoch.

"Aed? What is your opinion? This is why I brought you was for you to give an opinion?" Enoch asks looking at Aed.

"I would love to do more adventuring but not taking on dragons. I would love to move in with your three first of course." Aed responds sheepishly.

"Yes, we will be adventuring in South Jraconia just not on this scale. I would even love to go back to Koftan, but I doubt that could ever happen with three of us being banished from the tribe." Enoch says looking between the three girls. "Maybe see Alice's grave." Enoch continues as a tear forms in his eye.

"So, when do we get paid Angus?" Jennifer asks changing the subject.

"Your pay was the fifty coin at the beginning and whatever you got from selling dragon meat." Angus responds trying to hide as Jennifer scares him.

"He is telling the truth. I haven't been spending the money from the dragons for that very reason. I did however spend all the coin M and I made transporting goods from West Jraconia to South Jraconia on the Maul I used for this. Let us get headed back to Draconer's Grove." Enoch chimes in blocking Jennifer from attacking Angus.

Now back in Aibne's restaurant the group are at a table in the back where the lighting is dim. "So, what would the dragon slayers like to eat at my humble bar?" Aibne asks acting a waiter for the group.

"What is Aed's favorite meal here?" Enoch asks not showing any emotion.

"Well she loves the grilled yak steak with some grilled veggies. To drink she likes a nice mead most of the times." Aibne responds semi put off by the lack of emotion in Enoch.

"Sounds quite tasty. Just exhausted. Sorry for the lack of emotion. Had to use a heavy maul that is about as heavy as the dragon we brought you the other day." Enoch says sheepishly.

"Ok what for the rest of you?" Aibne asks looking at the girls.

"My usual." Aed responds chuckling.

"That sounds good." Maria says looking to her left at Enoch.

"I will take some of the freshest stew with a flagon of stout." Jennifer says looking around Aed at Enoch.

"Ok I will have the drinks out in a little bit the foods other than the stew will take a few minutes to cook up." Aibne responds jotting everything down before turning away from the group.

"Why did you want to try my favorite meal?" Aed asks looking at Enoch.

"You put forth the effort to try mine I should do the same for you. Plus, I am stewed out." Enoch responds squeezing Aed's shoulder before moving his right hand in a way Jennifer can sit next to Aed and have Enoch's hand on her.

"So why do you want to go back south?" Aed asks sheepishly.

"I would like to live in the house my father left me after he died in my arms." Enoch responds bluntly.

"Oh, I guess that is a good reason to want to go back then. I don't want to sell my house up here though." Aed says sheepishly.

"I don't expect you to just take as much stuff you can carry this trip." Enoch responds kissing Aed on the left cheek.

The group have finished with dinner and have moved up to the bar while Aed is upstairs in the room Enoch rented taking a bath. "Where did my little sister go?" Aibne asks looking right at Enoch.

"She went to take a bath. Is everything ok?" Enoch responds looking at Aibne funny.

"I have something for her. We once made a bet who would leave the grove first. Whichever one of us that moves first gets a present from the one that remains in the grove. Well it was looking like I would be moving first then you showed up. Well I will be leaving the grove in the next couple of years Aed is leaving before me." Aibne explains looking at Enoch.

"Why will you be leaving?" Enoch asks looking at Aibne funny.

"Looking to open a second location somewhere else. Was thinking of going local but I may just see if I can find a location in South Jraconia so I can see Aed every so often." Aibne responds as Aed comes down with her hair done and in her prettiest dress.

"Enoch, do I look pleasing to your eye?" Aed asks standing behind Enoch as he turns around.

"You look ready for your wedding day. Is that the ceremony you were talking about? And to answer your question you always look pleasing to my eye. Now you just look absolutely gorgeous and like I should be at the other end of an aisle waiting for you." Enoch responds smiling at the sight of Aed in a beautiful white dress with her wavy hair hanging down on her chest.

"Aed, you don't mean you plan to?!" Aibne asks looking at his sister.

"Yes, dear brother. I am doing the Jraconian blood oath to this were!" Aed responds looking from her brother to Enoch.

"Blood oath?" Maria asks confused.

"A blood oath is when someone of the Jraconian race wishes to spend the rest of their days with someone not of their race. When a Jraconian does a blood oath they shorten their life to match the person they took the blood oath with. So, for Aed to take a blood oath with me would make it so the day I die she dies not long after. I would push for her not to but if she has her mind made up nothing, I say will change it. I just hope she doesn't come to regret this decision. She is giving up nine hundred plus years she could live doing things that make her happier than living with me will. Where is your ancestral home?" Enoch explains before standing up to follow Aed.

"Follow me, Enoch of Koftan." Aed responds as she takes Enoch's hand.

Now at the site of Aed's ancestral home Enoch and Aed are standing before the sacrificial altar. "Enoch of Koftan do you take Aed Dundraillion to be your wife until the day you die?" Aibne asks looking at the duo standing there.

"I do!" Enoch says fighting the instinct to nod.

"Aed Dundraillion do you take Enoch of Koftan as your husband until the day he dies?" Aibne asks looking to his little sister.

"I do!" Aed says as Aibne hands her the familial ceremonial knife.

"You may now bind your blood!" Aibne says bowing as Aed cuts the palm of her hand before handing the knife to Enoch who follows suit and cuts the palm of his left hand before they grab each other's hand interweaving their fingers. "You are now married of the blood that flows through your veins. You can now kiss the bride." Aibne continues before he takes the knife back.

The duo kiss before they walk back down the aisle of the ancestral marriage grounds of the Dundraillion family.

Now back at the bar the duo is sitting at the bar holding each other's hands and conversing with the other two girls when Aibne returns with his parents and other siblings. "So, what is this I hear of my little sister taking the blood oath with a were who she just met?!" Isla asks walking into the bar.

"I didn't just meet him. I met him on our trip to Koftan when I was a little girl. He imprinted on me then. Not that you would understand as you have no love for your husband!" Aed responds getting upset.

"Aed, could you introduce me to your family?" Enoch asks looking at Aed with his right eye.

"So, the loudmouth you just heard is Isla my oldest sibling. The woman with a bit of a limp is our mother. The old coot ogling your other imprints is my father. As for my other siblings I doubt they could be bothered to show up despite not only is it my wedding day it is also the second to last day I plan to be in the grove." Aed responds pointing to each of the people she talks about.

"Hey old man. Eyes off my other women. One of which is my legal wife while the other is one of my finalized imprints." Enoch says looking right at Aed's father.

"Why are you already cheating on my daughter young man? My name is Brocagni!" Brocagni asks anger in his voice.

"I am not cheating on your daughter! I am a were who imprinted on many different females in my youth. Your daughter just so happened to be one of them. I can't control the fact she dropped her doll when I was around in my youth." Enoch responds annoyance in his voice showing.

"Enoch, it is best to not try and reason with my parents. They still don't like the idea that I opened this place despite they are the ones who told me that I should cook for the masses." Aibne says tapping Enoch's shoulder.

"Why did you have to tell them let alone bring them here?!" Aed asks whipping around to rip Aibne a new one.

"I was looking for Brody and Bonny to be honest. I found them but they said they may be a little late. Oh, and Brody said, 'About time Aed found her were!' so he may make some jokes." Aibne responds looking down at Aed. "Don't tell mom that those two are coming here. She is still mad that they sided with you on not marrying Angus." Aibne continues but in a whisper.

"Wait they sided with me, but they seem to avoid me!?" Aed asks shocked.

"You still talk to mother on occasion, don't you? They don't want anything they say to get back to her or father." Aibne responds even quieter than before.

There is a sudden commotion by the door of the restaurant. "Let me through you gawkers! Have you not seen some one carrying a present for their freshly married sibling?!" Brody hollers carrying a bear on his shoulder.

"Why did you kill a shadow bear, Brody?!" Aed asks looking at her older brother funny.

"Wait you have a brother who hunts?!" Enoch asks looking at Aed excitedly.

"I sure do boyo. So, you married my little sister? Here if you would help Aibne process this we can have a traditional Dundraillion marital feast!" Brody responds transferring the bear to Enoch's shoulder. "You look so beautiful little sister. So, does he actually know how to gut one of those?" Brody continues as Enoch saunter's away with the bear on his shoulders.

"Yes, he does. He brought in the dragon meat you can order off the menu. Would have brought more today but it was poisonous, and we didn't want to risk killing anyone here let alone ourselves. I didn't help kill the dragon today, but I did help keep morale up for Enoch." Aed responds turning to watch Enoch carry the bear away.

The bear has been processed and Enoch has come back down from a bath and while he was away Bonny showed up. "Is that the new member of the family?!" Bonny asks yelling.

"Aye, he is! He apparently has slain many dragons too! More than that hack mom and dad wanted Aed to marry!" Brody exclaims standing to meet Enoch halfway to shake his hand. "What happened to your eye, boyo?!" Brody asks shocked.

"I am an exiled were. I was exiled for not wanting to follow tradition. If I had followed tradition, I wouldn't have made it here and met your sister. Well I guess it is my second time meeting her but first in memory." Enoch responds sighing.

"Come take up your seat beside the bride. While we couldn't be present to witness the marriage hey at least you asked a family member to officiate it." Brody says motioning for Enoch to continue to the bar.

"So, what made you want to marry my little sister?!" Bonny asks looking right at Enoch as he takes his seat.

"Well she took the time to try my favorite foods, so I tried hers. Then when food was done, she went up to our room and cleaned up and got dressed in what she is wearing now then she mentioned taking the blood oath. I knew refusing would be bad for my health and hers, so I agreed to take the blood oath with her. I couldn't imagine doing it differently however." Enoch explains putting an arm around Aed's shoulder.

"You mean you were too coward to suggest it yourself!?" Bonny asks annoying both Enoch and Aed.

"Sister, he hasn't known that he imprinted on me even a week. He wants to leave North Jraconia for South Jraconia so, I sprung wanting to do a blood oath on him hoping he would go with it. Which he did. Those who are upset I didn't tell anyone about it I didn't even tell Aibne ahead of time. He had to leave the restaurant to his staff while he married Enoch and I." Aed responds annoyance showing in her voice.

"I am sorry I told everyone sister." Aibne says looking right at Aed.

"Don't be it was your duty as a member of this family big brother!" Bonny exclaims looking at her big brother in disgust.

"Ahem I would like to get everyone's attention. I will be leaving North Jraconia in two days. I would like my last day to be spent with my husband and his two marked were women. One of which he is legally recognized as having married. So, could we make this quick so Enoch and I can finalize the marriage?" Aed says standing up on the bar hoping everyone is listening.

"Short and to the point! One thing I love about my little sister! Well we have to wait for the food to be done!" Brody responds excitedly.

"Do you need help down sweetie?" Enoch asks standing up to offer a hand to Aed.

"That would be nice. If you could just stand in front of me and I will grab a hold of you, and you can help me down." Aed responds quietly as she wraps her legs around Enoch a long with her arms.

Now the crowd is leaving it is just Aibne, Enoch, Maria, Jennifer, Aed, Bonny, and Brody. "Enoch I am sorry for giving you guff, but my family expects me to be mean to anyone who chooses to join the family. I hope you make Aed happy. So, I actually was going to bring a gift but Brody one upped me with the bear on top of the gift he is holding behind his back excitedly." Bonny says looking at Enoch.

"Bugger off sister! So, I realize you are an adventurer who probably has a preference for their bow, but I made you a bow. I have been hoping the were Aed kept talking of would show his face so I could give him a bow. So here is your ash wood bow I have spent the last several years making for whoever the were that may turn up for Aed." Brody says excitedly as he hands the bow over to Enoch.

"I honestly don't have a bow, Brody. I didn't think having distance between me and my target was important till today to be honest. I could have just gone in and guaranteed my death today. Your little sister is why I didn't do that today. I chose to strategize how to kill the poisonous dragon today because I have three beautiful women who love me. When it was just M, J, and myself, I would have grappled the dragon and taken the fate of dying 48 hours from when I grappled the dragon. Don't get me wrong I love all three of my women equally but protecting my own life didn't occur to me till I found Aed. Something in her fiery personality draws me in and makes me want to ensure I can spend as long as possible with her. She reminds me of the only were I know I have marked and lost. M's older sister Alice. Yes, I witnessed M kill her sister twice, but

I still miss her. I wish I could return to my homeland and say my final farewell to her. I miss that girl." Enoch responds looking from the bow to Brody.

"You mean to tell me a were doesn't have a bow?!" Brody asks shocked.

"No, I never really thought they were more useful than my spear. With the magic leaving my spear I have been looking to other types of weapons. All of them up close and personal kind of weapons. I enjoyed grappling my enemies so I could slit their throat and feel the life leaving their body. I have killed my fair share of weres and other humanoids alike without batting an eye at the fact I am killing my kinfolk. Then again when a war is declared due to your absence not just once but twice yeah you get used to killing to keep your freedom. Hey, I think I should be heading to the bedroom with your little sister." Enoch responds looking at Brody. "Thank you for the gift. If you ever find your way to OxenDeValley in South Jraconia come find me. I would love to get to know you. I feel like we could become good hunting buddies." Enoch continues before heading upstairs.

Now up in the bedroom the four are looking at the fact the beds are separated into two beds. "I guess this is a better setup for Aed and I finalizing the blood oath. I know M is going to struggle to sleep unless when Aed and I finish we move the beds together and Aed sleeps behind me with M in front of me." Enoch says looking at the bed situation.

"I kind of did this while I waited for you to quit talking with Brody." Aed chimes in meekly.

"Don't be scared sweetie just remember that we don't get to sleep alone just you and me. I enjoy being surrounded by my girls. Let us get to what I have been saying we would do." Enoch says stripping.

Chapter 24

Several days have passed they have gotten all of Aed's stuff moved into Enoch's house in South Jraconia. They are all sitting around the table eating breakfast when there is a rapping at the front door. "Coming!" Enoch responds in a booming voice as he makes his way to the door.

The door swings open with a short slightly scarred female at the door. "Enoch of Koftan, I wish to return to your service." Yennifer says standing in the doorway.

"Yennifer, I haven't seen your face in quite some time. Though I remember it much less worn. I had a feeling you would be returning. Are you hungry?" Enoch responds stopping where he was looking down at Yennifer.

"Permission to enter the house, Enoch?" Yennifer asks looking at Enoch with tired eyes.

"Come in. Answer my question as well." Enoch responds before opening his arms to Yennifer.

"Aye! I am famished." Yennifer responds as Enoch lifts her into an embrace.

Now back in the kitchen area Enoch and Yennifer make their way in. "Who is this little woman?" Aed asks looking at Yennifer funny.

"She is my first imprint in memory prior to J jogging older memories. This is Yennifer the girl I had in tow when you and I imprinted. When is your brother coming today?" Enoch responds plating up food for Yennifer.

"I thought you two parted ways for good?" Maria asks looking at the duo funny.

"I never said for good. I had a feeling we would find our way to each other at least once more in the future. Well today is one of those times. So, what brings you here, Yeny?" Enoch responds sitting next to Aed and Yennifer.

"I miss adventuring to be honest. Well you are known for epic adventures. Kind of a legend all across the land Enoch of Koftan the dragon slayer." Yennifer says looking to her right.

"Remember you are on my blind side, so looking in that eye doesn't let me know what you are feeling. Also, I am taking a wee bit of a break from adventuring unless you count requesting permission to see the only imprint, I know of that has passed away grave. That is my next big adventure." Enoch responds not looking at anyone in particular.

"So why do you want to go on that suicide mission?" Jennifer asks shocked.

"Have you lost someone you love and then given up everything to revive them only to permanently lose them immediately after they come back to life?" Enoch asks as his right eye starts glowing yellow.

"No, I have not." Jennifer responds meekly.

"Well I lost Alice who I loved dearly. To save her I gave up my ability to go were. Then she went Demon grim werecat at my request and she had to be killed for me to keep my arm. She passed the Demon grim state onto me with her passing. I never got to properly say goodbye to her. I have all those I have marked that I can gather in my power here today. I could careless on the one who did as she was told. But I miss the one I lost because I hate being a member of the tribes." Enoch explains as his eye goes from yellow to purple.

"Uh your eye was just glowing yellow now it is purple." Aed says scared.

"Yellow is nothing to fear. That is my werecat state. Purple is questionable. It is my werefox state. Red and blue run. Werebear and werewolf respectively. White is just don't upset me and if you do don't stay standing directly in front of me. That is my were boar state." Enoch responds looking at Aed as his eyes go back to yellow.

"Why is werecat not dangerous?" Aed asks scared.

"Means I am aroused in an intimate manner." Enoch responds still looking at Aed.

There is a rapping at the backdoor of the house. Enoch gets up and heads to it. "Could you let me in? I am getting funny looks, brother!" Brody asks slight hint of worry in his voice.

"You chose the back door remembering how to get there takes a minute. Knock once! Checking a door." Enoch responds as Brody knocks on the door Enoch is at before Enoch opens it.

"There you are. Uh are your eyes normally glowing?!" Brody asks as worry creeps into his tone.

"Get inside and I will explain it. I don't have any food to offer. I only had made enough for one extra person not two." Enoch responds closing the door behind Brody.

Now in the dining hall the group are seated with some kind of beverage in hand. "I didn't think you would choose to show up so soon, brother?" Aed asks looking at Brody.

"Well our parents have broken my wish to stay away from them and as all of the family are wondering why you were in such a hurry to leave after taking your vows. It is customary to spend a fortnight with the families joined before departing after all. So why did you leave so quick?" Brody responds looking directly at his sister.

"Enoch wanted to return to the house of his father where you are currently seated at the table left to him by his father. I am merely a woman brought into the were life by Enoch." Aed says sighing.

"But you are a Dundraillion first and foremost!" Brody responds anger showing in his tone.

"Mother said that if I did find my were I 'lied' about that I would lose the right to be a Dundraillion. I found my were so I am no longer a Dundraillion!" Aed says anger rising in her tone.

"Well if you aren't a Dundraillion then why did you do the blood oath at our sacred altar?!" Brody asks as his voice continues to rise.

"Enough screaming and yelling! If you can't keep it a civil tone, I must ask you to leave, Brody!" Enoch exclaims chiming in.

"I had nowhere else to go to do the blood oath brother. As mother was forbidden from ever entering her original sacred altar when she defied her parents' wishes when she married father. Casting all of us from the family as well. If I knew of another altar that wasn't designed for those who are on their deathbed to extend their life, I would have done my blood oath there." Aed responds calming her tone.

"Consider yourself cast out from the Dundraillion family!" Brody yells getting up as Enoch stands up with the bow he was given in hand.

"Take back your gift. If you have the gall to cast out your own sister, then I don't need a gift from you." Enoch says handing Brody the bow he had given not even three days prior.

Brody just leaves taken aback unable to form words from the fact that Enoch had given the bow back.

"Why did you give the bow back that was a marriage gift from Brody himself he accepted you into the family with that bow?!" Aed asks looking right at Enoch.

"He just cast you out from the family. So, if my spouse isn't welcome in the family then am I?" Enoch responds turning to Aed showing his eyes are yellow.

"I guess not. But he worked on that for years for the guy I talked about." Aed says her tone wavering.

"He cast both you and I out, so the gift served no point. If it was to welcome me into the family only to cast me out less than three days later why give it to me?" Enoch asks looking Aed right in the eyes when his stop glowing and return to normal.

"He wasn't acting on his own wishes on casting us out. He was doing as my mother demanded. Have you not done something you didn't want to for your parents?!" Aed responds yelling.

"I have. It resulted in my father's death. I had just entered this town with sacks full of dragon meat. Only butcher that would accept the stuff was in the Misty market district. An anti-were riot happened to be getting out of hand in said district. My father asked for my help dispelling the riot. I went along because he was my father. I rush into the crowd in my bear state clearing all but one person who had tipped his weapons in belladonna berries and my father rushed this individual as his werewolf state. Next thing I know the coward is repetitively stabbing my father then I rush over grab the coward by his head and squeeze thill his puny skull pops in my paws. I return to my normal state as does my father. I scooped him into my arms and a few moments later felt him leave this plane of existence in my arms. Don't hold doing things because your parents tell you to over me. I think I have anyone on this plane of existence beat on that." Enoch explains before leaving the house and wandering off.

Now down at Enoch's pub of choice in OxenDe-Valley he is at the bar when Jennifer and Maria come in looking for him. "You didn't have to go off on her like that!" Jennifer exclaims before attempting to slap Enoch upside the head, but he grabs her hand.

"She was arguing that giving up a gift that served no purpose was disrespectful then she disrespected me asking if I had ever done anything I didn't want to because my parents asked while sitting in my father's house. How would you act when someone you care about disrespects you in the worst way imaginable?" Enoch responds revealing he has been crying causing Maria to rush to his right side to hold him in attempts to comfort him.

"You didn't have to just leave?!" Jennifer exclaims anger still present in her tone.

"I left for not just her safety but everyone in there's safety. I was struggling to hold back my demonic grim bear state." Enoch responds holding Maria from the side.

"You could have said you need time to take a breath." Maria says chiming in from Enoch's side.

"If I could have gotten more words out, I would have. I was on the cusp of transforming if I didn't leave." Enoch responds kissing the top of Maria's head.

There is a commotion as Yennifer bursts through the door. "Enoch of Koftan! You have a girl talking of taking her life if you don't get back there now!" Yennifer yells as she makes her way up to him.

"Of course, she holds my own life against me. If she dies, I die and vice versa." Enoch says sighing before getting up.

Now back in the house Enoch finds Aed hanging from a rope with tears streaming down her cheeks. "Get down this instant young lady!" Enoch hollers rushing to lift Aed up.

"Oh, you come when your life is in danger! Why should I live if you get angry at me and leave over the dumbest things?" Aed responds kicking her legs.

"I left not just because of the argument. I felt my control over my demonic grim bear state slipping away. If I didn't leave, I could guarantee all of us would be dead." Enoch says as Maria cuts the rope above Aed's head.

"You could have said you were losing control?" Aed responds as she drops down into Enoch's arms.

"I would have if I could. If I tried to tell you I would have lost control completely." Enoch says holding Aed as he loosens the rope around her neck.

Now everyone is back home, and Enoch is sitting in a chair in front of Aed who is sitting on the table. "You are going to have marks on your neck for a while, Aed." Enoch says looking at Aed's neck as she is leaned forward so he can look at her neck.

"I figured you wouldn't listen to Yennifer so I expected to die, and you wouldn't come to stop me." Aed responds meekly.

"As much as I was angry at you, I love you more than anything found in a glass. I am saying that you mean more to me than anything found at a bar." Enoch says touching Aed's rosy red cheeks that somehow her freckles still come through the redness.

"So, uh you aren't going to punish me for what I did? Considering our lives are linked I could have ended yours too." Aed asks meekly.

"I figure the bruising on your neck is enough punishment as you are going to have to explain you did this to yourself every time you are asked. I understand you were mad at me so you thought killing yourself would also punish me, but you were just being extremely selfish. You have to learn that I may leave at the hottest moment in an argument, but I am not avoiding conflict I am doing it because I still care." Enoch explains as he realizes that the other girls are sitting around them.

"Enoch, do you think we could get back into Koftan?" Maria asks meekly sitting directly to Enoch's right.

"Maybe. Currently focusing on making sure nothing in Aed's neck is actually damaged." Enoch responds still feeling around Aed's neck as she winces. "What was that, Aed?" Enoch asks looking up at Aed's face.

"I think someone got me with their knife when they cut the rope around my neck." Aed responds looking down in Enoch's eye.

"I didn't use my knife anywhere near your neck. I only used my werecat claws for that as I didn't want to risk hurting you as I cut the rope." Enoch says slapping Aed's neck causing her to wince again.

"It looks like a rope burn. Probably from when she made the noose to hang herself or when she kicked the chair out from underneath herself." Jennifer says chiming in.

"Another one of your punishments for attempting to kill you and me. So, who wants to head to Trawler's Wharf?" Enoch responds chuckling.

"For what?" Aed asks sheepishly.

"That is the nearest port with people who fly to Kof-tan." Enoch responds yawning before he stands up and slides Aed's rump off the table.

Chapter 25

The group have made it to Trawler's Wharf a couple of days later. Enoch is trying to cut a deal with the person in charge of the flying service. "No, I don't have that extremely heavy bag on me today. I left it at home now that I am taking a break from adventuring." Enoch responds annoyance showing in his tone.

"Why so many people this time when you request to head into the homeland of the war mongering weres?" the female pilot asks looking at the motley group of people.

"Because they wanted to join me. I am a bit of a legend apparently. Enoch of Koftan Dragon Slayer." Enoch responds sighing.

"Everyone will have to step on the scale. Especially the short scarred up lady." The female pilot says very loudly hoping everyone heard.

"What do you have against a dwarf?" Yennifer asks getting upset.

"I have nothing against your kind. Just couldn't tell if you were a woman at first. The scars made it hard to tell." The flight lady responds backing up a step.

"Let us not argue so we can get to Koftan at a decent time." Enoch says trying to get Yennifer to calm down.

Now back in Chaffington the group have just landed as the first sun starts to rise here. "Yeny, do you still own that house here?" Enoch asks looking at Yennifer.

"Technically yes I do." Yennifer responds.

"Let us see if our stuff is still there. I miss my mithril sword." Enoch says turning towards where he remembers Yennifer's house being.

"Enoch, technically the house is yours by the way. You paid for it." Yennifer says chiming in meekly.

"I paid off your debts and you bought the house before Alice helped me find you. If you want to get technical you belong to me, but I don't see it that way. I see that if you owe money as my marked woman, I owe money." Enoch responds putting a hand on Yennifer's shoulder.

Now the group is in Yennifer's tiny house. "Wow so much smaller than I have lived in a long time." Maria says looking around.

"It is the perfect size when it is just a dwarf and her other half." Enoch responds looking at the group.

"Here is your old bag. Here is mine. I never thought I would be back here after Maria had us kidnapped."

Yennifer says looking around at how she had decorated the house.

"She what?!" Aed asks shocked.

"I thought I was the only person he had imprinted on, so I sent some of Jenny's tribe to bring him to me." Maria responds sheepishly.

"Aed, drop it. If she hadn't done that, I probably wouldn't have gone down the path that has led to you. Plus, she saved me a good chunk of coin getting to South Jraconia." Enoch says annoyance welling up in his tone again.

"Let us get headed to the Koftan werecat tribe den." Maria says trying to get the subject off her previous actions.

Now on the edge of the forest that houses all the tribes of Koftan. "What are you doing here exile?!" A guard demands shouting at Enoch in particular.

"I would like to visit my late imprint Alice of Koftan at her final resting place." Enoch responds dropping all of his weapons to demonstrate he means no harm.

"Madison foretold of this day. We are to oblige you and whoever you have with you on this one-time thing. You will also be questioned by Madison herself." The guard says before letting out a heavy sigh.

"Will the only living were that marked me be present?" Enoch asks trying to look at the guard.

"I am right here dummy." Marley responds removing her helmet revealing Enoch has been speaking to her.

"Are you on my left?" Enoch asks blinking.

"Yes!" Marley responds.

"You blinded that eye Marley." Enoch says turning to face Marley.

"I wish I had the guts to disobey like Jennifer did. Maybe my life would be better than it is now. Pick up your stuff I need to get you to the den." Marley responds a hint of sorrow in her voice.

Now at the alpha's chamber the group are brought in while Marley stays outside. "What brings the three exiled weres here?" Madison asks looking at the group.

"I wish to say goodbye to Alice one last time." Enoch responds bowing.

"I would also like to say goodbye to my older sister." Maria says meekly looking passed Enoch.

"Oh, and has the news of my father's passing made it here?" Enoch asks looking right at Madison with his right eye.

"Zeke has passed away? What did you do?!" Madison responds anger showing in her tone.

"I didn't kill my own father. He did die in my arms though. He asked for my help to clear an anti-were riot in OxenDeValley Misty district. I went werebear and rushed in clearing all but one rioter. My father bit his arm off that held a sword. The coward pulled a dagger tipped in belladonna berry guts and repetitively stabbed my father over and over till I got to him. I grabbed him in my giant paws with my claws rupturing his eyeballs before flattening his head between my paws and licking some blood off my paw allowing me to go from grim state to the form you see before you. I picked my father up and offered to take him someplace he could have been treated but he told me that belladonna is were bane before dying in my arms." Enoch explains as his eyes glow following his emotions while he speaks so from red to blue.

"Marley take the group to Alice's grave. Enoch thank you for this information. Take your time saying your goodbyes." Madison responds taken aback at the information Enoch just revealed.

Now at Alice's grave site. "Here we are Enoch. Take your time. Welcome home by the way." Marley says as she walks past Enoch.

"Alice,

I have missed you so much. You meant so much to me. I actually was willing to go back if Maria hadn't done what she did. I wanted to marry you instead of Maria. But Maria just snapped over the years of bullying you did to her. I wish you hadn't gone after me when I revived you. Then maybe you would be here with me today. While I would be unable to go were, I feel I would still be happy having you by my side. You kept me sane when we were adventuring here in Koftan. I will always miss you Ally cat." Enoch says tears streaming down his face before he turns away from Alice's grave and walks to Marley.

"I miss her too. I also miss you." Marley says softly as she tries to comfort Enoch.

"Why couldn't life have gone differently? Don't get me wrong I am grateful for all the women I have imprinted on that I get to see on a daily basis." Enoch responds looking up at Marley to his right.

"I think you revealing you aren't limited to just what your parents were has told Madison something." Marley says looking down at Enoch to her left.

"Like what? What could the results of me begging the gods of life and death to bring Alice back to life reveal other than my love for Alice?" Enoch asks revealing how distraught he is.

"I have said too much. Plus, Maria is done with her goodbyes." Marley responds patting Enoch on the shoulder.

"We always have each other, E. I heard what you said about us. I understand. I am not upset." Maria says hugging Enoch.

"Ahem, has everyone that wanted to say farewell to Alice made their peace with everything?" Marley asks looking at the group.

"It was just those two. I only used her to hunt E down and Yennifer kind of always didn't like her because E loved Alice more." Jennifer responds looking at Enoch holding Maria and crying.

"Well then follow me!" Marley exclaims annoyed at Jennifer's bluntness.

Now back in the alpha's chamber. "So, Enoch I have a deal to make with you!" Madison exclaims standing up from her chair before climbing down from the platform her throne is on.

"What is it your majesty?" Enoch asks bowing.

"Quit with the pleasantries. They are reserved for actual members of the tribe." Madison responds annoyance sliding into her tone.

"Sorry kind of a force of habit as prior to being marked I did my best to obey the rules of addressing alpha's." Enoch says sheepishly.

"So, I don't know if you know of a prophecy among our people." Madison responds taking a breath. "There is a prophecy of a male were who can not only transform into the were states of his parents but the other weres as well. His eyes glow a corresponding color for each state. Now how he may have gotten this power is a subject commonly contested among differing tribes. But he is said to either eradicate all weres ending our existence once he finally dies or he will cement us forever into the fabric of this world. Your reputation points either direction as well. Though you will be remembered by the mortals as your reputation even reaches us here in the tribe. So, I am offering you to go on an adventure of a lifetime." Madison explains sauntering away from Enoch and the group.

"What is the adventure?" Enoch asks revealing he is excited.

"I will tell you tomorrow morning as the first sun is setting today. Do you have living arrangements in town?" Madison responds looking at Enoch as she sits down in her throne.

"Yes, but not with a bed big enough for all four of my marked women and myself. I would be lucky to fit two of us on the bed." Enoch says sheepishly.

"You can take Maria's old room. I will assign Marley as your guard. She is free to do as she wishes tonight as she should relax with the male who imprinted on her before he was exiled." Madison responds coldly.

Now in Maria's old room. "Why did you have such a large bed?" Enoch asks looking at Maria funny.

"I may have gone to sleep as the state I am in now, but I would wake up in my were state with the female assigned to me after you left also in were state next to me. So, I got a bigger bed because they got sick of hearing her growling and snarling at me when I pushed her off the bed." Maria responds as she nods at the door trying to get Enoch to look.

"Ahem, can I join you tonight, Enoch?" Marley asks standing at the door.

"I wouldn't be honoring how I was with Alice if I said no. So, come on in. Although is there any of the roast left?" Enoch responds unable to stand as he has both Jennifer and Aed's heads in his lap.

"Yes, but I don't know if you are allowed any. I could go ask." Marley says meekly.

"If they let us sleep the night here then they should let us eat. I will come help you." Maria responds climbing off the bed.

The duo have returned with two heaping full platters of boar roast. "Ooh I have heard the werecat tribe of Koftan boar roasts are to die for!" Jennifer exclaims excitedly as she clamors to her feet.

"I am the one who told you dummy!" Maria responds trying to joke with Jennifer.

"I will be assigning the mission tomorrow morning. I'd get some sleep if I were you." Madison says as she passes by.